ARK FOR THE BROKENHEARTED

ARK FOR THE BROKENHEARTED

SEQUEL TO ONCE TO EVERY MAN

ELIZABETH CAIN

ARK FOR THE BROKENHEARTED
SEQUEL TO ONCE TO EVERY MAN

This is a work of fiction. All of the characters, names, incidents, organizations, and dialogue in this novel are either the products of the author's imagination or are used fictitiously.

iUniverse books may be ordered through booksellers or by contacting:

iUniverse
1663 Liberty Drive
Bloomington, IN 47403
www.iuniverse.com
1-800-Authors (1-800-288-4677)

ISBN: 978-1-4917-5866-3 (sc)
ISBN: 978-1-4917-5867-0 (hc)
ISBN: 978-1-4917-5865-6 (e)

Library of Congress Control Number: 2015901925

Print information available on the last page.

iUniverse rev. date: 02/26/2015

author's note

This African story does not intend to exploit the differences between the characters because of their ethnic origins but to reveal how each one can heal the other when circumstances seem irreparable. But to understand the complexity of this story, you need to know who is black and who is white. Especially for readers new to these characters, I have noted the race of the main protagonists for a smoother transition into the heart of the novel.

Reena Pavane, later Patel, is a black Tanzanian who has been separated from her lover, Dakimu Reiman, for eight years. He is a black fugitive still on the run after crimes committed in 1985 and earlier. The story begins in 1993 with Reena discovering Dak's son by a tribal marriage in the 60s, Kiiku, who is also wanted by the authorities. Reena, in distress, reaches out to a white friend, the British journalist Jim Stone who had helped her through a difficult time years before. He is married to a white former missionary to Tanzania also named Reena Pavane, now Stone.

The focused pursuer of the black fugitives is British Major Fulsom Farley. Felicia, his white wife, has been damaged by a black man she says was the ruin of us all. *Safina is the black child of Reena and Dak. Suzanna is the white child of Fulsom and Felicia, or so she believes.*

Though "race" should not matter in this story, it does because of Tanzania's past dealings with other nations, some good and some bad. Today in that country, as I write in 2015, there is no color bar, and tensions have eased considerably, in my mind because of the example of men, women, and children like the ones who inhabit the pages of Ark for the Brokenhearted.

AFRICAN TRIBUNE, December 5, 1985

Dar es Salaam, Tanzania. TRIBAL WARRIOR FOUND GUILTY. Dakimu Reiman, former member of the militant Vitani, was pronounced guilty of the murder of two white citizens—David Sommers, son of Major John Sommers, who died in the Massacre of 1961, and Jason Highback, city police officer holding a warrant for the black's arrest for an earlier crime. They had tried to apprehend the native Tanzanian in the company of his girlfriend, Reena Pavane, local nurse, while they were parked at a popular city lookout on the night of December 1. Both men were shot point-blank.

It was rumored that Reiman had worked for the elder Sommers at the British Air and Ground Patrol station in Dar as Salaam prior to the black uprising in the sixties but had become enamored of the Vitani King Kisasi and joined in the senseless battle against blacks and whites alike, turning his back on his Christian roots, having been raised at the Pentecostal Mission at Huzuni.

During the trial, his white friends, Jim and Reena Stone, apparently lied for the accused, testifying that he was with them at the time of the killing, but his companion, Miss Pavane, stated under oath that she was in the car and saw Reiman fire a rifle at the men approaching them. Bullets from that rifle matched fragments recovered from the bodies of the victims and were used as conclusive evidence.

In a disturbing turn of events, the prisoner was awaiting sentencing when a young black called Kiiku, thought to be his son from an outlying village whose mentally challenged mother had also been in the courtroom, strangled two guards and broke Reiman out of jail yesterday evening. The only thing that remained in his cell was a Bible, which lay open to an underlined passage. The Bible was given to Mrs. Stone, who was the last person to see him before his escape. She and her husband are believed to have left the country.

AFRICAN TRIBUNE, September 10, 1993

Dar es Salaam, Tanzania. FUGITIVE DAKIMU REIMAN A PRIME TARGET. Local military and police investigators are still vigorously on the hunt for Reiman in connection with the 1985 murders of David Sommers and Jason Highback, of which he was convicted. The black's son, Kiiku, is suspected in the deaths of the two jailers found strangled outside his father's cell the night he escaped. Authorities explained that recent unlawful activity by the newly formed Chui Clan, of which Kiiku is purported to be a member, prompted their intensified search for the green-banded terrorist, hoping he could lead them to Mr. Reiman.

Repeated attempts to question Kiiku's mother, Reiman's first wife, who works at the market on Soko Street, have been unsuccessful. She had been called to testify against Dakimu in the 1985 trial but proved a disturbed and unreliable witness. Dakimu's girlfriend at the time of the killings, Reena Pavane, has not been available for comment. It has been observed that some have harassed her over the years for statements that led to the conviction of a person of her color. Police have decided that she has no current information to give them.

prologue

British Major Fulsom Farley slammed the newspaper down on the kitchen table. *That damn black*, he thought as memories of the last eight years plunged through his mind, giving him a fierce headache before he'd touched his coffee and store-bought scones. His wife lay in their bed, further than ever from getting up in time to make even a semblance of a decent breakfast before he had to report for duty, a duty that had not changed much in the last several months—find, capture, kill if he had to, that Dakimu Reiman and maybe the son, Kiiku, who had surely broken his father out of jail and hidden him from due justice.

The major had forgotten most of the other players in the drama in Dar es Salaam in 1985. But one woman's image remained, that of Kiiku's mother—a slender, retarded, almost mute Bantu, hovering in the dim light of the courtroom, rocking and mumbling incoherently. She had a stall on Soko Street these days but vanished behind a curtain when anyone in uniform appeared. He left her alone.

He had married the widow Felicia Sommers, who mourned the loss of her murdered husband beyond repair. She had been pregnant, and now he was raising her child, Suzanna, but he had never adopted the girl. Though he cared about the child, he wanted his own son or daughter more than anything in the world. But Felicia had only wed him to be a stepfather for Suzanna, not

1

to have any kind of sex that would result in her bearing another child. Yet he loved her. She was beautiful, even though she didn't take care of herself. She had a sweet temperament when she wasn't hysterical. She would caress his back at night, rubbing the knots out of his shoulders, and rarely, one hand would slip around and bring him to an explosive climax.

In spite of his loyalty to Felicia and his Catholic commandments, for many years he had enjoyed the attentions of a woman from another part of the country who quenched his sexual thirst and his need for an intellectually equal companion. He adored her, but she had never borne him any offspring of which he was aware. Their trysts were far apart and short-lived because of the circumstances of his career and his wife's unpredictable nature. He confessed his sin every week at St. Joseph's but knew he was doomed to repeat it until the woman barred her door. Felicia was his duty, his cross to bear, and he was determined to do it as graciously as possible.

Felicia made an effort for Suzanna, sewing pretty little-girl clothes and singing songs to her in a plaintive voice at bedtime. But once in a while, she cringed at the sight of the angry birthmark on Suzanna's face as if it shocked her back into the reality of her first husband's terrible death. Then Farley's ire would flare up at the black responsible for his wife's inconsolable and hapless life.

Farley's coffee was cold, and the two-day-old scone dry and tasteless. He thought of the weeks ahead. There was renewed vigor for the capture of Dakimu Reiman as a new clan of warriors had emerged, demanding more rights and property and privileges still reserved for whites and blacks with education and wealth. They called themselves Chui, Swahili for *leopard*, and one of the leaders, he believed, was Kiiku himself, the son of Dakimu, flaunting his status, wrapped in the green insignia of the clan, and seemingly unafraid of the army of searchers on his inscrutable trail.

"Find the son; find the father," Farley whispered to himself as he pulled on his riding boots. He'd be on the streets today, asking questions, probing abandoned neighborhoods, and watching for a flash of green.

one

She saw him the first time from the window of her second-story apartment on Soko Street. Normally, she wouldn't have looked that way that early in the morning, down toward the market. There would be few vendors setting out their wares on the cobbled alley in Dar es Salaam. Normally, she would be watching the sun light up the sea from the east, turning the dark layers of cobalt to aquamarine, the hard-muscled boys stacking their nets and beginning to push their little boats and homemade rafts out to the fishing grounds. But the figure of the agile, young black caught Reena's eye as he stepped behind a half-renovated building across the street, his bright green waistband flinging its color against the bland, gray cement and rebar splintering the fourth attempt to repair the structure.

There were places to hide in there. He didn't reappear, and Reena stifled a scream. The boy had been in her line of sight for an eerie and startling moment. Why was he here? It was so dangerous. Had he wanted her to see him? She barely remembered what he looked like, but his name sprang from her lips as he darted out into the open again, his white shirt, khaki pants, and green silk insignia of the Chui tribe now camouflaged by the nondescript dust of the abandoned edifice.

"Kiiku! Kiiku!" she cried with rising apprehension.

He couldn't know she lived there. She had moved three times

in the last eight years to avoid the animosity and suspicion directed at her over the horrific incident in 1985, the incident she had witnessed from the backseat of her car—her lover shooting two white men and after, the mad dash through the dark streets as she clawed at the seat covers. She had almost put out of her mind what happened next—Dak turning himself in, sitting in the defendant's chair haggard and ruined. But she would never forget Dakimu suddenly rising amid the chaos and embracing a beautiful black, who said as clear as the muezzin's midday call to prayer, "I am your son."

Then, in only a few hours—or maybe it was days—they had disappeared. Two jailers were strangled, and Dak's Bible lay open in his cell to a place he had underlined in Revelation—*And I saw a new heaven and a new earth; for the first heaven and the first earth had passed away, and the sea was no more.*

Now, here was his boy, more a man than the haunted youth she had met in the courtroom, surely in his thirties, who couldn't see her from the street, but she shivered. Kiiku and his father were still being hunted by the authorities. Once in a while, they harassed her, especially for information about Dakimu. *Has he contacted you? Do you know where he is? Are you hiding him?* But questioning her never got them any closer to their prey. She had no answers. Until today. Until the furtive young man below her window glanced up, and she recognized the face of Dakimu's son.

She looked away from the street, from the mystery that shook her to the core. She went to the door of a small room at the end of a short hall whose walls were lined with photos of lions and zebras and wildebeests and warriors that a white journalist, a friend, had given her. She had thought many times of removing them, but they were superb, after all. And it was *her* country. She turned the knob carefully and peered in through the semidarkness at a child curled up with a stuffed zebra, still asleep in nightclothes the color of the Indian Ocean. The girl whimpered for a moment and clutched the little equine more tightly.

"Safina, Safina," Reena whispered, not wanting to wake the

seven-year-old. "Oh, darling daughter, joy of my life, I think your brother is here."

She saw him again two days later at the end of a line of stalls where she had purchased tomatoes and mangos, avocados and sweet onions. Her cupboard was empty, and she was enjoying picking through the farmers' rich fare, reaching out for some ears of white corn, when Safina tugged at her tunic.

"Mama, Mama, look! A green ribbon!"

And there Kiiku stood, almost concealed by the colorful rows of fruits and vegetables, behind a woman polishing apples and eggplants and muttering to herself. He flinched but appeared fit and defiant as he stared at them. Reena paused at the stall. Safina cried, *"Hujambo,"* to the seemingly retarded woman and reached out her hand toward Kiiku.

"I did not come for you," he said in a dark voice, ignoring the girl.

Reena looked into his secretive eyes and then down at the woman hunched over the produce. *Yes, that is Kiiku's mother,* she thought, *trying to survive, helping out in the market, perhaps waiting every day for her son to come in from the hills.*

"I did not come for you," Kiiku repeated. "But I see I may have crossed a bridge I didn't know existed." And he removed the green sash Safina was still eyeing with childish pleasure and gave it to her.

"Tell me if I am wrong, mama," he said a little more softly.

"No … you are not wrong. But you are not safe around me. We shouldn't be speaking. Come, Daughter. Mama has enough now."

The boy and his half sister gazed at each other. They couldn't know. They must not ever know everything. Kiiku nodded and seemed to melt into a sheet of canvas draped behind the seller's trays and boxes.

"I like this," Safina said, curling and uncurling the green silk. "But it's dirty."

"Mama will wash it and put it someplace special."

"On me! On me!" the child cried hopefully.

"I don't think so, little one. There are reasons."

"What reasons?"

"Reasons a girl should never have to live with," Reena whispered.

"I still like it," Safina said. "And the man who gave it. Will we see him again, Mama?"

"I don't think so, precious," she answered, suddenly sad that the moment had been so brief.

Just then a white man rode by on a magnificent black horse, and the green ribbon was forgotten. Reena didn't trust many white people, but she didn't want Safina to be raised with bad feelings for white people or fear of them, so she beckoned to the soldier and asked if her daughter could pet the animal.

"Of course, mama. He likes petting."

"What's his name?" Safina asked.

"Resolute."

"Oh," she said, surely uncertain of that word.

"There are more horses at the Post. Would you like to see them?" he asked in a friendly manner.

"Oh yes."

Reena took the opportunity to hide the green sash in amongst her groceries. She wasn't certain why Kiiku was wearing the color of the Chui tribe, but she knew that symbol was not welcome to white eyes or to any in the military, the only men in her neighborhood who would be mounted, black or white.

Reena's feelings about whites were complicated. She hadn't known any white people until that day in 1985 when the Stones came into the hospital where she worked, were *brought into* the hospital really, by Dakimu Reiman—tall, handsome black, fierce as a prince and fiercely in love with the white woman, Reena Pavane Stone. She remembered the way the black had looked at the white woman in the waiting room while Dr. Mbulu had attended to her husband, Jim, suffering from, as it turned out, a bad case of malaria. The disease had troubled him for years, but that very day Dakimu had married the couple in a small village one hundred miles from Dar es Salaam.

She didn't know how official the ceremony had been because Mr. Reiman told her right away, almost defensively it seemed, that he was not a member of the clergy, but it had apparently been an emotional day for all of them, and special, even though Jim and his Reena had been together for more than two decades. The black man looked right into Mrs. Stone's heart. And she let him, but she did not look at him in the same way. Reena tried to steel herself from those emotions and from the light that gleamed in Dakimu's face, but she began to love him almost from that first meeting, and soon, he had possessed her and freed her at the same time from a deep loneliness. Then up at the Point one night while they were savoring the swift, African sundown over Dar es Salaam, he killed two white men who rushed them with guns as she and Dak held onto their blackness like armor. Those whites, Reena hated.

Safina was still stroking the horse. This white man was perhaps being too familiar. The bitterness of past years in Tanzania was over, the years when the British had dominated the natives' lives, controlled the government, families' education, and freedom of movement, but suspicion and grievances remained, as did injustices and acts of racism. Her child invited a kind of gentle tolerance.

The soldier was saying, "You can come tomorrow."

"No, sir, we have church," Reena said promptly.

"Well, in the afternoon? I'll give you a tour myself."

"Mama, please. I want to see the horses," Safina begged.

Reena hesitated. She had never left Safina with a stranger, much less a white stranger. The man with three gold bars on his blue jacket, an important man she decided, seemed to recognize her discomfort and said, "Oh, mama, it will be quite safe. A group of children from the public school across town will be here to see the horses and watch a small demonstration of equestrian skills put on by some of the troops. Your daughter can fit in with them. I assume she won't know any of them. She attends school closer by?"

"Yes. The Light of the World Catholic School."

Something changed in the soldier's eyes. He looked away briefly. "Ah yes," he said. "It's where I would like my daughter to go. She would be starting second grade this year." He still did not look at her but said, "She has … difficulties. But she is bright and can read. I think she could easily catch up with the others."

Reena didn't tell him Safina would be in the second grade that year. She didn't want to be involved any more than she had to be with white difficulties. The odd circumstances of her becoming involved years ago with the white journalists, Jim and Reena Stone, still plagued her. Yet she had loved them. She felt slightly faint remembering how close they had been.

The soldier was giving Safina a gold-edged card. It read Major Fulsom Farley. "This will get you onto the Post. Your mother can park by the school bus. The children may already be in the barn. Just enter the aisle way and join them. I'll try to meet you, but I may not be able to stay."

Safina jumped up and down with anticipation.

The major leaned over and spoke conspiratorially to Reena. "I am charged with finding a fugitive of many years. He is becoming careless in his movements. I may be following a lead on him tomorrow."

Reena's heart stopped. She should have nothing to do with this man. But she decided, looking at her daughter's eager face, that perhaps one time couldn't hurt, and maybe it would distract Safina from wanting to know more about the black man with the green sash, her own half brother.

Major Farley wheeled the horse smartly away, but Reena felt off balance as she took her daughter's hand. She had seen this man before. *Yes, of course.* He had been at St. Joseph's a few times, her Catholic church, but he had never spoken to her. She would ask Father Amani what he knew about him.

She squeezed Safina's hand. "What did you think of the soldier?"

"He was nice. But the best thing about him was the horse. Re—so—lute. What does that mean?"

"Staying strong in the face of great odds," Reena said.

"What does *that* mean?" Safina asked.

"I hope you never have to find out," Reena answered.

They reached the door of their apartment building. Reena glanced back down Soko Street as they entered. Was she looking for Kiiku, long-disappeared son of Dakimu running from the likes of Major Farley, or was she hoping to see the retreating shape of the commanding soldier who could use all of their identities against them? But then she realized, the man had not even asked their names.

The next morning, almost the first words out of Safina's mouth were, "Where's the green ribbon?"

"Why?" Reena asked.

"I'll wear it to church," she answered.

"I haven't washed it yet, baby. Maybe next week."

"Okay, Mama, but can I tell Father about it?"

"Why, Safina?"

"He'll know what it means. If it's a sign from God," her naïve child answered.

He'll know what it means all right, Reena thought.

They finished dressing, climbed in Reena's Citroën, and drove through the quiet Sunday streets of Dar es Salaam to St. Joseph's Cathedral. Safina ran up the steps. Father Amani had seen them come in. He hugged Reena and kissed her child on the forehead.

"I have a secret, Father," the seven-year-old said.

"You do?" the priest said. He bent down on her level. "What is it?"

She whispered something in his ear. He straightened up startled, and Safina bounded off toward one of the Bible story classrooms.

"Reena, what's going on?" he said. "Who gave her a piece of green cloth?"

"It was Kiiku," she said, hardly believing it herself. "He was in the marketplace yesterday."

The priest made the sign of the cross and said, "This cannot be good."

Reena remembered how Amani had counseled Dak and believed in his redemption after the murders. Perhaps he had even aided Kiiku in smuggling his father out of the city. She didn't really want to know, so she tried to downplay the meeting in the market.

"He said he was only here to see his mother. And she was there … at one of the produce stands."

"You spoke to him?"

"Not really. But I let him think what he would about Safina. I couldn't deny him that."

"And if he goes back to Dakimu with this? If he's still with Dakimu."

"I don't know, Father. I always imagined Safina and Dak would find each other someday. This knowledge would mean so much to him, but I don't want him to die for it," Reena answered.

The priest clasped her hands and said, "You must be careful, dear one, for the sake of your daughter."

They parted, and the service began. Reena noticed how many more blacks were in the church now. Some of them surely recognized her and guessed who Safina's father might be, even though Safina herself did not know. A lovely Maasai woman sang a beautiful anthem in Latin, only half of which Reena understood, and then the altar boys prepared the sanctuary for communion. But the sacraments did not calm her heart, and when the children came out to rejoin their parents, she was still keyed up.

Apparently Safina felt some nervous energy too as she immediately asked about going to the base to see the horses. "Please, Mama, please," she said, pulling on her mother's skirt while Reena was trying to discuss with another nurse the problems of a house-bound patient, someone she was going to see that afternoon.

"Stop whining, child," Reena said in a firm voice.

A hint of a storm whispered around them as they all stood on the steps of the church. The priest was ushering parishioners to their cars through the gauntlet of beggars who gathered after services. Reena dreaded leaving the relative safety of the crowd of the faithful and Father Amani's protection.

But soon they were on their way through the colorful streets of Dar es Salaam, *port of peace.* Reena thought of the storms she had weathered right there in the old city, once the capital of Tanzania. Now there were rumors of terrorist groups whose long arms reached across the whole world. These were not the warriors of Dakimu's time who raged against British control or overzealous missionaries. These were, in Reena's mind, deranged people who could never be caught or reasoned with.

She and Safina were approaching the military compound with its imposing guard towers and mounted cannons poised to annihilate intruders. In light of the violence she had seen, Reena was grateful her child only dreamed of stroking horses, not imposing her will on her own countrymen or the world.

A uniformed man stopped them at a closed gate. "Papers?" he said in Swahili when he saw she was black.

She handed him the card Major Farley had given her with his personal invitation for them to drive to the horse barn.

"Follow those signs," he said, reverting to English. He pressed a button that started the gates sliding on rollers and gave them access to the Post. There were children, black and white, playing on sparse lawns and dry fields, but not together. They had separate teams, separate languages. Safina watched, taking in the unfamiliar scene.

"Where are the horses?" she asked.

She is more at home with these half-wild creatures than with humans, Reena thought. *Is it because the animals can't speak, strike her with profane words, or turn their backs on her because of the color of her skin?* Major Farley was waving from the end of a long row of corrals and shelters. Beyond that was an ornate barn where, Reena supposed, the favored mounts were kept.

"You can leave her awhile, mama," he said, after they got out of the car. "It'll take some time to see them all," he continued.

Reena thought again, *He doesn't even know who we are.*

"I want to learn all their names," Safina said matter-of-factly.

"I have to take some meds to a patient who lives close by. I'll visit with him for a short time and then return," Reena said, feeling chilled.

"She'll be fine," Mr. Farley assured her. "See? There are the other children just ahead."

Reena was not comforted. Even though this man's job was to serve and protect, that didn't always extend judiciously to black and white alike. And Reena didn't like her daughter being around all those guns. But the girl had disappeared into the dark barn without a backward glance. Reena got back in the car and drove slowly out of the compound, her heart fluttering.

§ § §

Inside the stable, Safina breathed deeply. The hay, the horse sweat, and the leather saddles and bridles gave off the scent of a secure life. The place was warm and quiet, save for the easy munching of equine mouths on timothy and oats. The stall doors had names on brass plates screwed into the mahogany.

"Cloudy … Sergeant … Resolute," Safina said aloud as she passed each door.

Mr. Farley's eyebrows went up. "What grade are you in?" he asked.

"Second," she told him. "Trooper … Flame … Mlinzi."

"I don't even know what that last one means," Farley admitted.

"It's Swahili for *watchman,*" she said.

"Smart little thing, aren't you?" the major said, not unkindly.

"I can read, and I can make up songs," she said.

"*Can* you now?"

Then they went by a stall with the nameplate *Jester*, but Safina gasped at the sight of the animal. He was cut and bruised, legs swollen, and head drooped low. She grabbed an empty bucket, turned it over, and jumped on it to peer over the half-door at the poor beast. The horse was hanging in a wide band slung around his belly. He could reach hay and water but barely.

"What's wrong with him?" Safina asked.

"Besides the broken leg? And some edema? Oh, he's tranquilized."

"What's that?"

"We gave him something to make him sleepy so he wouldn't struggle in his restraints and make things worse," the man explained.

"Oh. Can I talk to him?"

"Yes, but don't stay too long. You should join the others. I must attend to some duties."

"Okay."

When the soldier left, Safina unlatched the gate and crept closer to the sad, brown face, closer than the soldier would have permitted had he still been there she was sure. The horse put his nose out toward her. She kissed it and blew into his nostrils. He seemed to like that. She didn't reach for him. She let him reach for her. Then she began to say words, prayers she'd learned at St. Joseph's, parts of hymns, soothing, healing words.

"*Ho, everyone that thirsteth, come ye to the waters …*"

The horse nickered softly.

"Are you thirsty?" Safina asked.

His water bucket was almost empty. Safina could not lift the hose very easily, but she found a measuring cup and managed to turn the faucet on. Little by little, she filled the container with cupfuls of water and pushed it closer to the horse's lips. He drank.

Suddenly, she was not alone. A few feet away stood a young girl maybe a little older than Safina. She was white, but one side of her face had a red mark that crossed one eye and flamed over her right cheek.

"Does that hurt?" Safina asked, holding her palm out so as not to point at the damaged skin.

"No," said the girl, "but it's ugly."

"Oh, I don't think so," Safina said. "I think God chose to paint you with his hand."

"Really?"

"Really."

"What's your name?" the white girl asked.

"Safina."

"What does that mean?"

"It means *ark* in Swahili," she said.

"Like from the Bible?"

"I guess. What's your name?"

"Suzanna."

"That's pretty. Is this your horse?"

"No. He belongs to the regiment. He broke his leg crossing the river, but he's a 'specially good horse everyone says, so they're trying to fix him."

"Maybe we can help," Safina offered.

"How?"

"We can talk to him and sing to him so he'll stay quiet and not have to have that … bad medicine."

"Could you come play with me too?" Suzanna asked.

"Okay."

"Where's your mother?" the white girl asked.

"She's helping a sick man. She's a nurse."

"Maybe she can take care of my mother," the girl said.

"What's wrong with her?" Safina asked.

"No one knows. She gets things mixed up and sometimes doesn't get out of bed or eat all day." Suzanna hesitated and then said, "She has headaches that make her scream."

"I'll tell my mama about her."

"Sometimes she screams when she looks at my face," the white girl said, barely above a whisper.

Then Safina dared to touch the dreadful mark and said, "It's nothing to scream about. Maybe she should scream about something else."

"Maybe," Suzanna said. "Why are you here, anyway?"

"A nice soldier on our street let me come see the horses."

"My father is a soldier. He told me to check on the black girl in the barn because he had to leave on a special mission. I heard him on the phone. He wanted to know why some man would show up in Dar and that he'd find him."

"He must be a very important soldier," Safina said.

"Yes," the white girl said. "I hope I can be as important when I grow up. But I know to be important, I have to go to school." She rocked from side to side on her chore boots. "Do you like it?"

"I love school," Safina replied, "but I don't have any best friends yet. I think I need a best friend."

Just then Reena pulled up to the barn opening. Safina and Suzanna met her halfway down the aisle. Safina greeted her mother, whose face had the look of surprise or maybe disapproval, but she did not let go of the white girl's hand.

"Mama, Mama, this is Suzanna. She lives here. She knows the horses. She wants me to play with her," she blurted out all at once.

They stepped out into the sunlight, and Safina saw her mother swallow hard when she noticed Suzanna's birthmark, but she only said, "Hello, Suzanna. That's very nice of you, but perhaps I should talk to your mother."

"Well, today is not a good day. She had to have tranquilizers."

"Like Jester!" Safina exclaimed. "We could sing to your mama too! We could help her be calm."

"Oh yes, I think she'd like that. Can you come back tomorrow?"

"Where's your father, Suzanna?" Reena asked.

"He was here, but he's out on patrol now. He'll be home tonight. We live in bungalow number eight. I fix dinner for the three of us, and then he works on his reports. I'll ask him to call you. It might be a few days, with my mom and everything."

"That's all right, dear. I have to work this week. I'll look for your father at the patrol stations. What's his name?"

"Fulsom. Fulsom Farley."

"Major Farley is your father?" Reena asked.

"Yes, ma'am."

"We have met. Safina and I saw him on his black horse near our street. He generously allowed Safina to visit the horses today," Reena told her.

"Oh, he's the soldier Safina meant. I think he asked her to come more for me than for the horses. He wants me to have friends." She looked across the compound as if expecting someone might hear her. "I haven't gone to school yet. I don't know anyone."

"What about the children who live on the Post?" Reena asked.

"None of them have ever touched me ... like this," she said, holding out her hand that was in Safina's.

Safina was reluctant to let it go and whispered something in Suzanna's ear, right next to the terrible mark.

"We need to go," her mother said. "It's getting late."

"I'll be back," Safina promised the girl.

§ § §

When the white girl smiled, she was really quite beautiful, Reena thought. She drove off the Post and maneuvered through the late afternoon traffic, lost in thought. There were so many things to consider. Kiiku was out there, perhaps running from Major Farley while his half sister wanted to be part of the major's life, his daughter's friend. Darkness descended upon them before they reached home.

"Mama, can I stay longer next time?" Safina asked.

"We'll see. I don't think Mr. Farley should have left you girls alone with the horses."

"Suzanna told me he was called out on a special patrol. He sent her to check on me because he couldn't."

"What kind of patrol?" Reena asked with suspicion.

"She heard her father on the phone. He said something like, 'Why would he come here?' and 'We'll get him.'"

Oh God, Reena prayed silently. *Maybe if Safina is Suzanna's friend, she can find out things, things that will help Kiiku. Wait! What am I thinking, putting my child in this crossfire? We should run as far and as fast as we can ...*

"Mama, you're not listening," Safina complained.

"What, child, what?"

"Maybe Suzanna can come to our house. Maybe she likes dolls too and making doll clothes. You have some old scraps, don't you, Mama? There's the green ribbon. We could use that."

"I wish you'd just forget about that green ribbon," her mother said.

"Why?"

"Because I don't like it."

"But why?"

"It's something you will understand when you're older."

Reena didn't know if the tribal insignia was taught in the mixed-race school her daughter had been attending for two years. Certainly it was a part of history, these rebels and their demands. But how much they exposed the children to she didn't know. Dakimu's history was another story, perhaps too recent to be in any textbook, but he was still a fugitive and probably hiding with his own son's clan, the Chui—if she was right about the green scarf.

Did she still care what happened to Dakimu Reiman? She thought of that day at the beach with him, walking along the shore at low tide, finding coins and shells and pieces of life that still flowed in after hundreds of years. She remembered Dak telling her about one of his friends who had found a set of rusty leg irons dating back to the East African slave trade. The man had sold them for two thousand dollars. Dak believed it was enslaving another human being to do that.

Then he had stopped right where they were, the tide starting to roll in again, washing up against their ankles, then their calves, warm and inviting, but Dak trembled as he encircled her in his arms and said he could only love her, that the white Reena had been a fantasy, a jealousy, wanting what belonged to Jim Stone because Jim had betrayed him years before. And he said, "I'll only ever really love you." Of course, she still cared about him.

When she and Safina got home, the girl raced ahead to a pretty package by the front door. It was tied with a thin, green ribbon.

"Safina! Be careful! We don't know what's in there," Reena said.

The child backed away from the little gift apprehensively.

Dear God, I can't let my daughter grow up with fear, Reena thought, and she reached down and tore off the wrapping. It was a bag of ground coffee from one of the plantations near Arusha, according to the label. She lifted the sack to her nose, and the sweet aroma filled her with a sharp vision—Dakimu on his hands and knees in one of the shadowy rows of coffee beans. *No one has the time or inclination these days to walk through three hundred acres of coffee trees row by row! No one will imagine Dak is in such a place!* In this way, her suspicions began.

Reena pocketed the green ribbon and opened their door. Safina seemed hurt that the present wasn't for her.

"Let's have those corn cakes you like so much for dinner," Reena said to appease her.

"Okay, Mama," the girl said.

Later, they sat on the couch from which in the daylight hours they had a superb view of the Indian Ocean. Now the city lights glittered between them and the coal-black water beyond. Safina told her mother about the brown horse in the sling and how she and Suzanna had comforted him.

Reena got up and turned the television on. The set was to the right of the big window so it would never block the sight of the city and the splendid sea. Reena wasn't paying much attention, but suddenly the whole screen was filled with Kiiku's face! Underneath his beautiful countenance that looked more like Dakimu's than ever, bright letters at the bottom of the screen read—*Have You Seen This Man? Reward for any information leading to his capture.* This was repeated in Swahili and in a few other languages.

"Mama! Mama! We saw him at the marketplace! He gave me the green scarf!" Safina cried. "What did he do?"

"Nothing for you to worry about, sweetheart," her mother said. "A few years ago, he broke the law, but it wasn't a very big law." Her lips tightened as she thought that if he had killed those jailers, it was a pretty big law.

"Is that like not a very big sin?" Safina asked.

"Maybe."

"But God forgives us if we say we're sorry and don't do those bad things again," the child, fresh from Bible school, reminded her mother.

Reena was silent. This was intolerable. Whatever she said, there was going to be hurt in it. But she couldn't let Safina lead the police or the soldiers to Kiiku, so she took a chance.

"Safina, I want you to promise me you won't tell anyone you saw that man in the market and that he gave you that green sash."

"Do you know him?"

"Yes."

"I liked him," Safina said.

"As well you should," Reena said, still hesitating to reveal more. Finally, she went on. "He is your brother."

"I have a brother? Why doesn't he live with us?" Safina asked, her eyes filling with tears.

"He's your half brother. You and he have different mothers but the same father."

Now that this much was out, could the child understand any of it?

"Then who is our baba?"

"Someone I loved a long time ago. He'll never come here. It's best to forget him," Reena said, knowing as she spoke that it was a careless thing to say.

Before she could soften her words, Safina said, as calmly as any child who had heard such news could, "But I might want to love him."

"And he needs your love, I am sure, but it's dangerous right now to have anything to do with him."

"What's his name?"

"I can't tell you that, Safina," she said, "because if you slipped just a little, mentioned his name to anyone, especially to Suzanna, you perhaps would never see your father."

"What did he do?"

As shocking as the answer was, Reena could not lie to her child about this. She said, "He killed two white men."

"Were they bad men?"

"One was the son of a man your father killed many, many years ago, before I even knew him, in a shameful war. The other was a policeman with a warrant for his arrest. They were angry and not thinking straight. They approached the car with guns." She had slipped unintentionally into the actual event. "One man might have taken a shot, I don't remember, but I do remember seeing your father raise the rifle and pull the trigger."

"But how could *you* see that? How could *you* know what happened?"

"Because I was in the car."

"Oh, Mama, oh, Mama," was all she said.

Reena lowered the TV sound and looked into her daughter's eyes. "You are not to worry about this," she said.

Then they walked silently hand in hand to the girl's bedroom. The room was a haven of stuffed animals, market trinkets, and statues. Next to a plaster-cast image of Mary and the baby Jesus was a paint-chipped, black horse. Reena tucked her daughter in bed for the night, and they joined their hands for a prayer. Safina said, "I'm going to pray for Baba … and my brother."

"That's good, baby. And God will answer it."

"That's what Father Amani says, but I don't know if I believe it," Safina said.

"I want to believe it. I used to believe it, but what I believe doesn't matter. I'll tell you something else … your father is Catholic … like we are."

"But do they have Mass where he is? Can he confess his sins there?"

"I hope so, little one. I truly hope so," Reena said. And then she leaned down and whispered in her ear, "Your brother's name is Kiiku."

two

*R*eena went back to the living room and stared at the television. The reporters were speculating above the crawl that read *Breaking News*. Some thought Kiiku had already escaped the city. No one was going to find him. The military horses and dogs couldn't do as well at night, and the sounds of the animals might drive him deeper into hiding, so they'd suspended the search.

Reena's anxieties went beyond that. Kiiku may not even know he'd been sighted in Dar es Salaam and could make a simple mistake, show himself as he had to her. Suddenly, she feared that Kiiku might think she and Safina had tipped off the police after they saw him at the market. He could feel betrayed if he noticed the widespread manhunt developing. *I have to warn him*, she thought. *But if the authorities can't find him, how can I?*

She paced the room, not wanting to stop her feet, wanting to move until she found the right direction, the courage to reach out to Kiiku, because she was pretty sure she knew where he was. She passed by the phone and impulsively picked up the receiver. There were seven rings before the priest said, "Father Amani here."

"Father," Reena said desperately. "Don't say my name. I must speak to the son."

"How did you—"

21

"Lucky guess. It's important."

Kiiku came on the line.

She spoke quickly. "Someone saw you. There are mounted soldiers and unmarked police cars going down all the back streets. You must go."

"*You* saw me," Kiiku said.

"I know ... but I would never tell anyone. I would never betray the son of my only love."

"Hah! You betrayed *him*."

"I know. That's why I won't do it again."

Reena's past flew into her face—the day she told the court that she was with Dak in the backseat of the car and that he had to kill the white men who had seemed bent on killing them.

"Why didn't you lie? It would have changed everything," Kiiku said, bitterness still in his voice.

"It has consumed me for the last eight years. So now I *will* lie, and now I have to teach my daughter to lie," she answered.

"My father's daughter, yes?"

"Yes."

Father Amani had grabbed the phone. "You must stop talking now. There are five police cars outside the church. I will intercede. It's the best I can do tonight," he said and hung up.

Reena supposed it was better that way, just that brief exchange, that warning for the son of Dakimu Reiman, that small piece of restitution for her larger crime of making his father flee from the ones he loved.

She couldn't sleep after that, so she was wide awake when the policemen began banging on doors, flashing Kiiku's photo in people's faces, questioning their movements, their social activities. Had they seen anyone in their neighborhood wearing a green sash? Reena froze when she heard that. She had cracked her door open so she could find out what the men were saying. She thought quickly. The sash was in her sewing kit. Would they look there? They didn't seem to be going into the apartments. If they found the sash, she would say her young daughter had picked it up on the street. But they didn't enter; they just stood, finally, in her doorway, pressing the photo of Kiiku closer to her face.

"Do you know this man, mama?" they asked.

"I've never seen him," she lied.

"Where do you travel in the city?"

"I'm a nurse at the Hospital of the Good Samaritan," she said.

"Where do you worship?"

It seemed they were lingering at her door longer than anyone else's.

They pursued her with their questions. "Do you know Father Amani?" they asked, even though she had not said she attended St. Joseph's Cathedral.

"Yes. I've been going to St. Joseph's since I was just a little older than my daughter."

Why did she say that? They didn't need to know she had a daughter.

"What's this?" one of the officers asked, noticing the bag of coffee on a table just inside the door.

She didn't flinch but said, "It's a gift from a friend who owns a coffee plantation."

"Which one?"

"I don't know for sure." Luckily she had removed the potentially damning label from the package.

"If you see this man, you must call it in," another officer said.

"Of course ... but what's he done?"

"Years ago, he broke a killer out of jail, a man who had killed white citizens. The man was his father. The extent of the boy's crimes is unknown, but he could lead us to the murderer."

"Oh, I had no idea. I don't follow all the things that go on at the courthouse."

"Well. Okay. Sorry to bother you, mama."

They trudged back down the stairs and out of the building. Reena checked on Safina and stifled a gasp. In the girl's hand was the dusty and faded green sash that belonged to her half brother. She gently unwrapped the cloth from her tightly clasped fingers without waking her, carried it out to the kitchen sink, struck a match, and burned it to ashes.

"I smell smoke," Safina said the next morning at the breakfast table.

"I got rid of something that could harm us."

Safina looked at her mother for a long time before she said, "It was the green ribbon, wasn't it?"

"Yes, it was. Someday I'll explain it to you."

"It was my brother's," she said.

"Yes."

"The man on television last night."

"Yes."

"It makes me sad that my brother is a bad man."

"Sweet child, really, the police have made a mistake. I'm sure your brother has not done bad things. I hope someday you can know him."

§ § §

On Monday, Major Farley took Resolute and rode out to the block of the abandoned buildings near Soko Street. He hadn't been able to finish his search the day before because of the interest of the black child—he didn't even know her name—in his horses. And he had been distracted by a vague memory of the child's mother. He had thought about it all night, whenever Felicia woke him in her breathless nightmares. He would almost figure it out and then drift back to his dreams of the woman who waited for him hundreds of miles away. Maybe he should take a break from his hunt for the fugitives and give in to his deep longing for—no, he would not say her name, even to himself, in the bed of his wife.

A motion shook him from his musings. His horse arched his neck and reached for the bit, ready to feel his master's hand directing him. Farley took up the reins and halted him. There! At the end of Soko Street. A young black was almost running into the dilapidated housing behind the market. Something seemed off about the man. He was not dressed in city clothes. He kept glancing behind him and looked uncomfortable with the market crowd. He had no green about him, but Farley became suspicious when he turned into an empty building and did not reappear.

Resolute was nervous under him. He was used to standing quietly on street corners or prancing in parade formations. He slipped a little as the major forced him down the uneven footing of the deserted alleyway and resisted trotting. Farley dismounted and tied the gelding to a fence that still stood in the rubble of a torn-down apartment and continued on foot. He noticed a hand print in the dust on the side of a still erect structure and reached for his weapon.

Where could the black have gone?

Overhead, someone opened a window. A shard of glass from the broken pane fell at his feet. He jumped back and peered upward. The sun was in his eyes, but a dark figure leaned out, then darted back inside. Farley stepped into the crumbling doorway and waited. Perspiration ran down the back of his neck although it was not a warm day. The black had no place to go, and Farley would catch him and question him mercilessly. This black may not be the son of Dakimu but could know him, could be a Chui in town to steal or cause havoc among law-abiding citizens. His actions were too bizarre, fleeing the market as though—yes!—as though he had seen the major on the tall, black horse coming toward him.

There was a rush of footsteps behind him, but Farley did not see the arm that swung the two by four at his head. When he was conscious again, it was much later in the day. He got up slowly, smelling the blood before he saw how it had soaked one sleeve of his shirt, and lurched out into the open. The surrounding buildings seemed empty, no motion, no voice, and when he made his way to the wider street, his horse was gone.

§ § §

Kiiku galloped the black horse hard until he reached a Chui camp a few miles out of the city. His tribesmen greeted him with cheers when he came in on the military horse. Kiiku saw that the gelding was afraid at first of the odd shacks and open fires and unregimented barracks, but everyone admired the animal and treated him with respect. Only Kiiku would ride him, but many young men offered to feed and groom him, so the fine horse would be secure, though no one knew his name.

Kiiku retreated to his tent. He had stolen the sturdy structure the year before from an abandoned army camp. He heard that the soldiers had all contracted malaria and were transported to Dar es Salaam for medical attention. The tent was waterproof and not as exposed to the wind as the thatched huts his companions lived in. He lay in a hammock like the one his father had in his own hiding place and pondered the last few days.

Safina! He had a beautiful half sister that he already felt he would give his life for. He drifted in daydreams of secreting her to their father so she could know him in her childhood, as he himself had never known him. When he was growing up, his father was a citizen of the world. He had wandered the streets of London waiting for his white friend, Jim Stone, to recover from severe dehydration and malaise from malaria. He had tracked a notorious British colonel who toured America oblivious to the black shadow who was Dakimu Reiman, the shadow who ultimately killed him in New York. He returned to Africa, a fugitive even then.

Of course, all of this Kiiku learned later and not from his mother. He sought out the priest, Father Amani, at the church where his father had become a Catholic. He wanted to know about the heart of the man he would be breaking out of jail. Everything he was told only made him love the man more. Dakimu was a warrior who knew how to kill and knew how to love. But as much as Kiiku tried, he could not find the man's god.

A light breeze tossed the door flap open, and the figure of a white soldier stood there. "I have come for my horse," he said, but then shifted into the shape of Jim Stone, who held out his hand but did not speak.

Kiiku woke suddenly when the storm rattled pots and pans stacked outside and the shouts of men scrambling to tie things down and contain the livestock reached his ears. He rose and went out to help, shaking his head and wondering why those white men had come to him in a dream.

§ § §

Reena was exhausted. The hospital had a crush of patients that week, and she barely had a moment to herself. She would pick Safina up at the base, and they would go straight home, her daughter chattering the whole way about adventures with Suzanna. The girls groomed the horses together, polished tack to a fine shine, and ate their lunch that Major Farley had fixed before he left for his duties, side by side under a huge baobab tree in the courtyard.

One day in the middle of the week, there was another brightly wrapped package by the front door. This time Reena let Safina open it. The gift was a lovely beaded bracelet. Perhaps Kiiku's mother had made it especially for the little girl who had spoken to her so sweetly in the marketplace. It was a work of art. In between every six beads was a circular piece of tinsel that made the whole thing sparkle in the sunlight. And in every group of six was one green bead.

"Oh, I love it!" Safina said, and she slipped it on her wrist. "It's better than the green ribbon. Do you think it's from my brother?"

"I do."

So he had not left Dar es Salaam yet or else had gone and then returned with the present. He had taken a huge risk coming to their door, and Reena loved him for it.

Safina was dancing and twirling and called out to her mother once as she swung past the big window where the light captured the tinsel dividers, and flecks of silver danced all over the ceiling and the walls.

"I'm going to dance right up into heaven," she cried. "I can't wait to show Suzanna."

"What will you tell her?" Reena asked.

"I'll say an old friend of my mama's gave it to me, but I don't remember her name."

"You are wise beyond your years, my girl."

The doorbell rang. Fulsom Farley stood there ready to take Safina off to play with Suzanna. They had big plans with the horses. Reena didn't know all the details, and her mind was on other things. She kissed her daughter good-bye, thanked the major for providing a way for the girls to be friends, even with all the reasons they should not be, and closed the door.

She was leaving Safina with the white people until the next day so she could take the night shift. The children seemed bonded like sisters. Reena wondered if her daughter would be tempted to give Suzanna the bracelet. There were few things the girl kept if giving them away brought some pleasure to someone else.

Reena thought she shouldn't have let Safina wear the bracelet until she knew more about it. In a hollow she had carved under the floorboards in her bedroom, she had already buried one strip of the green sash that she could not bring herself to burn, the sack that had held the sweet coffee, and the red leather volume of Jim Stone's *Memoirs* he had signed for her in 1985, a volume that had been revised and updated with pages she had not yet read. They were clues, or perhaps petitions, for a different kind of justice, a justice she had never been able to give to Dakimu.

Reena finished her housework, washed her hair, and left for work early in the car her mother had given her before she died in the cancer ward at Good Samaritan. She was grateful the Citroën still ran well. Many of her friends had to take the bus everywhere, running to clamber on as the vehicle slowed at intersections. It was terrible and dangerous, but many blacks did this day after day while whites drove by in air-conditioned privacy.

She suddenly remembered that Jim and Reena Stone had rarely used a car but walked or hired the local taxis and paid way over the usual charges. They knew their drivers by name and often bought gifts for their children. The Stones were Africans at heart and had taught Reena something about love. She thought of the way Jim looked at his wife as she wiped the sweat from his face when he was so sick with malaria and held his head when he could do nothing but retch after the least amount of water he had swallowed. "I'll never forget your hands," he had said to her.

Traffic was light, but Reena didn't hurry. She had about an hour for her errand, the only place she could think of to go in her unsettled state of mind. The bells at St. Joseph's were pealing out their song of mercy. A legless beggar was huddled against the outer masonry wall. She put two American dollars in his basket. He was mute and could only nod his head. The pain of the world fell down on her shoulders.

Reena stepped into the confessional and took a deep breath. "Bless me, Father, for I have sinned," she said to Father Amani, her priest and friend.

"And what is your sin, Reena?"

"I don't want my daughter to get involved with a white family."

"Oh, my dear, that is perhaps politically incorrect, but I don't think it's a sin," the priest said gently.

"It's what's in my heart, Father," Reena said, trying to compose herself. "Mistrust ... judgment."

"Judge not lest ye be judged," Father Amani quoted.

"Those white men ... back then. They were going to kill me," she whispered, the fear still languishing in her voice. "I can't even remember their names, just that they were white."

"What about Jim and Reena Stone? You loved them," Amani reminded her.

"Maybe only because they loved Dakimu. After they gave up their friendship with him to save his life, they forgot me."

"Maybe they were saving your life too," the priest said.

"Maybe … Give me my penance, and I'll try to be more open about the white people at the base," Reena said.

"The military base? Be careful, Reena. Those people have long memories," Amani said.

"Those *white* people, Father."

He sighed. "Yes, some things are complicated. You are forgiven, my dear."

They met outside the little room, and the priest hugged her. She rushed out of the cathedral to get to the hospital for her night shift. The African darkness came swiftly when the sun passed the horizon. A hand caught hers as she reached for her car door.

Kiiku said, "Tell me her name."

Reena wheeled around. "Why?"

"His heart is breaking. Her name could give him hope."

"Hope for what? She doesn't know anything about her father," she lied. "I have to go to work … please."

"Hope for a future. I am not enough for him," Kiiku said.

"Perhaps you should find his other Reena, the white one," Reena said, unable to hide the sarcasm in her voice.

"*She* doesn't love him the way you do. *She* doesn't have his child. Give me her name."

"Safina. Her name is Safina," she told the determined Kiiku.

He squeezed her hand. "Look more closely at the bracelet," he said. He disappeared behind a row of cars. Reena almost believed he'd not been there, that she had been dreaming this face from the past. Maybe she would find Reena Stone herself. Wherever she was, she was surely being watched. The *long memory* would stretch across the sea to England, to America, to wherever she and her husband might go.

She pulled into her parking space and turned the engine off. Dr. Mbulu would know where the Stones were. He had become quite close to the couple while Jim had been his patient. Did she dare ask him anything about Jim and Reena? She glanced down the street where the Imperial Arms used to be, where Jim and Reena had spent a week together over thirty years ago and then again for a time eight years ago, where she herself had first slept with Dakimu.

The hotel was called something else now, the rooms redecorated, but she remembered the wide window where one could look out to the Indian Ocean, see the storms building and the white caps rising against the cobalt sea. It was the reason she had found a place with almost the same view. Could the Stones still be there, hanging onto their memories, their truths, as everyone else fled from place to place to be safe. She didn't want to know, and yet …

"Miss Pavane, you working tonight?"

It was Mwuzaji Dharani. He'd been asking her out for weeks, but she wasn't attracted to him. Perhaps she wouldn't be attracted to anyone again, after Dak.

"Trying to will my feet that way," she said.

"Yeah, nights are tough. Do you want to have coffee later?"

"Zaji, you know I have to pick Safina up the minute I get off."

"How's that beautiful, little girl doing?"

"She's okay. But she met this girl who wants to play with her," Reena said.

"Well, that's good. A child gets lonely when the parent works, needs friends," he said.

"The girl's white."

"Oh," he said. He paused. "Shouldn't matter to you. You had those white friends a few years back."

"Yeah, there are exceptions. It's the rule I'm worried about," Reena replied.

"You'll do the right thing, Reena. Do you like the girl?"

"She seems sweet." Reena stared out at the traffic, the high cross on the church in the distance, trying to avoid saying too much. "But she lives at the military base. You know a Fulsom Farley?" she asked.

"Sounds familiar. Do you want me to find out something?"

"I'm not sure, Zaji. I'm a little afraid of what you might discover."

But the military knew how to put up walls. No personal information was ever given out. *To blacks*, Reena told herself, even though blacks worked and lived at the base along with Indians, Chinese, and a few Afrikaners from Johannesburg trained in crowd control. She should listen to Father Amani and his *Judge not* …

For herself, she did not care. She had seen the worst there was to see. But for her child, she longed for a perfect world, no one close enough to break her heart. She was secretly proud that Safina had chosen the white girl with an unavoidable disfigurement and a probably mentally ill mother. Suzanna certainly needed Safina more than Safina needed her. Reena would watch where things would go.

After her twelve-hour shift, she was relieved that her daughter was with the Farleys because she was so tired that all she wanted to do was sleep. She stumbled up the dim stairwell toward her apartment and almost missed the small scrap of paper stuck in a plant by the door. She took it inside and held it under a brighter light. It read—*You must remove one foil in bangle. K.* The chances that boy was taking! Reena had no idea what that cryptic note might mean but resolved to figure it out when Farley brought Safina home the next day.

She collapsed in her bed. She dreamed and hardly knew she was dreaming. She felt Dakimu's arms around her, his mouth holding hers as they rocked together in their own sweet dance of love. Her back arched involuntarily when, in the dream, Dak put his hand on her sex and made her come. She woke crying his name and thanked God their daughter was not there to hear.

When the morning light played on the turquoise field of the Indian Ocean, Reena dressed and sat on the couch, holding a cup of coffee from the beans of the plantation where Dakimu might be. She watched the roadway for the military jeep and breathed more easily when she saw it turn onto Soko Street.

Major Farley saw Safina to the door and said, "Those girls talked all night, mama. I'm sure your daughter will need a nap today."

"Thank you, Mr. Farley. May I pay you for keeping Safina?"

"Oh, no, mama. I'm glad to help you out. Jobs are so hard to get these days, and my Suzanna has never had a friend like Safina. My wife is confused and disapproving, although she has only heard the strange voice in the next room, but to me, Safina is a gift." And he rushed away as if he had said too much.

Safina was soon asleep on the couch by the bay window. Reena spread a blanket over her and slipped the shiny bracelet from her wrist. The girl barely stirred. Reena examined the bangle under her reading lamp. She turned each piece of foil over and over, looking for marks or words. After twenty painstaking minutes, she unfolded one of the last silver foils and grabbed her magnifying glass. There, printed in tiny letters, was the word *Shanga.*

Shanga! Jesus, Joseph, and Mary, Reena cried to herself. It would be perfect. A black warrior with a handicap—the name of a killer—hidden among the mentally and physically disadvantaged habitants on the outskirts of Arusha. No one would look for him in a place like that. He could move with ease among the artisans and their caretakers. He'd help them. He'd honor them. He might be only a long day's drive from her, and she was sitting there with the daughter she thought he could never know. By then, perhaps, he even knew her name.

Kiiku seemed evasive and yet led her to these enticing discoveries about his father. Had he promised not to tell anyone where Dak was hiding but couldn't keep silent after meeting Safina? Did he enjoy making a game of the mystery? She would question him more closely when she could.

Reena made the sign of the cross for herself and over the resting body of her child. She pulled the foil off the bracelet and buried it with her other forbidden objects. Would Safina notice one foil leaf was missing? Had she seen the word *Shanga*? Had she heard of that place from someone at church or in the market?

It was almost time for school to begin. Surely she would learn many things of the world, the good and the bad. But that her own father was one of the bad people, Reena did not want her to know. She pulled her child's head onto her lap. Outside, the sky had turned gray, and the sea a dull green. It had lost its blue luster, its shining whitecaps their pure white. Dar es Salaam, port of peace. *Not today*, thought the mother of the daughter of the most wanted man in Tanzania. *Today the sea is spoiled.*

Reena thought of Kiiku, perhaps safe now, but for how long? And then she had an astounding idea. She would find the Stones. She would beg them to gather their black friends together again and give them asylum in their own white country. She suddenly believed that they would rush to help her and Safina, even though they had seemingly disappeared from Africa in 1985. Her instinct was to trust them. It overwhelmed her doubt. She slipped the bracelet back on Safina's wrist and got up to make lunch.

The following weekend, Reena had Saturday and Sunday off. Safina begged until her mother relented and allowed Suzanna to come over for both days. She imagined Fulsom Farley didn't like it any more than she did, but Suzanna's mother had been hospitalized for some tests. She hadn't been eating or keeping herself clean. Farley told Reena he was trying to spare his daughter the details and thought if she spent the time with her best friend, it might help.

People in the apartment building stared at the pair of seven-year-olds climbing the stairs hand in hand. Were they aghast at Suzanna's terrible mark or at the fact that the girls were touching each other? Reena glared at her neighbors and was glad when they lost interest in the children and closed their doors.

Safina and Suzanna played with Safina's dolls. "I've never seen a black doll," Suzanna said once. "Can I hold her?"

"You can have her. Maybe I can have one of your white dolls."

"Oh yes, that would be fun. But they can be friends ... like us!" Suzanna said.

Reena left them to heal the world. In a few minutes, she was speaking with the manager of the old Imperial Arms, trying to find out first if he remembered the Stones.

"Jim and Reena. Of course. Haven't seen them for a few years, though."

"I'm a friend who's lost touch with them. Just wondered if they were still in Africa." Reena tried to sound casual while her heart raced.

"I'm not sure. Let's see. I believe they left a forwarding address, but I have no idea if they're still there. They've been gone six or seven years."

He read off a name—*Homestead Highlands, Selous Wetlands, Tanzania.* Reena's hopes sank. She was certain there was no such development. They had been afraid to reveal anything of their new life, their journey without Dakimu. They could be any place in the world.

She called Father Amani. "Father, just say yes or no. Please," she said.

"If I can," he replied.

"Do you know where Jim and Reena are?"

There was a long pause.

"Father?"

"You know I can't answer that nor should you want to know."

"They are my only chance," she said.

"Chance for what, my child?"

"To save everyone," she said.

"Reena, you can't save everyone. For some it's too late. You know that."

"But what if it's not, Father?" She hesitated. "Just tell me this then. Did they keep their promise? Did they leave Dak alone?"

"Yes. That I can tell you. And you should leave him alone too. You must think of your daughter," the priest said.

"I am thinking of her," Reena said, raising her voice slightly. "I'm thinking of giving her a family in another country!"

"No, Reena. Just leave everything the way it is. Some things cannot be fixed."

The children skipped through the room laughing.

"Who's there?" Amani asked.

"Just a girlfriend of Safina's, the *white* girlfriend."

"They sound happy. That is working out then?"

"Mostly. They have no idea how close they are to being brokenhearted."

"So, promise me, Reena, you won't rush that very possible outcome."

"I can't promise, Father." She hung up more disappointed than ever. There seemed to be no place else to go.

But there was some place she had not been yet—into the pages of Jim Stone's little, red book. She had to be careful. Many people were afraid of the things that had been revealed in that book, about both blacks and whites. The book was banned in many parts of the country, and people had been questioned for owning it.

The girls were galloping the room with toy horses and being dutiful soldiers, rounding up lawbreakers and sentencing them. They never spoke of the color of the outlaws' skins, only the crimes they committed—stealing from the market, spray-painting vehicles, jumping a bus ride and not paying, starting a fight. She fixed them some lunch and decided the red book could wait. She couldn't take a chance on the girls seeing her hiding place.

Later, she heard her daughter say to Suzanna, "My father is alive, but I don't know where he is. Your mother is alive, but you don't know where she is either, in her mind."

"That's why God made us friends," the white girl said.

This talk of fathers and mothers unnerved Reena. She already feared a rogue wave rising up behind them all, a missing piece of information that she would not be able to hide under the floorboards of her room.

On Sunday, they got ready for church. Safina told her mother almost every week how she loved hearing the Bible stories and watching Father Amani bless his parishioners with his gentle, black hands on their heads. But Suzanna seemed nervous listening to Safina going on and on about the activities at St. Joseph's.

"Do you feel all right, sweetheart?" Reena asked her.

"Yes … but my mother and father fight about the Catholic Church, so I'm confused," she said.

"What do they fight about, my dear?" Reena asked. She had thought perhaps the girl wasn't comfortable in a crowd of strangers, but this disagreement between her parents was troubling.

"My father is Catholic. He says that thousands of years of learning and praying have made priests closer to God than anyone, and we must believe them so we can go to heaven. Mother says the priests are wrong to forgive people of terrible sins, sins that have brought grief and pain to other people, and that we should not believe them, ever."

"What do you think?" Reena asked.

"I don't know," she said. "Father enrolled me in the Light of the World Catholic School this year, and Mother didn't come out of her room and cried for days. I'm afraid to go myself. I have learned to read, but I'm poor at arithmetic and hate my face."

"Oh my, Suzanna. I am so sorry," Reena said. "But sometimes you have to do things you think you can't do. A famous American lady said that, the wife of a president. You can just sit with Safina. You'll feel safe with her, won't you?"

"Oh yes," the girl replied. "But if I hear the Catholic words, doesn't that make me a Catholic?"

"No, dear," Reena promised her. "The words can't change you unless you want to be changed."

That day, holding tightly to Safina's hand, Suzanna entered St. Joseph's Cathedral. It was a bright day, and the stained-glass windows depicting scenes from the Bible leaped out as though real over the congregation below.

"Oh, I didn't know it would be so beautiful," Suzanna whispered. "Is God in here?"

"God is in you, child," Reena said.

The girls went off to Sunday school, and Reena sat in the back pew where she had first sat with Dakimu as he struggled with his own *terrible sins*. The choir was singing that song that always lifted Reena's spirits—*Ho, everyone that thirsteth, come ye to the waters … and ye shall go out with joy.* She always wondered what kind of water—holy water? Baptismal water? The renewing water of the Indian Ocean? Then there was the flooding water of the Rufiji River, but that was another story of another time. Not her story and not her joy.

After church, they went to a market three times as big as the one near Soko Street. Reena bought spring flowers, fresh ocean perch, and some material to make Safina's school uniform. The girls never let go of each other's hands. Shoppers here were used to more radical sights. There was even a booth where, Reena was sure, one could buy a gun. She wasn't clear on the laws about guns, but she prayed she would never have to own one.

When they got back to the apartment, Reena fixed a delicious meal of pan-seared perch breaded in corn flour, slices of sweet mango, and a coconut pudding that had been her grandmother's recipe. Later, the girls played a spelling game and then curled up on the couch for a nap. Reena thought again of the red book in its secret place and considered reading it while the children slept, looking for clues to finding the Stones. But before she could get to her bedroom, there was a knock on the door. The girls tumbled off the couch and came toward Reena arm in arm. She supposed it might be Farley, but when she opened the door, a bulky, white soldier stood there stiffly.

"I am here for Major Farley's daughter, ma'am," he said formally. Then he noticed the children.

"What is this?" he asked. "I thought you just had Suzanna by herself for daycare. Who is this black child?"

"This is my daughter, Safina," she answered. "The girls are friends. They play at the base too."

"I've never seen the black girl. This is not proper, them touching."

"I guess *Major* Farley believes it proper enough," Reena said.

"What's your name?" he asked in a surly tone.

"Reena."

"Last name?"

"Just Reena to you," she said. She turned to Suzanna. "I guess it's time to go home, dear."

And right in front of the racist soldier, Safina and Suzanna kissed each other on the lips.

The moment Reena had not yet planned for seemed at hand. The soldier had wanted her last name. How could she say *Pavane*? It hadn't been so long that people would have forgotten the Reena Stone with the maiden name of Pavane who had lied for the prisoner Dakimu Reiman. She herself would forever be connected to those events, even though no one blamed her for the deaths, and she had told the truth. But her name was suspect. Even when she registered Safina two years ago for the preschool class, she had not given a last name.

Now she would use a name and let the school officials and anyone else think she had married. That was more believable than never admitting a last name.

She watched her child innocently lining up her dolls and horses by sizes or some other construct of the girl's mind. Safina was saying to herself, "Now, *these* children and *these* horses have mamas and *babas*, and *these* are missing one or the other." At the last minute, she switched a white doll with a black doll and put her most beautiful horse in the group with only one parent.

"Mama? What about the people who are missing a *child*?" And she moved her ebony stallion into a place by itself. "I will call you *Baba*," she said to the imposing statue.

"Safina, come here, girl, I need to talk to you," Reena said. She held out her arms to her jewel of a daughter.

"What is it, Mama?" she asked.

"I have to explain to you why you must, from now on, break a rule," her mother said.

"Which rule?"

"The one about lying," Reena answered.

"Oh, no," Safina said. "God will be mad."

"I don't think so, little one. Now listen. You are going to have a new last name—for school, for church, for wherever you are. You cannot be Safina Pavane. Your last name will be *Patel*."

"Is that my father's name?"

"No. It's a common Indian name. You can say your father is from India and travels there a lot on business. I swear that is the only lie you will ever have to tell." Reena hoped to God that was true.

"But, why, Mama?"

"Safina, there are some bad people in this world, people who want to kill your real father."

"Do you know where he is?"

"No, love, but I do know that if you have my name or an African name, you might not be safe." *Or the name of your real father, Reiman,* she thought but did not say aloud. "I'll tell you more of the story when you're older. For now, you just need to understand that you must say you are of the Patel family. Promise me."

Safina looked away. Her mother knew this was hard for her. The child had been taught never to lie.

"Will I have to confess my sin to Father Amani?"

"No, my sweet. He already knows why we must do this."

"Why would the bad people want to hurt me?"

"They might think you could lead them to your father." Reena stopped. She couldn't tell her that some bad people might threaten her with more than curses to get her to reveal something she didn't know, that some might hold her captive to lure her father in.

"But I've never seen my father. What could I tell them?" Safina asked.

"Someday you might know where he is," Reena said. She thought of the sack of coffee Kiiku had left her with the label from a plantation near Arusha, the foil-sparkled bangle with the name of Shanga on one silver piece. Her father might be closer than he'd ever been.

"Someday I'm going to find him," Safina said.

"Oh, baby, just forget him. It's too dangerous to speak of him. Now, practice saying your name."

"Safina Pa ... tel."

"Good girl."

three

Suzanna hid in her room while her mother wailed.

"Don't make her go. Don't make her leave me," Felicia cried.

"Mother, we must think of her life," Farley said. "She needs an education."

"But the *mark*! What will people think!"

Suzanna crushed the pillow around her ears. What *will* people think? She wanted to run away. But she knew there would always be mirrors. She remembered the first time Safina had touched her face. Even though she knew the mark was still there, inside, in her deepest self, she almost believed it was gone.

She could barely hear her parents' voices. The sound swelled and receded like the restless tide out on the Indian Ocean. Their exact words were lost now, buried like little shells under the drifting sand.

She let herself float on an imaginary sea. From the moment the black girl had put her hand on the birthmark, Suzanna knew she was meant to live and to have a place in the world, an important place. She could never be the beauty that Safina was. She could never actually heal people. She wasn't sure she even believed in that, but she had seen Safina do it.

That first Sunday Mama Reena had taken her to St. Joseph's, Safina had tossed some coins in a beggar's box by the front steps of the church. But the raggedy man had wanted more. He had waved his hand almost blindly in front of her, trying to touch her, trying to *see* her. When Safina took his hand, he cried, "Ah, you are just a little girl. You are black. You have on a purple dress and a bracelet of green ribbon. You are not blurred and formless as all the others are. I don't know why."

And he picked the coins she had given him out of the box and told her to give them to someone less fortunate than he. He only needed to see a little better to get a job doing dishes at a café down the street. "You did that for me," he said.

"All I did was give you all my coins instead of putting them in the collection plate for the church," Safina said.

"And now you can give them away again!" he said.

"You do it," Safina offered. "You might know who needs them the most."

"I might. But if you choose, the beggar will get more than coins."

Suzanna could not forget those words. Had God given her the birthmark so one of his children could take it away? She had never longed for anything as much as having a friend like Safina. Maybe that friendship was already worth more than all the coins in the world.

§ § §

One day in the middle of October, Reena waited downstairs for Major Farley to arrive in his camouflage-painted truck. He often took the children on his days off, sometimes dropping them at the stables to watch that poor horse with the broken leg. Reena foresaw a bad ending there, but the girls believed so much in that horse. If the songs and prayers that Reena heard them say could heal, the animal would surely live to carry his soldier again.

She had planned to ask the major about the school situation. He had driven the girls to a safari park out of town, and it was past time for them to be home. She thought it was strange that he was so comfortable with his daughter's friendship with Safina.

Yes, Suzanna's first day of school was drawing near, and the major needed his daughter to face this challenge. Maybe he was depending on Safina to help her. But he showed affection equally to the girls as if they were sisters, as if they were the same color. There was nothing inappropriate about his behavior, just something secretive. She paced nervously, not wanting to think about her own secrets. Finally, she saw the military vehicle coming slowly up the lane.

Farley called out right away when he stopped where she was standing in the street, "So sorry, mama. The girls wanted to go on the loop twice. They got to see a zebra birth. It was quite wonderful."

The girls were both asleep in the backseat, curled up like puppies, one black, one white, arms and legs and hearts entangled, trusting and pure. Reena forgot what she was going to say and let the major drive off unquestioned after he helped the tired Safina out of the truck.

When she thought of school, Reena thought of the lie she had asked Safina to tell. Who knew the name Pavane? She couldn't remember the last time she actually used that name. Even the time card at the hospital just said *Reena*. She had changed to that single name when Mr. Stone became a patient because his wife was known as Reena Pavane. Her own mother had named her after the white missionary from the village of Huzuni, but Reena was so different from that white woman. That Reena was not Catholic. That Reena had known Dakimu for twenty-five years. That Reena had lied in court for him, saying he was with *her* when the killing occurred.

Reena had sat in court and gasped at the way Dak looked at the white Reena and began to disavow her own last name. She knew Dak had gone through many transformations since those early years in Huzuni before he ever met the white Reena Pavane that he would come to love so desperately. He and that Reena had shared something neither one would speak of. Not even in Jim Stone's red book could she find the details of Reena and Dak's relationship. But both of the Stones had loved him, an odd triangle in anyone's eyes.

But between that Reena and Jim, there was a divine light. They had been together more than three decades now, with a strange eight-year separation after Dak had let Jim believe she was dead. How could such a betrayal be forgiven? That took a profound love among the three.

All at once, Reena missed her white friends. They had stood with her at Dakimu's confirmation and for his first communion at St. Joseph's. She remembered Jim embracing Dak and saying, "Much peace to you, my dear friend." Later that night, Dak killed the two white men, and his peace was shattered forever.

While she helped Safina get ready for bed, she tried to figure out what words she could use to find the Stones. She could write something for the newspaper like— *Found: red, leather book on Kipele Street. Will return to author only at St. Joseph's Sunday mass* or *White patient left wallet in room 110. Call R. P. to identify.* Heaven knows there hadn't been very many white patients at that hospital. If the Stones still read the news from Dar es Salaam, wherever they were in the world, would they dare answer? How many lives would she be putting at risk by doing this?

"Mama, what are you thinking?" Safina asked. She snuggled under the soft covers made by her grandmother who used to live in Huzuni but whom she never knew.

"I'm thinking of school and all the wonderful things you'll learn, the friends you'll make," Reena lied.

"I only need Suzanna," her daughter said.

"Oh, no, baby, you'll need lots of friends, black and white."

"I don't think so. Suzanna is my sister from another life," she said with confidence.

"Who told you that?" Reena asked.

"That slow lady at the market where we saw my brother."

"Safina, you shouldn't speak to her!"

"But, why? She's sad and lonely. She likes us. Sometimes she gives us treats that she makes at home with green candies on top.

Sometimes I brush her hair. Suzanna is afraid of her, and the lady keeps her head down. She won't look at anyone, but she looks at me. When I have my fingers in her hands, she smiles."

"Oh, Lord, Safina, won't the world spare you?"

"Spare me what, Mama?"

"Its terrible secrets," Reena whispered as her innocent child lapsed into her own dreamland, where green meant grass and big trees and plant-choked estuaries on the Indian Ocean, never the sign of the fierce and unknowable Chui, the Leopard people, of whom her half brother was probably one.

Later, Reena could not sleep. She dug out the red book from its hiding place and opened it to a random passage. Jim was describing the days when he first contracted malaria and could only find help among the blacks he had come to know while photographing their village life and documenting their ways of hunting, building huts and schools and churches, and caring for their families. One scene was so powerful Reena read it twice, not because it was so vivid but because it showed the depth of Jim's insight into the country he was sent to journalize.

He had been very ill, unable to eat, but he was aware of the natives, one or two, with him at all times. They caressed him with cool cloths. They helped him swallow a cure made from the bark of the ironwood tree. They built up the fire when he shivered and kept robes as soft as velvet over him. He didn't know their names, but they held his head and murmured words in a language he barely knew.

One day, I was able to walk around the camp. I felt like crying. They were so poor, but they would be dancing in marvelous skirts of reds and purples and golds. They would be roasting rabbits and corn and sweeping the dirt around their huts. I felt poor in comparison. Then I was startled into another reality when the men who had carried me and bathed me, each one at different times would catch up to me on my slow traverse of their world and take one of my hands. We would walk along together like that. I was surprised, then honored, then loved, then accepted as a brother. I can never give back what these Tanzanians gave me. I can barely understand it, but if ever I can show mercy to any one of them, I shall lay down my life to do it.

Reena found tears on her face. *Oh, I must find Jim again*, she thought. His wife had tried to tell the black people a story of salvation, a story of a white God, but Jim had let the blacks heal him with *their* stories, *their* prayers. He was the one who could help her now. Her hand flew to the gold cross around her neck. *Oh, that is not fair*, she thought. *I am a Christian. I only find things to criticize in the missionary because Dakimu loved her!*

Reena typed out the message on her old typewriter and put a leopard stamp on the envelope. These words would be seen in the *African Tribune—Need mercy now from author of the red book, room 110, Good Samaritan Hospital.* She would ask Mbulu if they could leave that room empty for a week or two. She would open that door every day with ardor and hope.

§ § §

Suzanna Farley waited for the school bus on the designated corner a few feet from the entrance to the Post. She stood alone, shivering in the early morning air. Even children she knew were huddled in little groups that seemed closed to her. Someone laughed and pointed her way. Her breakfast came up in her throat, but she was able to swallow it down.

Safina would be on the bus already, as it stopped at Soko Street first. With Safina she'd be okay. They had planned for this day, Suzanna's first day at the Light of the World Catholic School. Safina had promised to stay with her as much as possible, but Suzanna knew the black girl already had other friends who would want her attention.

Suzanna had taken some of her mother's face paints and practiced mixing the right color to mask the birthmark. But this morning in the dim light of her bathroom, she couldn't see to get it right. Nothing would truly ever hide the blistery red that marred her face, marred her heart. When she was with Safina, she almost forgot about it. Now she ached for the school bus to appear. There were some parents on the corner fussing over their children, checking backpacks to make sure they hadn't forgotten anything, and tucking their white blouses or shirts into navy skirts or pants. They ignored her too.

Earlier, Suzanna's father had left on patrol after wishing her well and giving her a quick hug, but her mother lay mumbling to herself and pushing toast around on her plate like a spoiled child.

"Where are you going then?" she asked in a petulant voice.

"I'm going to school."

"You don't go to school," Felicia said. "Who will take care of me?"

"Mrs. Vinton from next door, remember? Father made arrangements for you. You shouldn't worry."

"But what will people think of you?"

"I don't know, Mother, but I'm going. I can't stay in this bungalow the rest of my life."

She had waved her hand at her daughter as if in dismissal, and Suzanna turned and fled. Being in school could never be as bad as being in that room. Maybe she should have stolen one of her mother's pills, as she herself felt anything but calm. That was thirty minutes ago, and the bus still had not come.

"I hope she sits in the back," a boy said.

Suzanna pulled the hood of her sweatshirt halfway down over her face and decided to go back home. She couldn't do this. She tried the hardest she ever had not to cry because she was afraid tears might wash off the makeup. Then the yellow vehicle rounded the corner and rumbled toward them.

Everyone lined up at the curb, jostling each other to be first through the door to get the best seats. Suzanna went to the end of the line. Then she looked up and saw Safina's face in a window. Her hair was braided and tied with a thin, green ribbon. She would find out later that Safina's mom had burned a whole scarf of green, but Safina had already cut off a small strip and hidden it under her pillow. When Suzanna finally climbed on the bus, Safina was holding her hand out to her and wouldn't let anyone else sit next to her.

"This one's saved, this one's saved," Safina said over and over until Suzanna reached the seat and clasped her hand with relief.

"Are you okay?" her friend asked.

"I'm okay now," she said, and did not let go of Safina's hand until they were going down the school bus steps and walking toward the massive buildings of the Catholic institution.

Suzanna noticed the odd sensation of becoming aware of her birthmark the moment Safina released her hand. Then the nun who was to be their second grade teacher tried to separate them by seating Safina in the front and Suzanna in the back of the classroom.

"No," Safina said. "She's with me."

"I think you'll do as I say," the sister said firmly.

"No! This is her first day at school ever. I'm her best friend," Safina said, and grabbed her hand again to the astonishment of the white nun.

"All right. All right," she said. "Please yourself … this time." She gave them a hard look.

Suzanna let Safina find her a place at the end of one row, and then she took a seat directly in front of Suzanna as if she would be a shield, a shield from too many questions, a shield from the eyes of strangers, a shield from the remarks of insensitive children. Suzanna felt the birthmark blend a little better into her white skin, and she knew then that no matter what happened, she would always love the black girl.

§ § §

Reena answered a call from Major Farley quite early one morning just as the long rains started. He sounded frustrated. He said that Safina better not come over after school that day, that Suzanna's mother was quite unwell. Reena could hear his daughter crying in the background.

"What is wrong, sir?" Reena asked.

"We don't know for sure, mama. Something she read in the paper set her off, made her ... inconsolable."

Maybe it was the woman who was weeping.

"What could she have seen?" Reena persisted.

"Well, it doesn't make any sense to me. All she'll say, between gasping for breath, is 'The red book lies, the red book lies.' The doctor is coming to sedate her, and I have to go out in this damn rain with a search party. Suzanna will have to stay with Felicia," the major said matter-of-factly.

"Felicia?" Reena said hoarsely.

"Yes ... my wife."

"Oh, I'm sorry, sir. Can I help?"

"Well, in a week or so, we're going to take Jester out of the sling. Felicia should be better by then, and I know Safina wants to be here to see the horse walk on his own. Perhaps you could bring her out Saturday afternoon.

"Yes ... I'll do that."

Reena hung up the phone and sat in stunned silence. Then she got up and walked deliberately to the closet where high on a shelf she kept the reports from *that* time. She sat right there on the floor and carefully turned the pages in the old notebook where she had pasted the news articles until her eyes found what she was afraid to see—that name, Felicia, staring back at her from the print, from the story of the widowed *Felicia Sommers*, devastated by the loss of her husband to the murderer Dakimu Reiman, being held without bail for killing David Sommers and Jason Highback. In the photo, the woman looked about six months pregnant.

"Oh, sweet Jesus," Reena whispered. She had suspected *something*. She had dreaded *something*. She had not wanted to know. The woman was now the wife of Major Fulsom Farley. Suzanna was the daughter of David Sommers. There was the unequivocal truth of all their lives.

Reena scanned the rest of the articles, but it was never mentioned, the reason David Sommers had been at the Point that night. Dakimu had killed his father, John Sommers, during the Massacre in the early sixties. War is war, and gruesome things happen, but David had arrived in Dar es Salaam twenty-some years later with vengeance in his heart.

"Mama! Mama!" Safina was crying.

Reena rushed in to her. "Baby, what's wrong?"

"I had a dream about Suzanna! She was black, all black, but her birthmark was white! It was awful. I got scared."

"Why, baby?"

"I like Suzanna just the way she is. I don't want her to change."

"Safina, it was just a dream. Dreams don't come true. You'll be all right," Reena tried to assure her. But she knew that things could change without warning.

The day Jester came out of his stall was a near disaster. It had been raining for three days, and the ground was muddy and slick. The girls stood close by hugging each other against the bitter air and their fear for the horse. That was all Safina had talked about that morning.

"What if Jester can't walk? What if he falls down? What will they do to him?" she asked.

Reena knew the answer to that all too well. In this country, animals that could not work were put down, but at least their flesh might feed the poor or the dogs. Now, as the moment arrived, Reena stayed in her car some distance from the scene, trusting Fulsom to watch out for their girls.

But at first, everything seemed to go well. A soldier, maybe Jester's personal rider, led him down the long aisle between the stalls, then turned him into another stall, and Reena lost sight of them for a moment. The horse had moved soundly, Reena thought. Then Jester appeared in the open doorway and stepped cautiously out into the slippery footing. Reena threw a hand to her mouth. Safina and Suzanna were sitting on his back! Fulsom was on one side, and another uniformed man was on the other side, steadying the children as they crossed the yard.

Jester behaved properly and importantly carrying his two little nursemaids with contained joy. But no one counted on Mrs. Farley. She raced out of her bungalow still in a nightdress that flapped crazily in the air and startled the recovered horse that had seen nothing for months but four wooden walls. The woman was screaming.

"Who is that black child? Get her off of there!" she cried.

But she needn't have asked because the horse obliged, swerving excitedly and spilling the girls to the ground. Reena reached for the door handle, but Safina and Suzanna scrambled to their feet laughing and covered with mud. She could hardly tell them apart. They were both a nameless brown.

Felicia screamed again. "Get that black away from Suzanna! Now!"

No one hurried to obey, and the girls stayed as tight as ever in their sisterly way. The men were trying to calm the horse, seeing that the children were okay. Major Farley said to his wife, "Felicia, go back inside. You're only making things worse."

She ignored him and said wildly, "Suzanna! Get away from her. Why are you touching her?"

"Because she's my friend."

"Friend? No black can be your *friend!* What have I taught you all your life!"

"You taught me to hate," Suzanna said, "but I can't do it."

"Why? Why? If you knew—"

"Because I love her," Suzanna broke in. She began to wipe the mud from Safina's face with one edge of her own blouse that was still clean.

Felicia Sommers Farley had been maimed by the deeds of a black man. That was certain. But for her to rail at Safina was almost more than Reena could bear. She wanted to strangle the woman but couldn't move. She must never let this mad woman see her. She must never allow her to know the identity of the black child in her yard.

Major Farley was shepherding the girls toward the barn

where there was a warm shower and possibly some robes they could wear until their clothes were washed and dried. Did Farley wonder why she hadn't gotten out of the car? Did he think she should be helping the girls?

Felicia was circling in the rain that had begun falling again and raising her fists to the sky. "No, no, no," she shouted.

The soldiers avoided her and vanished when her husband finally took her, resisting and hitting at him, back to their bungalow. Then Fulsom Farley came out and walked directly toward Reena where she remained motionless in the driver's seat. He got in the passenger side of the car but looked straight through the front window.

"I have been wondering about you for some time now. When Suzanna told me your name was Reena, I started remembering things. I remembered your face, your voice. But if you had stepped out of the car when the girls fell and my wife made a scene, I would have thought you were just any mama concerned for the safety of her daughter," he said softly. "But now I am reasonably sure that you are Reena Pavane, and Safina is the child of Dakimu Reiman."

"Oh God," Reena said.

"Here, now, in this car, you are going to tell me the truth. For the sake of our children. I will not repeat it." He paused. "Have you seen the boy Kiiku?"

"Yes," she said. "Not so much of a boy anymore."

"I suppose not. Do you know where he is?"

"No."

"Have you spoken to him?"

"Yes … in the market. His mother works for a vendor there. I believe she thinks fondly of our daughters."

"Hmm. She has never given us answers of any use."

"I'm sorry, Mr. Farley. I tried to keep Safina from getting so close to Suzanna. They seem bonded by something we cannot imagine," Reena said, feeling braver.

"Yes. I married Felicia before Suzanna was born. David's friends have left Tanzania. Most people, including the girl, believe

I am her real father. I love her, of course, as if she were mine. I knew David slightly. I did not approve of his witch hunt for Dakimu at the time, but the law did seem to be on Mr. Sommers' side. And then, he was killed."

"I was there," Reena reminded him. "Dak shot those men in self-defense. Suzanna's father would have killed us both."

"I suspected as much," Fulsom said. "I love my wife. Understand that. But I have no love for the black people of the Chui clan who stir up trouble, stealing and … I believe that boy took my black horse, Resolute."

"I've heard nothing about that," Reena said.

The major held up his hand and continued. "What I have seen between our daughters, however, is worth the world to me. Your child put my child's heart back together after years of Suzanna hating herself, her mark, being shy to make friends, to show herself in public. That Safina should be the daughter of Dakimu is not upsetting to me. I welcome the girl. But it would kill my wife. We are on a tightrope, you and I, so hear this, Miss Pavane. I will protect the children at all cost, even if that means ignoring your movements that might show me the way to either fugitive."

"Then you must not call me Reena Pavane," she said. "I have given Safina the name Patel to use in school. You could call me Mrs., or Mama, Patel."

"That I will do," he said. "I'll bring your daughter home when her clothes are dry."

"Thank you. Will the horse be all right?" Reena asked, not wanting the conversation to end just yet.

"I believe so. It was foolish of me to put the girls on him," he said, but didn't get out of the car. "I am praying for a good outcome for everyone, Mrs. Pa … tel. Truly."

"So am I, sir."

"Is there anything else you should tell me?"

Their warm breath in the small space was fogging up the windows, and the two of them, black and white, were enclosed in an elusive shelter.

Reena didn't answer right away. She felt she should tell him *something* but something that would not be damaging to anyone she loved.

"Mr. Farley … what Felicia saw in the paper … about the red book … that was my doing. I am looking for Jim Stone."

The major was silent for a moment, so Reena went on. "He's an old friend of mine, someone who helped me when I was floundering years ago. I … may need him again, to keep me focused on what I should do for my child in this … situation."

Finally the man looked at her. "Thank you for your honesty. I will keep my promise," he said. He stepped out into the drenching storm. He did not say good-bye.

In a few hours, Major Farley brought Safina home. The girl was in heaven over getting to ride Jester and seemed to have forgotten Mrs. Farley's ranting. But just before bed, Reena sat with her daughter for prayers, and the girl said. "Lord, please heal Suzanna's mother. I think only you can do it. And guard my brother, Kiiku … and my father, wherever they are. Oh, not the pretend *Patel* father, my *real* father. Amen. I'm too tired to say more, Mama."

"That's okay, dear one. You did fine. God knows what's in your heart even if you can't say all the words," Reena said.

Safina made the sign of the cross and crawled into her safe, warm bed. Somewhere in the night, her father and her brother, the wandering Chui, as Reena now understood, slept, aware that this Safina, this Ark, was not available to them.

four

$\mathcal{I}$n the morning, Reena asked her daughter if she thought she should stay away from the Post for a while. The girls seemed to be settling into school and avoiding Felicia, but Reena still could not process what had happened at the Post. She felt as if she were at the precipice of a crumbling cliff with no handhold, no rope to draw her away. Was that what she wanted Jim to be? A lifeline? She would do what she could in the face of Jim not appearing at all.

Safina said, "Mrs. Farley doesn't like black people. But I think I am all people."

"What on earth do you mean, child?"

"I have an Indian name, a black mother, a white sister, a black half brother, a slow-minded stepmother, a—"

"Stop! Safina, you are mixing things up. Can't you just be my black daughter?"

"Only if you tell me who my baba is."

"This is a secret. You can't tell anyone," Reena said.

"Okay, Mama."

"I am looking for a man who knows your father, even better than I do. I want him to speak to you about your baba."

"What's his name?"

"Jim Stone. He's an old friend who loves Africa very much, especially Tanzania," Reena said.

"Is he black?"

"No … he's white."

"Can I take him to meet Suzanna and Jester?"

"Well, maybe, but today I want you to stay with Father Amani after church while I go to work. He has some school things to give you. The sisters have been collecting notebooks, used uniforms, and colored pens and crayons."

"I only need green," Safina said. The subject of her father faded into the gray day. No surprise, Reena supposed, with all the directions her bright mind could go these days.

At Mass, Reena looked for Major Farley, and then she had a startling thought. What had he told Father Amani in his confessions? The priest could never tell her, even if it were vital to her safety. She supposed the man had a life that had nothing to do with her. How many promises had he broken? How close was he to finding Dakimu without any revelations from her?

She walked up the aisle toward the communion rail. Farley was not in the church. She took the bread and the wine faithfully, but it did not settle her as it usually did. Who was it? St. Paul, who had a thorn in his side? She crossed herself and went slowly back to her pew. She always sat in the last row where she and Dak had first touched and whispered words of love, made promises before he ever knew he had a son and that he would flee with him into the African wilds and leave her behind. Her truth ultimately sent him to jail where she had never had the chance to tell him she was sorry or that she was pregnant.

The service was over. Safina came out of Sunday school to give Reena a quick hug before her mother had to leave for Good Samaritan. When she looked into her daughter's eyes, she knew if she ever found the girl's father, she would never betray him again.

§ § §

Major Farley hated one thing above all others—betrayal. He'd been riding at the perimeter of the city for most of the day on a horse not nearly as tuned to him as Resolute. He swore out loud about losing that black horse. Now and then, his eyes turned toward the west, toward the montane forest and the place where his lover made her meager life. He missed her. It had been over a year since he'd climbed into her bed and allowed her to work her magic with her lips and hands and endearments. How easy it would be to swerve off the main track and ride in the shadows until he reached her modest dwelling.

It was a betrayal for sure—this heady and dangerous love—a sin against Felicia, his Church, his God. And so he was loathe to perpetrate another—to break his promise to Reena Patel that he would turn a blind eye to her activities and destinations. But oh how he wanted that Dakimu, to see him suffer as his family had, to see him pay for his crimes.

He was near a black settlement. A stooped, old man pushed a cart full of vegetables down a dirt lane strewn with trash. Emaciated dogs fought over an old bone. A woman marched proudly past him bearing a water jug on her head. And then there were the children, running in ragtag gangs, thin as the dogs, wide-eyed, the girls holding hands. *Holding hands,* he thought suddenly, remembering the last time he saw his white child holding Safina's black hand. Even though there seemed to him to be little blatant racism in this country he had called home for half his life, it was still an incongruous sight. But the black girl had drawn Suzanna out of her shell, and for that, he was grateful. For now, he would honor his bond with the girl's mother, but if he found that she was his best or only lead, he would follow her to hell itself to have Dakimu behind bars.

He thought of Reena reaching out to Jim Stone. He remembered the man vaguely, mostly because he had written an amazing book that no one knew whether to believe or not. Someone told him once that Stone had reported that British commanders had put Tanzanians who had fought side by side with them against the Nazis in World War II into concentration camps when they returned home. Farley hated that that might be true. Talk about betrayal. He didn't like looking back too far in history. Some acts could not be reconciled.

He was struggling with the facts of the crimes of two blacks a mere eight years ago. It was all he could do to chase after Dakimu and Kiiku and hold his little family together, support Suzanna as she met challenges at school, support Felicia when the pain of the past became too much for her. His own comfort would have to wait. He turned his horse reluctantly toward the base, missing the floating gaits of Resolute.

§ § §

On Thursday of that week, Reena arrived at Good Samaritan early. Dr. Mbulu was waiting for her when she entered the hospital. He led her to the uninhabited room 110, touched her cheek with one hand, and left her outside the door.

She opened it cautiously. *What is happening?* Jim Stone was standing at the window. He turned, and Reena reeled at the sight of his aging but still beautiful face. He was alone, and he waited for her to speak. She put her hand to her heart and could only say, "Jim."

"My dear Reena … what can I do?"

She collapsed into the nearest chair and put her hand over her eyes. The sight of her old friend approaching from the window with the African sun streaming in behind him was overpowering. She didn't know where to begin. He sat down opposite her and put his hand on hers.

"Oh, Jim, Safina is asking about her father," she said, and then she realized Mr. Stone had no idea what she was talking about.

He smiled. "Is there maybe another thing you should tell me first?"

"Dak and I have a child. Of course, you wouldn't have known that. The thing is I can't shelter her forever. There are so many truths I don't want her to hear. Oh, Jim, I can't bear this anymore."

He asked her to explain what she must bear and what she

needed him to do. He told her he had only a few days. He was on a special assignment and was meeting his wife in Amsterdam that week.

"Are you both well?" Reena asked. She shouldn't think only of her problems.

"Yes. Sometimes the malaria flares up, but there are good meds now," he said.

She squeezed his hand and then looked into his eyes. This white man she loved. Maybe that was all she needed to know, that she could still love the white man who drove her black love from her forever.

"Tell me more, Reena," he said.

"Safina has a friend she loves like a sister … a white friend."

"And?" Jim said

Reena held his hand even tighter. "She's the daughter of David Sommers."

"Oh dear God," Jim said. He seemed to have trouble breathing for a moment. "Does anyone else know who Safina is?"

"The girl's stepfather, Major Fulsom Farley. He's promised to keep it to himself for the sake of the children … and for his deranged wife, Felicia Sommers! But I don't have a good feeling about it. Safina should hear about her father from *you*, not from some old news reports or some history lesson at school. I don't understand Dakimu the way you did. I don't even know where he is."

"I don't know either, Reena. And I couldn't tell you if I did because another betrayal could kill him, literally. Does he know about his daughter?"

"I think he does by now. We saw Kiiku in the marketplace, quite by accident. He gave us presents and wanted to know her name. Then later, I told Safina he was her half brother."

Jim stood up and paced the room. He seemed to be wiping tears from his eyes. Then he said, "Reena, what are you most afraid of?"

"I'm afraid she'll try to find Dakimu. You see, she's beginning to fill her life with the brokenhearted. She'll think her father is one of those … even if he isn't."

"Take me to her," he said.

"I'll be off at three today. Can you come home with me?"

"I will," he said. "Shall I wait here? I'm a bit weary from the flight."

"Of course. I'll bring you some tea and something to eat."

Reena spent the day in a haze of fear. Putting her daughter and Jim Stone in the same room held unpredictable consequences. The only white adult Safina knew was Fulsom Farley. He had been tolerant of her but not personal. Jim would tell her about her father. And he would love her instantly, just because she was Dak's child. *Will he tell her the whole truth*? she wondered.

The day seemed endless, but at last she signed out, and she and Jim drove to her apartment on Soko Street. They climbed the stairs, and as soon as they were inside, she called the base and asked if someone could bring Safina home. Her daughter had been going home with Suzanna in spite of Reena suggesting the girls spend some time apart. They had their own ideas about friendship.

In a few minutes, she and Jim heard Safina in the stairwell. She was laughing at something a neighbor said. "Oh, I wish her father could hear that sound," Jim said.

Reena opened the door. Safina ran into her arms. "Mama! Mama! Who is this?"

"My friend, Jim Stone."

"You knew my father!" Safina said to him.

"Yes. Your father was like a brother to me," Jim said, but he looked uneasy, wiping some sweat from his brow.

He surely would not want to lie to a child, especially the daughter of Dakimu, the man with whom he had exchanged many lies in their past.

"Do you know *my* brother?" Safina asked.

"Not as much as I'd like to," Jim answered.

"Do you know his name? Do you know about his clan of the green ribbon?"

"Safina, I've told you that for your brother's safety we should not mention the green sash. Neither should you speak his name," her mother warned.

She dropped her head. Jim Stone reached out and took the girl's hand. "Tell me about your white friend."

"Oh, I love her … and she needs me. Her mother is … like a sad horse."

"A sad horse?" Jim looked at her quizzically.

"Yes. She has to take pills that keep her quiet. I don't think she likes me, but I'm thinking of songs to help her."

"What kind of songs?" Jim asked.

"I sang hymns to the horse, and he got well. So I could sing to Mama Farley and make her well," Safina said.

"What was wrong with the horse?" he asked.

"Oh, he had a broken leg."

"Perhaps not as easy to heal a broken heart."

"I can do it," Safina said confidently.

If anyone can, maybe Safina will be the one, Reena thought.

There was a long silence.

"Can you stay for dinner, Jim?" Reena asked.

"That would be lovely," he said. "I see you have a place to view the Indian Ocean, just as my wife and I did at the Imperial Arms."

"I couldn't get that scene out of my heart," she said. "We've moved several times since I last saw you, but when I found this apartment, it brought back so many good memories."

He nodded and turned to Safina. "Shall we sit together over there? I'll tell you more about your father."

"Oh yes!" she cried.

Reena stayed in the kitchen slicing vegetables to pan fry with plantain and rice, but she caught words about proud warriors resisting white control, kings and children of kings defending their traditions. *The story of the world*, she thought. She heard again his personal feelings about Tanzanians and the selfless things they had done for him, which she well knew. Then Jim told

Safina about her father bringing him medicine for his malaria and saying that he had a black heart.

"What does that mean?" she asked him.

"It means we were truly like brothers at that time. But we each told a lie to the other and didn't see each other for many years."

"Were you sad?"

"Very sad, darling. But our reunion was so wonderful. We hugged and hugged and cried together."

"Where were you?"

"About a hundred miles from here where there stands a big cross in a mission village."

"Oh, that means you forgave each other. You loved each other."

"That we did, my girl, that we did."

And then Reena heard details that even she didn't know—that Dak had wanted to kill Jim and his white Reena in America, but instead they helped him escape to Africa and threw the gun in a big river. And of this story, he asked Safina not to remember the words *kill* or *gun* but the word *love*.

"*Upendo*," Safina said. "The love made up for the lies and saved you all."

"I'd like to believe that," Jim said.

"Will you find my father now?" she asked.

"I'll try, but only if it doesn't compromise his life."

"I don't understand," Safina said. She had moved closer to him on the couch, Reena noticed as she set the dinner plates on the table in the living room. Was she really too young for this conversation?

"I won't tell you where he is if he might die because of it," he said.

"I'll find him myself," she said.

"Safina," Jim responded quickly, "your father loves you and can send you that love from far away. There will be a day for you to meet. You must ask your god to keep your voice and your feet still for now."

"My god? Isn't he your god too?"

"I don't know, sweetheart, but I do know your father became a Catholic. My wife and I were there with him as well as your mother. He took communion and knelt at the altar at St. Joseph's. If you listen very carefully in the sanctuary, you might hear him say, '*Kyrie eleison. Christe eleison.*'"

"Oh, I will!" she said, and then she threw her arms around him.

Reena went over and caressed his shoulder. He tried to keep the tears from falling but couldn't in the end. He told her he'd put his African life behind him and felt helpless in many ways. He said his wife had done the same. "We lied to save Dakimu, and then he was spirited away. We look at each other and wonder what we could have done differently. There are never any good answers," Jim admitted.

"But what about you and Reena? Still so deeply in love?" she asked him.

"Our love is our salvation," he said.

After dinner, he said he should go, he had calls to make but that he would come to them again and give them what they wanted if he could—a pathway to Dak.

Two days passed and no word from Jim. But one night, there was another package at their door. Reena let her daughter open it, supposing it was from Jim, that he had missed them somehow. But it seemed to be from Kiiku, who must still have been prowling their neighborhood and in severe danger. Safina gasped when she found the plush toy leopard in its plain, brown box. The animal's eyes seemed to match hers. There was no note.

But they had no time to figure out that mystery as there was someone pounding on their door. Reena opened it partway. Major Farley stood there trying to hold Suzanna who was limp in his arms.

"Mama Patel, can you help her? I can't take care of Felicia and this sick child. You are a fine nurse, I have heard. Just for a few days. She must be well for school. She is so far behind."

"Of course, Mr. Farley. Leave her with me."

"I'd be pleased for you to call me Fulsom," he said.

There was only one bed besides hers, and that was Safina's, so they took her down the hall lined with Jim's photos and laid her gently on the fresh, white sheets. The girl lifted her head and said, "Safina."

Reena's daughter instantly put her new leopard in Suzanna's arms before Reena had a chance to hide it under the floorboards. Safina had already brought cool cloths from the bathroom and had pressed them to her friend's feverish forehead. Then she began to tell her a story about the stuffed animal in a comforting voice.

The adults stepped back into the kitchen where Reena set out some ingredients, modern and tribal, for a healing soup. Helping the girl would be easy. Farley was an unknown factor. Helping him could only be a generous thing that perhaps he would remember in times to come.

"Mrs. Patel," he began formally, "one of my men saw a white man here a few days ago."

"Yes."

"Does that mean anything?" he asked.

"It was an old friend," she said.

They looked at each other through the steam rising from the pot on the stove.

"Can you tell me his name?"

"I think you know. He's leaving the country in a few days. It wouldn't make any difference. He doesn't know what you want to know."

"Are you sure?"

"Yes. Because if he did, I'd be on my way there at this moment," she said.

"You still love that black fugitive?"

"I have his child," she said simply, as if that would answer all his questions.

"I'll go then. Thank you for taking care of my child. Her mother was shrieking and hallucinating. I'm not sure what she would be like if she knew where I had brought Suzanna," he said.

"Is there no hope for Felicia?" Reena asked.

"To bring her husband's killer to justice, I suppose. For her child to know the truth that she doesn't know how to tell … or has forgotten, pray God," he said.

"If I can't help Suzanna, I'll take her to my hospital," Reena said.

"God bless you. I am indebted."

"No, sir. We shall remain equal in all things."

"Goodnight then."

"Goodnight."

Reena stirred the shaman's soup and prayed to her Catholic God. *We are not exactly equal,* she thought suddenly. *I will not tell all I know, but I will give more than you expect.*

She went back to the bedroom.

"Mama, Mama, Suzanna's tummy was sick, but I cleaned it all up and gave her a little water. She's sleeping now."

Safina embraced her friend as if she might break, pressing the soft covers around her and letting her own black, unbraided hair fall over the birthmark on Suzanna's right cheek. It was a scene Reena would cherish.

In the morning, the white child seemed better but still couldn't keep any food down. Safina held her so many times that Reena was afraid her daughter would be sick too, but she wasn't. She remained strong. One time she said to the prostrate Suzanna, "This is how you do penance for lies, suffer with someone you love." Reena was sure Father Amani had never told her such a thing.

The girls slept together and seemed to find ease for their separate sorrows. They said the Lord's Prayer, Safina in Swahili and Suzanna in English. Reena heard Suzanna say, "I wonder how many languages God knows."

Her daughter said, "He knows all the words in all our hearts."

She has learned that well, Reena thought, turning the lights out on the fourth night. At the end of the fifth day, Major Farley appeared again.

"Your daughter is well, sir," Reena said.

"I knew she would be," he said.

Suzanna came out of Safina's bedroom with the stuffed leopard.

"Oh no, dear, that is Safina's. You must leave it," the major said.

"She gave it to me," his daughter said, clutching the animal to her chest.

"There are reasons—" he began.

"I believe it is a harmless toy," Reena said to turn Farley in another direction.

"Perhaps because it is a *gift,"* he relented.

"Yes … no one will think anything of it," Reena said.

"Only the Chui in the hills," he whispered for her ears alone.

"Maybe."

"Mrs. Patel, I know you've not been letting Safina come home with Suzanna every day, encouraging them to make other friends, but would you reconsider? Felicia is on heavy medication. I believe I can keep her from seeing your daughter and causing a scene. I know you need someplace for her to go after school while you are working besides St. Joseph's."

Reena felt trapped. She had thought of having Safina go to a daycare center instead of the church, but it was very expensive. Being at the Farleys put Safina so close to a painful truth. But there was just as terrible a truth Fulsom must keep from Suzanna.

"I will agree to try it again," she said at last. "And, Fulsom, you may call me Reena."

She imagined she saw a flicker of understanding on his face—that they needed to trust each other for the well-being of their children.

§ § §

School had only been in session a few weeks when Safina heard a commotion near the perimeter of the playground. She raced to the chain-link fence where Suzanna huddled against stinging pebbles and insults, her arms already cut and bruised, her face wet with tears.

"Witch!"

"Cursed-face!"

"Monster!" children called in cruel unison, black and white alike.

Safina burst through their ranks, stepped purposefully in front of her friend, and threw her arms straight out to her sides. She looked like a little brown cross planted in the ground, defiant and holy.

"Get away from her!" Safina cried, dodging small rocks and sticks that battered against her.

Suddenly the missiles of torment started falling short of the two girls, and that scared the bullies into a grumbling retreat.

"Who is that black girl anyway?" someone asked.

"Safina Patel. She's a half-breed," another answered derisively.

"She's a troublemaker."

"She's crazy."

"I think she's brave, taking those rocks for the white girl," one of them said.

Safina led Suzanna toward the nurse's station. The white girl seemed to be in some kind of shock, so when Sister Abigail saw the girls and demanded, "Safina, what have you done to Suzanna?" she couldn't say a word. The nurse shook Safina hard and called for an aide to help clean Suzanna's wounds. Some were quite deep. Reena's daughter did not cry or defend herself.

Finally, Suzanna grabbed Sister Abigail's arm. "She saved me," she managed to get out in a choked voice.

"What?"

"She ran between the boys and me. The stones hit her too—look!" And Suzanna pointed to a bloody place on Safina's cheek.

"Oh my goodness, what is wrong with those boys, attacking little girls," the nun cried.

Safina did not want to mention the birthmark or the racism that made most of the children wary of her friendship with Suzanna. But Safina finally spoke up, now that she seemed to have an adult's attention.

"Sister Abby," she began, "some of the nuns and the teachers are always trying to separate us. We're not allowed to sit together in class or eat lunch at the same table. There are black groups and white groups for everything, never mixed together. I had my arm around Suzanna one day when her tummy hurt. The black kids always steal her food or make her eat something off of the floor. The white kids told me I'd better stop hanging onto her or 'You'll be dirtier than you already are.' Those are their exact words. We're best friends, like sisters almost. Why is that bad?"

The nun, who was white and not a racist, tried to explain to the girls that the school had rules for segregation because the parents wanted it that way. They were afraid of people who were different and thought it best for each child to associate with his or her own color. "I don't believe in that myself, but I am only one voice," she said.

"Now there are three," Safina said quietly.

Sister Abigail called Mr. Farley to come get them, and when he arrived, the white principal, Mr. Keppler, known to be an authoritarian and insensitive man, rushed out of his office to greet the important major. Safina smiled secretly when she saw that Suzanna's father did not take Keppler's outstretched hand and shouted at him, "Are you trying to set our culture back decades?"

At the Post, he half-carried both bandaged children into bungalow number eight and said, "Children, Mrs. Farley is asleep now. If you play quietly, she won't know you're here together. And Safina, Sister Abigail told me how you stood between Suzanna and those bullies. I won't forget it," he said.

Safina sat on the couch holding Suzanna's hand. "We will be leopards," Safina whispered, and they both reached for the stuffed toy that had been kicked absently to the foot of the sofa. When they looked up, Suzanna's mother was leaning over them. They skittered apart, leaving Safina with the leopard in her hands.

"Who *are* you?" Felicia demanded.

"I am Safina Patel," she lied coolly.

"Why are you in my house?" Her voice was steely but not crazed.

Suzanna got up carefully. "Mama, Safina is my best friend."

"How can that be? A black man was the ruin of us all," she said, her words as cold as ice.

Safina remembered her saying those words before. Felicia continued to stare at her. "I think you've been here before, with Suzanna, on the horse!"

Just then Major Farley came in.

"The ruin … the ruin," his wife was mumbling.

"Now, Mother," Farley said, "the girls don't need to hear all that. It was a long time ago. It has nothing to do with them. Let's go lie down." He gently guided her back to bed.

Suzanna threw her arms around Safina. "I'll tell Mama what you did for me. She can't hate you then," she said.

"But what about what the black man did? Maybe she'll always hate him," Safina said.

"I don't care. Daddy said it was a long time ago."

"It was before you both were born," Major Farley said, reentering the room. "I explained to Mother how Safina took those rocks for you today, Suzanna. She said, 'I have misjudged that girl. What a brave thing to do!' So she will not forbid Safina to be in this house."

Suzanna grabbed the stuffed animal from Safina and tossed it at her father. "Who is the *chui* now?" she bantered.

Fulsom froze. "Where did you hear that word?"

Suzanna laughed. "It means *leopard* in Swahili, silly," she said.

"I know what it means," Farley said, and his voice seemed colder than his demented wife's. He turned and asked Safina, "Where did you get this anyway?"

"It was in a box by our front door," she said, unaware of his intent.

Then he softened. "I'm glad you gave it to Suzanna. It is safer with her."

"But who would want it?" Safina asked, confused.

"No … I mean Suzanna is safer having it than you."

"Why?"

"The Chui is the name of a tribe who may be harboring a criminal," he said.

"The *black man*?" Safina asked.

"*A* black man," he answered. "Maybe not *the* black man. Now, go play. Mrs. Patel called and will be late from work. You are to have dinner with us, Safina."

The girls clapped their hands, the day's trials all but forgotten. But Safina watched Major Farley escape to the kitchen and pour himself a large glass of whiskey.

At school, things got better. A few children who admired Safina, black and white, began to follow the girls around and wanted to know their secrets. Some of the boys told Safina and Suzanna they were sorry they had thrown the pebbles at them. Safina noticed one day in the yard that a small, black boy with one leg shriveled by polio was steadied at the baseball plate by a big, white boy. The black could hit. The cheers of the crowd and his team brightened the crippled boy's eyes while another boy streaked for first base in his place. Black and white and Asian teachers began eating together in the lunchroom.

One day, the white girl with the glaring birthmark said to her black friend, "I think those rocks were worth it."

Safina put her hand on a place on her friend's arm that hadn't healed properly and bore a deep scar. "I was only trying to save you, not the whole world," she said.

After that, Safina turned her mind to the horse. She and Suzanna brushed Jester and took him for walks every day. Safina asked Major Farley if they could have riding lessons on one of the older mounts.

The major's eyes twinkled. He said, "Why not have lessons on Jester? It will help fit him up for service, and he's a gentle creature."

"Will Mother scare him again?" Suzanna asked.

"I think not, dear. She's quite amenable to my wishes these days. We should take advantage of that."

After Mr. Farley dropped her off at home, Safina raced up the stairs wanting to spill the whole story to her mother about all the things that had been happening, but Reena had not even noticed the marks the rocks had made on her arms when she'd endured the bullying for Suzanna or the roughness of her hands from holding Jester's grooming tools day after day. Safina sensed that her mother was lost in some inner trouble and decided to save those words until another day. *I have my own secrets now,* she thought.

five

Reena ached for the signs from Kiiku. She made her way up the stairs after her shifts at the hospital, averting her eyes from her door until the last minute, collapsing against the frame if there was nothing there. It was her only tie to Dakimu, and she hoped, sooner or later, that the gifts would come from his own hand. But when there was a package or a box tied with a green ribbon, she made a sudden gasp and rushed to pick up the offering from Dakimu's son. At the same time, in those moments, she dreaded what that contact with Kiiku might mean for her daughter.

One time, she was startled to find a torn piece of paper with faint words shakily printed on it—*I saw what Safina did in the schoolyard. She's a Chui. Get the leopard back. K.* Reena crossed herself, went quickly inside, and buried the scrap in the cache under the floorboards. Then she sat on the couch and watched the Indian Ocean disappear in the sharp equatorial slide from day to night. She didn't want to know what happened in the schoolyard, about Suzanna's problems with her mother, or about that horse at the Post. She was being drawn out of her child's world by the inexplicable mystery of Kiiku.

Get the leopard back, Kiiku had written. *Why?* she thought now, in total darkness. And then, quite suddenly, she knew. There was something inside the stuffed animal, something that could lead Major Farley to Dak! And the toy was there in the man's house.

Safina was staying with the Farleys that night because the girls had a field trip the next morning, a long bus ride to a new Safari Park. The leopard would be safe mixed in with Suzanna's toys one more day.

As she lay in bed later, still restless and despairing, an idea began to form. Field trips. The Catholic School was known for taking its students on unusual tours, sometimes traveling hundreds of miles and spending the night with mysterious tribes or at historical missions. What if a trip to Arusha could be arranged? There were many attractions in that city—the Cultural Museum full of African artifacts and art; a National Park with the shy Colobus monkeys, elegant giraffes, and colorful flamingoes; and the renowned Shanga market, where handicapped artisans lived and worked, the place where Reena believed Dak could be.

She planned to get Father Amani involved, ask him to let her dress as a nun and accompany the children. She was sure the group would be followed, as the authorities knew the priest had a certain loyalty to Dak. Besides that, the routines of the Light of the World School were always noted.

The phone rang. Reena's heart began to pound. It was midnight. She reached for it and said into the receiver, "Jambo."

"Reena, it's Jim Stone."

"Oh, Jim, you scared me."

"I'm sorry … I didn't call you before I left Africa. I just wasn't myself … fever or something. Reena reminded me after I'd been home a few weeks that I was supposed to give you a message. She got a note from Dak about two years ago, the only one she ever received. It read—*In the cathedral are many perfect candles shaped of healing light; in one place stands a twisted pillar of wax whose flame shines not as bright.*

"Wait, let me write it down," she said.

He repeated the phrase—half poem, half clue to where Dakimu was hiding, she knew. But he had told Reena! His white Reena and no one else that she knew of. Her heart ached.

"Why, Jim? Why did he tell *her*?"

"I learned long ago not to guess what is between them. We

have to hold onto the love they have for us … always," he said. "Now I have to go. Love to you and Safina."

"Wait. Jim, are you all right?"

But he had hung up.

Reena did not read the lines from Dak again that night. She stuffed the paper, where she had carefully copied the words, into the hiding hole to save it for a day when its secret would jump off the page, maybe tomorrow, maybe in a year. She slept at last with her hands upon the gold cross she always wore around her neck.

She woke with the first light, thinking, *I have to get the leopard back.* Oh, those girls wouldn't understand. Maybe she could buy another one and switch them. Would the girls know the difference? She could put the one from Kiiku in the safe place, which had very little room now with all the surprises from him, Jim's red book, passports for herself and Safina, her nursing certificate, and a piece of sea glass from that day on the Indian Ocean, a reminder of Dak's embrace.

She need not have worried long. Safina and Suzanna had made up a new game that brought the leopard right into her hands. The girls both loved the animal, so they decided to give it back to each other when either one did a good deed. Sometimes the leopard changed hands more than once in the same day—when Safina showed Suzanna how to read new words; when the white girl fended off questions about Safina's *Indian* father; when one befriended an outcast or the other chose a misfit for the best side in a schoolyard game.

Those girls will change the world, Reena thought, *if it's not too late. They will change me, at least.*

After the Safari Park trip, where the friends had cried seeing a free, wild leopard that paused to look back at the children as he crossed the trail in front of the jeep, Safina came home with the stuffed leopard. She had moved over so a smaller child could see the amazing *but not scary, Mama,* beast. But Reena had to go to work, and by the time she returned thirteen hours later, Safina had given Suzanna the toy back for whispering in a teacher's ear that a new boy was afraid to tell her he couldn't see the blackboard from the last row.

Only Father Amani knew about the leopard game. Reena heard him tell the girls one Sunday that leopards were feared and that they should play the game quietly, not draw attention to themselves. She knew he was referring to the Chui warriors, the double meaning lost on Safina and Suzanna. But they complied as best they could, still obviously excited about helping people and each other. Reena could swear the white girl's terrible mark was fading.

Near the end of that school year, Safina set the leopard on her bed and told her mother that Suzanna wanted her to have it because of what she had done, something Suzanna herself could not do.

"What was that?"

"Mrs. Farley had a terrible headache today when we got home from school. Mr. Farley said we had to stay outside. But I asked him if I could see Suzanna's mama," Safina explained. "Mr. Farley took me to her bedside. She couldn't open her eyes, she felt so bad, so she didn't know it was me. I got my hands very cold under the water in the bathroom and put them against her head. I sang to her, but in just a few minutes, she reached up and caught my hands. 'Are you a nurse?' she asked. 'Are you an angel?' I was afraid to answer, but I leaned down and kissed her cheek. Her eyes flew open! Then I told Mr. Farley to bring me some lavender and red pepper leaves from the garden and burn some in a bowl. The smoke filled the room, and she asked me if I could also heal a broken heart. I said only God could do that. She sent me out to play with Suzanna, and just outside her mother's door, Suzanna gave me the leopard."

"How did you know about those herbs?" Reena asked.

"From Kiiku's mama," Safina said.

"Praise be to God," Reena replied.

Now Reena had the leopard before her, and she didn't know what to do. The girls were in school, and she had two days off. "Little leopard," she said, "tell me your secret." She turned the plush toy over and over. Her fingers seemed to feel a rough spot, perhaps thicker thread under his front legs, which were curled such that one paw lay slightly over the other.

She went to her sewing basket, collected small scissors, dark gold thread, and reading glasses. It would be fine work, stitches that had to be put back exactly as she had found them. She worked carefully. Slowly she opened a hole in the gold and black chest. Some stuffing fell out. Reena collected it and put it aside. She reached into the fake, fierce leopard, exploring with her fingers. She almost stopped, but there … just a bit deeper, she found the edge of something. She pulled. A rolled-up shard of brown paper came out with her trembling hand. She flattened it, and then she read—*In the cathedral are many perfect candles …*

"Holy Mother of God," she cried into the empty room.

She quickly sewed the hole in the leopard back to its original shape and placed the animal back on Safina's bed. Then she pried up the floorboards and retrieved the paper upon which she had written the words Jim Stone had given her over the phone. She lay the notes side by side and read the puzzling words again. They were exactly the same, except the one she had just discovered was signed *D.*

It wouldn't matter who had possession of the leopard now. Its secret was revealed and would be hidden with all the other evidence she had collected. She memorized the lines, running her hands over the words Dakimu had written with his bold strokes. How long had this clue resided in the innocent leopard? How long would Dak wait for someone to find it? Interpret it? Make the journey to *his* hiding place?

She would tell Father Amani in the confessional so he could not be forced to expose the cryptic rhyme. He could help her make sense of it, decide what to do. She gathered her purse and a long-sleeved sweater, and in a few minutes was in the rush-hour traffic of Tanzania's main port city. *Haven of peace, haven of peace,* she kept saying to herself amongst the hordes of shoppers, street sellers, taxis, buses, homeless and poor asking for alms, disfigured and lame begging for … *Christ! Disfigured and lame! A twisted pillar of wax … whose flame shines not as bright! Shanga! Dakimu is at Shanga!* If she didn't know it before, if she had only guessed at the clues, she knew it now.

Brake lights flashed in front of her. She came so close to hitting the taxi. Tears blinded her, and she almost turned around, but she needed to tell Amani this. She couldn't keep this secret alone, this dark knowledge of where the killer was, the father of her only child. She drove around the block several times, where St. Joseph's stood as an oasis in the teeming city, praying for a parking place. There was one quite far from the church, but Reena swung into the space, paid a slender, black youth to guard the car, and walked toward the cathedral with her head down. She was not in the mood to talk to friends or look strangers in the eye.

She entered the sanctuary and knelt at the last pew. There was a line outside the confessional, parishioners coming in on their lunch hour seeking a moment with the priest. Reena was anxious but did not stand with the others. Finally, the church was empty. She stepped into the chamber of confession and said, "Bless me, Father, for I have sinned."

"And what have you done, Reena?"

"I have found out where Dakimu is, and I have a plan to see him."

"That is not a sin," the priest said.

"My plan involves deceit … on your part too," she said.

"There is very little I can do then."

"It's a small request that will give Safina a great chance of meeting her father."

He sighed. "Tell me."

"I think Dak is at Shanga, living with the disabled. Safina's school, as you know, is always searching for good places for field trips. The children have never been to Shanga. It would open their eyes to so many disparities of life."

"I agree, but how can you and I go there?"

She told him her plan. He would begin to accompany the

students on a few outings so traveling with them to Shanga wouldn't be suspect. He would give her a nun's habit and treat her as a sister, perhaps along for training or taking the place of a nun who couldn't go that day. "I don't have it all worked out yet," she said.

"Reena, how did you find him?"

"Do you think you know, Father?"

"I do … but I believe I was given only half a clue," he said.

"What was that?" she asked.

"One line of a poem scratched inside a copper bracelet with designs on the outer band that are often seen on Shanga products. It was put in the collection plate last year, I don't know by whom. The line was, *In the cathedral are many perfect candles, shaped of healing light …*"

"*In one place stands a twisted pillar of wax whose flame shines not as bright,*" Reena finished without hesitation. Then she said, "Copper's tarnished color is green."

"Aha. It all fits now. I will help you and then confess to the bishop when he is here again."

"Can you trust him, Father?" Reena asked.

"I dearly hope so," the priest answered.

But the school year ended before any field trips could be arranged. Reena despaired. To have the clue and not be able to follow it haunted her waking and sleeping. Every day Safina met Suzanna at the Post. They rode the horses that were safe for them and spent hours with Jester. The big, brown gelding became part of their fantasy stories. One of the girls would say, "Jester won a race down to the sea and back!" The other might add, "We galloped in the waves and then tied him to a big piece of driftwood." The horse rose to every occasion they could dream up. His coat glistened with daily grooming.

His own soldier would come to exercise him and find that his gaits were strong and sound, his temperament settled and reliable. Reena was surprised when Fulsom allowed the girls to start riding him. The major went through several instructors before he was satisfied they could handle Jester and not be pushed too fast. The lessons seemed to consume them.

Reena wished she could have the same focus in her life, but imagining Dak somewhere near Shanga ate at her resolve to wait until the next school year. It also made her want to question Kiiku openly about what he knew about his father. She would not spare him any pressure.

She found him one day in the market helping his mother lift some boxes of vegetables from a truck. It seemed careless that he was showing himself like that. Reena knew Fulsom was keeping an eye on Soko Street, but that day he had taken Suzanna and Safina to an art gallery that had a new children's exhibit. How Kiiku would know that, she wasn't sure. Maybe he had a comrade at the base—a maintenance man or a gardener. Whatever the reason, Reena decided to take advantage. She stepped behind the curtain at his mother's stall, and he followed.

"Is Safina all right?"

"Yes, Kiiku, but I am not," she said.

"What's wrong?"

"I need to know where your father is. I mean it, Kiiku. He sent clues. You led me to clues. Why can't you just tell me where I can find him?"

"I took a vow," he said. "But I'll do anything for Safina."

"Well, he's always been absent to her. She hardly knows what she wants. She has an exaggerated idea of who he is. I loved him," Reena said. She glanced around to make sure no one had heard her, especially Kiiku's mother, who perhaps hated him.

"But do you *still* love him?" Kiiku asked.

Reena didn't answer. She had told herself she still loved him when the possibility of seeing him became likely after a distressing almost nine years of silence. She loved the man she remembered, but who was he now?

"I don't know," she finally said.

"Let's find out!" Kiiku said. "Get in the truck."

"What?"

"Get in the truck now! No one is watching. It may be your only chance. We're going to Arusha. It's a hard trip, many hours on the road. You can't tell anyone."

"Safina is with Major Farley," she said, stalling for time.

"I know," he said.

"I'll have to call him, say I'm with a patient, can he keep Safina for a few days. He'll be suspicious."

"It's risky. Can you do it?"

"Let's go," she said. She hardly understood why she agreed. She felt dizzy and disoriented. She looked at her clothes. She was dressed for the market, presentable but not how she would clothe herself to meet Dakimu after all these years.

As if he read her mind, Kiiku said, "You look beautiful."

§ § §

Safina asked Major Farley where she could get water. "I don't feel good," she said.

"What is it?"

"I need my mama."

"We just got here," he said. He shook his head.

She and Suzanna and Fulsom were standing in a line in front of an impressive art gallery. Neither girl had ever been there. A huge sign announced the special children's feature—Artists from Eight to Eighteen it read in bright colors. Safina focused on the green letters and felt better. The major had brought her some bottled water, which she swallowed gratefully in big gulps.

Mr. Farley had been promising them since school was out to visit the gallery. Safina didn't want to ruin her friend's day with her father. She would give anything to have one *hour* with her own father.

The line was moving now. Safina tried to concentrate on something else, to push the thought of a father far down in her consciousness. It made her sad to think that if they saw each other on the street, they wouldn't recognize each other.

"Shall we see the children's exhibit first?" the major asked.

"Oh yes," Suzanna said. "We have art next year. It will give us some good ideas."

Her father looked at Safina.

"Yes. I'd like that too," she said. "Thank you for the water."

He squeezed her shoulder gently, and she smiled at him. He was a caring father, she decided.

§ § §

Reena was given a burka and put between the Bantu driver, who everyone knew delivered vegetables from Manyara weekly as far as Dar es Salaam, and Kiiku, who kept one hand on the passenger door and the other on a semiautomatic rifle. They rocked along in silence until they were safely past military posts and armed checkpoints.

Then Kiiku said softly, "You might not like what you find."

"It doesn't matter now," she said. "I'm committed. But I have to call from the next town."

"Who will you call?"

"Dr. Mbulu. He can make my excuse sound real when he contacts Fulsom."

"And what excuse will you give the good doctor?"

"I don't know yet," Reena said.

"And wait a minute, you call the major *Fulsom*?" Kiiku asked. She saw him grip the rifle more firmly.

"Yes."

"God, woman. You don't know who you're messing with!"

"I know him well enough." She stared out over the grassy plain moving in its own sea-like way to lap against the montane forests far beyond. It calmed her.

The men bantered in Swahili. The driver, whose name she had not been told, drank a beer, but Kiiku reached over her and put his hand on the man's arm when he tried to open another.

"The truck will be returning to Dar in four days. Will that give you enough time for your errand?" Kiiku asked her.

"Leave me a mile from where he is. I'll find him," she said.

"I'll take you practically to his door. I make no guarantees after that."

"I must be crazy," Reena said.

They pulled into an isolated petrol station.

"Make your call," Kiiku said, "but be quick."

Dr. Mbulu, whom she had always known secretly cared for her, would deny her nothing.

"Of course I'll do as you ask. But we need you here," he said.

"I'll be back in a few days. Please don't worry."

"I always worry about you, Reena."

She glanced over at the two men who were delivering her into the unknown.

"I'm in good hands," she said.

They entered the outskirts of Arusha just before midnight. They had stopped several times to pick up men and boys, some with guns. The rough-looking people climbed in the back seemingly unaware of her.

"Are they Chui?" she asked Kiiku in a whisper.

"Most of them," he said. "You're safe with me. What'd you tell Mbulu?"

"That I was with a trusted friend," she answered. "I didn't say your name, of course."

"I may like you after all," he said.

She dropped the face veil in the darkness of the cab. "Kiiku, I couldn't lie … back then … at the trial," she told him.

"I guess you'll learn to lie now."

"Yes."

"You can't see my father tonight. I'll take you to my quarters. Tomorrow go to the glass blower's shop at Shanga. I have a job to do. You're on your own. The truck stops at Shanga on the way back to Dar at 6:00 a.m., Tuesday morning. Be there … no matter what."

"I will," she said. "Thank you."

"Don't thank me yet."

They pulled up to a small barn at the back of a coffee plantation.

"The owner is Chui. No one knows. In the morning, follow that path." He pointed to a trail leading through a grove of eucalyptus. "It comes out near some worker huts at Shanga. Someone can direct you to Dakimu's station. I hope you find what you need … for Safina's sake."

The truck rumbled away. Reena was so tired she didn't mind making a bed in some clean straw. Kiiku had given her half a sandwich, some bananas, and a carton of juice. There were some animals close by. They smelled like goats. At first she was cold, but the hay warmed her, and she fell asleep.

When the sun came through a dusty pane on the east side of the structure, Reena awakened instantly. She found a pump just outside and washed her face with sweet well water. She was hungry but too excited to eat. She brushed pieces of straw from her blouse and skirt. She was glad she had just had her hair cut because it was cropped close and didn't need much fixing. She knew that style made her eyes more noticeable and the shape of her face more attractive.

She found the trail easily enough and approached Shanga with eager steps. She could hear the artisans in the distance setting out their wares and greeting each other. She didn't have to ask. She located the glass blower's stall and sat down on a bench across the path from its open entrance. But there was no one there.

An hour passed. Her heart raced. Then she saw a tall, superbly dressed, beautiful native woman pausing outside the door. Reena looked away, but the woman spoke to her. "May I help you?" she asked.

"I am waiting for the glass blower," Reena said.

"Why?"

"Why should you care?"

"I am his wife."

Reena stopped breathing. She could not think what to say. The woman drew closer.

"Do I know you?" she asked.

"I don't suppose so … I am a friend who has not seen Dakimu for many years."

"But why do you think he is here?"

"I was told by someone who knows," Reena said, still marveling at the woman's beauty and her own disappointment.

"I can tell you that he is not here. He's been gone for several days. I do not know where. He has his private life. But I do protect him from strangers," she said.

"I'm not a stranger," Reena said, getting braver.

"Then who are you?"

A sudden breeze swept through the compound, shaking the wind chimes into sound and upending a cart full of beaded baskets close by.

"I am the mother of his child," Reena answered.

"That's not possible," the wife said. "I would know."

"Well, I didn't know about you. So you didn't know about me."

"I will have to wait for Dakimu before I can believe you," she said.

"I'll come every day, but on Tuesday, I will be gone."

And so the vigil began. The woman never told Reena her name. She sold glasses and bowls and ornaments to tourists. She brought food and water to Reena twice a day. Her demeanor softened, but distrust showed clearly in her eyes. Dakimu did not appear. Other shopkeepers asked her why she was there.

"I'm praying," she would say and show them her rosary, the prayer beads fashioned from sea glass that she and Dak had collected on the shore of the Indian Ocean. Of course, they couldn't know that, but they left her alone.

On Monday afternoon, the glass blower's wife sat down next to her and put an exquisite bowl in her hands. It had a stripe of green flowing through it like a jungle river twisting and turning around the glass. Reena was startled and ran her finger along the ridge of green.

"Did not a Chui bring you here?" the wife asked.

"Yes."

"Well then, he must know your child," the woman said, her eyes shining.

"Yes, and my daughter loves green. I'll give this to her," she said, knowing that the gift would probably go in the vault beneath her floorboards.

"Will you tell her who made it?"

"I don't know. Will you tell Dak I was here?"

"What's your name?" she asked.

"Reena Pavane."

"I thought Reena Pavane was white," she said.

"There is a white Reena Pavane. He knew her first. I was a poor substitute."

"I doubt that," the elegant woman said. She paused for a moment as if choosing her next words carefully. "Kiiku does not tell you everything. Neither have I told you everything. You should come back, if you can. Trust me," she finally said, and put her hand over one of Reena's that clutched the green-etched bowl.

Early the next morning, Reena hesitated by the empty glass blower's shop before she made her way to the entrance of Shanga where the rusty truck idled. She got in the passenger's side and placed the burka over her head and her arms through the black cloth. Some men were loading crafts in with the vegetables to be sold in Dar es Salaam. She watched but didn't see any boxes labeled glassware.

She fingered the bowl beneath her heavy garment. Dak's mouth had blown the unique shape, and his hands had added the green pigment. *Neither have I told you everything*, Dak's wife had said. Oh yes, Reena would return.

six

The field trips began when the girls started third grade. Sometimes Father Amani accompanied the children and sometimes not. Reena had not told him yet of her impulsive journey to Shanga or that she knew Dak was the glass blower there.

By the semester that began in February 1995, Safina and Suzanna had sailed on a dhow to Zanzibar, climbed in the foothills of Kilimanjaro and dug their own bits of tanzanite that had been formed three million years before when the mountain had been an active volcano, and stared into the diggings at Olduvai Gorge where perhaps all humans, black and white, had remains of common ancestors. Safina and Suzanna told Reena and Fulsom how that history made them feel like *real* sisters. They were all standing in the school parking lot with the tall cross at the entrance casting a shadow on them. The two adults peered over their children and looked at each other with despair. One child's father had killed the other's father and grandfather. Could even *sisters* encompass that into their love?

About that time, Felicia Farley began to ask about Safina's mother. Safina told Reena that she made excuses for her, saying her mother was too tired, she had a headache, or she had a long shift at the hospital. Reena had to ask her daughter why she didn't want the two women to meet. The girl couldn't know the reason herself.

Safina said, "Kiiku told me you would scare her for reasons he couldn't explain, just promise to keep you away from her. Do you know why?"

"No," she lied. "But maybe Kiiku knows something I don't." That was surely true and maybe would cancel the lie.

"Okay, Mama," Safina said.

"When do you see Kiiku anyway?" Reena asked. She had assumed Dakimu's son was out in the hills with the Chui clan, perhaps hiding with his father, not so often in Dar es Salaam. He had not left presents for months.

"Suzanna and I are friends with his mama. We take her leftover food from the school cafeteria and material and buttons the nuns don't want. If Kiiku is there, he always speaks to us. He speaks to us as one. We have no secrets from him," she answered.

Oh, that can't be true, Reena thought.

Safina went on explaining. "Suzanna knows that her mother might be afraid of you. But she thinks it's just because you are black. *I* know there's another reason."

"What if you couldn't be friends with Suzanna?" Reena asked, daring to approach a dangerous possibility.

"Oh, that will never happen! Mrs. Farley likes *me*. She doesn't see my black skin. Just my heart," she answered quickly.

"Which is perhaps the best heart the woman could see," Reena said with pride.

Just then, Reena remembered a line from Jim Stone's red book, *Memoirs on an African Morning.* He and Dakimu had become very close as prisoners of a famous warrior king in the early sixties. According to the account, Jim had treated the people in the village as friends, as afraid as he was of the demonic leader. One day, barely recovered from a devastating bout of malaria, he had helped a little girl carry a heavy pot of water from the river to her mother's hut. The jug had slipped once out of the child's hands, broken, and cut her foot. Jim wiped her tears, cleaned and wrapped the injured foot, and went back to the river with another vessel to fill for them to take to her mama. He'd chosen a place on the river where he could have vanished into the thick brush and escaped, but he came back, in some pain himself, and got the girl and the water jar safely to the mother's kitchen. Jim nearly collapsed by his own hut, and that's when Dak had said, "Sometimes I think you have a black heart." Jim had told Safina her father had said those words, but Reena hadn't remembered the whole story.

Could the words of that old journal be playing out in the lives of Dak's children and the white child who was the most innocent and yet could become the most brokenhearted of all?

"Safina," her mother began, "I believe I would frighten Mrs. Farley because I might remind her of that bad time in her life. But you should be her friend if you can. She must be very lonely. And I would never take you away from Suzanna. Sometimes things happen to friends as they grow up. I just don't want you to be hurt."

"Okay, Mama," she said. She scooped up the leopard and skipped away.

Reena could hardly think straight the rest of the day.

The rest of the year was not any easier. Safina could play openly in Suzanna's house, have meals with Felicia Farley in her prisonlike bedroom, and ride the beautiful Jester. She pictured the white girl catching Safina in her arms as she dismounted from the tall animal. Half of her longed to pay attention to her daughter's life. "Mama, we put up jumps today! Mine were a little higher than the ones for Suzanna, but the riding master said Suzanna had the best form over the fences. Jester loved it!" Half of her was poised for signs from Kiiku and distracted by the plans for the field trip to Shanga that she had devised almost a year ago.

Father Amani constantly checked with her about the details of the scheme. "We'll have two layovers," he said one day on the phone. "One in Arusha the first night and another in Dodoma on the return trip at an old Catholic mission between Arusha and Dar es Salaam. The first day will be a difficult eleven- to twelve-hour drive, so we'll have to depart at four in the morning."

Reena felt exhausted already but grateful too that the priest had taken charge. It would be the last excursion before school closed, the end of the third grade for Safina and the beginning of a life with a father.

"The children will have to bring pillows, sleeping bags, snacks, and a liter of water. The church will provide six vans and extra bottled water," Amani continued.

Reena's thoughts wandered off. She would never get away with this. That one time with Kiiku was dangerous enough. Dakimu could be captured or killed. Oh, why did Kiiku have to break into their lives and be so likeable, lovable really?

"Reena, are you hearing me?" The priest raised his voice.

"Yes, yes, go on."

"Don't you think we should limit the group to about thirty students but no preschoolers or first graders?" Amani asked.

"Yes, probably," Reena answered, knowing a lot of children would be disappointed.

"Are you still prepared for this, Reena?"

"Oh, absolutely. I'm just tired … and worried about the risk."

"Yes, so am I, but God will guide us," the priest said.

"Of course, Father. Can we talk later? Safina will be home soon."

"Yes. I'll come by the hospital tomorrow. I have to see a parishioner who is dying. What's your schedule?"

"Ten to three all week," she said.

"All right. Pray for us all, Reena," the priest said by way of good-bye.

Just then Safina burst through the door clutching a bag of limes.

"From Kiiku's mama!" she said excitedly.

Behind her was Suzanna.

"Girls, girls," Reena said. "Didn't you two have riding lessons today?"

"Yes, but there's a special trainer at the Post this week preparing the horses for a stressful mission," Suzanna answered.

"The horses need to work on ditches and steep hills, not our soft, level footing, my father said."

"But he also said the jump course we do on Jester has helped his condition," Safina added and then went on with hardly a breath. "Mama, we have to write a story for English. We've been assigned as partners, and we have to bring something real from the story, even though it's made up. Can we use the green ribbon from Kiiku's last package?"

Suzanna had gone into the bedroom and retrieved the leopard. Reena was about to say no when the white child cried, "Let's use the *chui* for our project!" The birthmark flamed in the afternoon light.

"Okay," Safina said.

Reena looked into her daughter's big, dark eyes and rested her hand on a black braid that had a green strip woven in. The girl had delicate features like an Ethiopian and a thin frame. *She could be a model,* Reena thought. Far from racism, poverty, and the story of violence that she surely would hear someday. Oh, for the means to give her that choice!

The girls began to create their tale of a leopard that must choose between his own kind and the lives of some human friends. Reena made them some icy limeade with mint and chips of banana crushed in. One time their black and white hands met over the back of the toy, and they didn't let go. Reena marveled at their innocence and their love.

At the Good Samaritan the next morning, Father Amani signaled to her to meet at the chapel at noon. She moved from patient to patient in slow motion and witnessed the priest giving last rites to the woman in room 45 who had been suffering for months from a rare cancer. Father Amani's voice sounded like God himself offering the gift of heaven and a healed afterlife.

At twelve o'clock, Reena freshened up in the bathroom and went wearily to the small chapel that had one stained-glass window depicting Jesus holding a lamb. Father Amani was there. They prayed for a moment together, and then the priest laid out more of his plans for the field trip.

"We'll choose the top students from each grade but make sure there are black and white children, black and white nuns and teachers. The drivers will all be black and armed."

"Is that necessary?" Reena asked.

"I think you know that it is," he said.

Suddenly, it seemed to Reena that the priest who would lead them all on a camouflaged mission to find Safina's father had no color, although he was black. He knew everyone's secrets, everyone's sins, but no one except the veiled nun—she herself—who would ride with him alone in the sixth van knew his.

A few days before the event was to take place, Reena had to tell Safina that she would be going with them disguised as Sister Kimya, which meant *silence* in Swahili.

"This is a grown-up secret. We can't behave like mother and daughter. Lives are at stake."

The girl nodded. "Mama, am I going to see my father?"

"I think so, my little one. You can't tell Suzanna, though."

"But ..."

"I mean it, Safina. But I will promise you this. Someday you may tell her. There will be a time for such things. It is too soon. Maybe even too soon for us to see him, but I have made the decision knowing what can happen in this world. I would never forgive myself if something kept you from ever meeting your father."

"Does Father Amani know?"

"Yes. He's the only one. He's doing this for you. You must promise to never speak of this."

"To lie?"

"If you cannot lie, you may stay home. But I am going," Reena said.

"I hate lies," Safina said.

"I know ... but there's no other way."

"I wish Mr. Stone was here."

"So do I, my sweet child," Reena said. "He is a white man with a black heart, but even he lied to his best friend."

"My father?"

"Yes, as Jim told you. Now, go finish your homework. Things will become clear in time."

The morning the chosen students of the Light of the World Catholic School gathered in the parking lot, there was some tension. Children had forgotten permission slips or their personal snacks or pillows. Father Amani flitted around, borrowing from some and making phone calls to others to help so that they could get an early start on their long day. Thus it was after four thirty when they pulled onto the highway out of Dar es Salaam.

Traffic was light, and they made good time. Most of the children slept. Reena and Father Amani were silent in their van. The driver probably assumed they were praying, and perhaps they were, each in a unique way, one for the safety of the outing, the other for the safety of her fugitive love.

After about five hours, they stopped to rest in Dodoma at a park with a giant fountain. Some smaller boys rolled in the grass; girls combed each other's hair or traded jewelry. Safina and Suzanna sat on the edge of the fountain in their own fanciful world of horse stories and leopard stories. No one approached them. Reena feared for their future. They should have other friends, other dreams. They should not touch as they had as seven-year-olds. Suzanna was nine already. Their hugs seemed naïve enough, but it was a worry for Reena that the girls might not fit into accepted society. She didn't believe women being together was sinful, but she didn't want Safina to feel the pain of rejection by her peers or by Suzanna herself, who was so dependent on Safina now but who might mature and slide back into her white world, leaving Reena's daughter adrift in a friendless sea.

The priest signaled everyone to load up again, and in another six and a half hours, they entered the outskirts of Arusha. It was almost three thirty in the afternoon. They visited the Cultural Center before it closed and ate dinner there. Then they wound through the dusty streets lined with little grocery stores, car repair shops, people roasting corn on small grills, furniture makers building beds in their lawnless front yards, uniformed children hiking home from school, and the colorful variety of humanity along the road to an orphanage. There they gave other children gifts and played together in the darkening compound with strange smells surrounding them, goats and neighboring families wandering through the narrow alleyways.

When it was completely dark, a strange thing happened. The orphanage was bordered on one side by a main road still heavily congested. There were no street lamps or traffic signals, and many cars had only one or no headlights. So when Safina suddenly walked out into the unlit lanes, Reena gasped in horror.

Her daughter moved quickly, as though she could *see* and grabbed a black boy out of the path of an oncoming car. He screamed and struggled, but Safina would not let go. Finally, she brought him into the yard and asked him his name.

"Joshua," he said, seeing that it was just a girl about his own age and not a kidnapper or a terrorist.

"Safina, how did you know he was crossing the road?" Sister Kimya asked, breaking her vow of silence. "How did you even see him?"

"I don't know, sister. God gave me eyes in the dark," she said.

After that, the boy wouldn't let go of her hand.

Reena checked on the children at midnight. When she got to the room where the third graders had been assigned, she found Safina and Suzanna in the same bed with the orphan, Joshua. The white birthmarked girl and the fatherless boy were curled against Safina. How many poor hearts had her daughter collected in her short life?

The next morning, both girls were talking excitedly to some of the others about asking their parents to adopt Joshua. Safina glanced at her mother. Reena looked away quickly, hoping her daughter would remember that she shouldn't speak to Sister Kimya. After a breakfast of thin porridge, the children from the Light of the World School hugged their new friends good-bye and scrambled into the vans. Joshua held one of Safina's hands and one of Suzanna's until the very last minute. He did not cry but would not let go. One of his care providers had to pry his little hands from theirs and try to explain why he couldn't go with them. It was an emotional omen for the day.

About ten o'clock, they pulled into the flowered grounds at the Shanga Center for disabled craftsmen and women. A manager greeted them with a welcoming smile and showed them where each of the neatly swept pathways led. The children formed their groups of six as they were instructed to do and gathered around the nun or teacher who was chosen to accompany them with a Shanga tour guide.

The smell of rich, country food made Reena feel faint, as the morning meal had been so meager. But then she realized the true source of her discomfort. Dakimu could be staring at her right at that moment from his workstation. It was an overwhelming possibility to consider. Reena had agreed with Father Amani that she would shake her head no at every black artisan she encountered, so if investigators were watching, they wouldn't know if she had discovered Dakimu. It was highly unlikely detectives had followed them. She could only hope Fulsom might have the power to stop such a move because his daughter was in the area.

At first, no one noticed that many of the workers were handicapped. The array of crafts—jewelry, handbags, home decorations, glassware, tools, dresses, baskets, gems, and leather goods—astounded Reena's senses. On closer inspection, she saw that almost everything was made from recycled materials. In a necklace could be pieces of glass, strands from tires, plastic, buttons, wooden beads, strips of metal, and burlap. She had never seen so many colors all at once. People of different ages applied a mastery of skills in booth after booth. It was quiet except for the Catholic school's own chattering children.

Then a white boy in Safina's group screamed. She grabbed him and slapped her hand over his mouth. There, on the ground next to his mother or aunt, was a young black man whose body ended someplace just below his waist. He was slowly placing one bead at a time on a necklace. No, not a necklace, a rosary. Safina bent down and said something to the woman attending him. The little white boy from Dar es Salaam hid in Safina's skirt. She got out the purse that her mother had made for this journey in case they were separated. It held some money, a candy bar, tissues, and Reena's sea glass rosary.

Safina lifted the sparkling rosary out and showed it to the crippled youth. He made sounds no one could understand. But Safina put the sea glass loop around his neck. His guardian clapped her hands. The black boy, who seemed to be about seventeen, slipped the last bead on the rosary he was creating and pushed it toward Safina. She persuasively unwrapped the trembling white boy from the folds of her dress and told him to accept the offering. White hand touched black for a moment, the privileged, whole body receiving the gift from the broken, black body unable to even lift himself from the dirt floor.

And then the damaged Shanga youth said, "A ... san ... te sa ... na."

His companion took a sharp breath. "He has not spoken clear words ever!" she said. Then she translated for the children and the tourists who might not know Swahili. "He said, 'Thank you very much.'"

Reena could not react as a mother might at the tender gesture of her child toward the handicapped boy. The youth had made such an effort because of Safina's gift—rosary or love, it didn't matter. Reena had to remain in her disguise as a nun. But many people noticed and thanked her daughter as she passed by other vendors and their crews with similar but perhaps not such serious disfigurements. Reena followed another group of six with her veil over her face.

The older girls bought scarves and bangles; the boys liked the forged tools and knives inlaid with African turquoise and agate. Some of the teachers bought tanzanite rings and baskets woven with multicolored beads. And then she saw the glass blower hidden behind his protective mask. It could be anyone. He was bent over, dressed in oversized overalls with gloves on his hands. She wished she could see those hands because she knew she would remember the hands that had brought her so much joy.

She walked toward his table anxiously and reached out for a bowl the size she had needed for a while. It had swirls of yellow and blue and purple and felt so good in her hands. She reached for some bills. He raised the visor on his headgear. She gazed straight into the eyes of Dakimu Reiman. She became unbalanced, and he caught her as she fell forward. She remembered to shake her head no for Father Amani and then stood up and lifted her veil as though to better see the glass maker's products.

"Oh Lord … oh my sweet Lord," he whispered.

"You are here," she whispered back.

"Reena … you …"

She spoke quickly, barely recovered, "I am not a nun … just not wanting to lead anyone to you," she said. She picked up another bowl to inspect. "I must see you alone, or I shall die right on the spot."

He stirred his fire, breathing deeply. "Yes. I am overwhelmed," he said. "If you walk over the bridge past the dining area to the fourth hut on the left, we can be safely together for a few moments."

Reena bought the first bowl and watched him wrap it carefully in recycled, brown paper with the hands she had not forgotten. Then she went to Father Amani, who was close by, and spoke softly. "Father, I will need something to eat, or I will faint. Could you do without me for a half hour?"

"Of course, sister," he said.

She walked unrushed toward the café to give Dak time to close up his shop and go by a different path to his quarters. Her heart would not be still. Even so, she arrived first and entered the modest *kibanda* without hesitation. As soon as her eyes adjusted to the darkness inside, she was standing face-to-face with his wife, more beautiful than ever. Reena stepped back, not knowing what to say.

"Shh, mama, it is okay. He told me who you were. You wait." And she guided Reena to a woven reed chair.

In a minute, Dakimu rushed through the door and pulled her up into his arms. Her headdress fell off completely as he put his mouth on hers. He kissed her as if no one else was in the room, as if ten years had not passed, and it was over way too soon.

He grabbed her shoulders and held her at arm's length. "Just as lovely as ever," he said.

The woman said, "I will return later."

When she was gone, Reena wouldn't let him kiss her again. "You are married!" she said.

"She is my wife, but we are not … together. We married because single men are questioned more often by the police. She has a partner, a woman in hut ten, but her tribe does not approve of that kind of love. The arrangement works for both of us."

"She is very striking," Reena said, and thought, *She loves a woman. That is the everything she would not tell me.*

"As is her companion … but no one knows about them. The other woman lost a child and is barren, so no man will marry her. She's an outcast who found work here, but I believe she and my wife are very happy."

"Dakimu, I swear I didn't know for sure if you were here. I never tried to find you all these years. But Kiiku … Kiiku kept leaving us gifts—coffee from that plantation next door, exquisite bracelets I recognized as Shanga-made, and a toy leopard, and then he brought me here last year, but you were gone."

"I know. He shouldn't have been so reckless … but if he had not seen you on Soko Street before that, I would never have known about Safina. Oh, Reena, would you have kept me from her forever?"

"No … I brought her today. She's …"

"The girl who traded her rosary!"

"Yes."

"Oh, I recognized something in her. The way she looked at that poor boy and then showed the white boy how to not offend him. A generous spirit. Safina, an ark for the brokenhearted."

"Yes," Reena said. She closed her eyes and sought his lips again in the dark hut.

Then he led her back to the chair, brought over another one, and sat close to her. He clutched her hands again. "I didn't want to leave you, to lose you, Reena, but I didn't want to die. I had to trust God and Kiiku. That's all I had when I first escaped from Dar es Salaam. I learned a trade. I hid in the coffee trees in the pouring rain. I had wonderful days with my son."

"Are you Chui?" she asked.

"No ... I am only Catholic. These young Leopards. They live to fight and dream big dreams of controlling everything. I long for the Mass, the singing of the Litany, the bells of St. Joseph's ... and you," he said. His face showed her the truth of his words.

A woman stopped outside the door. "The priest will hear confessions," she said and moved on.

"Oh God, Reena, can you take Safina's hand and stand where I can see her?"

"I'll try. I have to be careful." She paused. "You didn't ask about the Stones."

"They disavowed me."

"To save your life!"

"But I never felt the same after that," he said.

"Well, I saw Jim last year. He said they were both devastated losing you."

"I still think of them. It was a difficult time. So many years wasted hating and then being broken by circumstances so soon after reconciling," Dakimu said, glancing away from her.

"The years loving were not wasted," she said.

"Even those. I was too angry to love the young missionary Reena properly. And she loved Jim. How long have they been together now?"

"Over thirty years, I think."

"If I turned myself in, maybe you and I and Safina could be a family. I might be acquitted. Someone must know the killing was self-defense besides my black brothers."

"Someone does," Reena said. "Someone you will not believe. Someone white."

"Who could that be?" he asked.

"Major Fulsom Farley at the International Military Post."

He looked amazed. "Do I know him?"

"Maybe. He married Felicia Sommers before David's baby girl was born. He is Suzanna's stepfather."

"And who is Suzanna to you?"

"She is Safina's best friend."

"God in heaven," he cried as if he could not take another shock.

"The major and I have a pact. He still wants you, but he will not sacrifice the friendship of our children, or so he says."

A crowd was gathering at the picnic grounds not too far from where they whispered in secret.

"I have to go," Reena said. "Dak, find a small bowl you have made or a drinking glass with only green in it. Safina loves green. I didn't have the nerve to give her the one your wife gave me when I was here before. Bring something to her where we are grouped for lunch. She'll know who you are. Don't look at me."

It wasn't long before everyone found a bench or lawn chair and then was served a delicious meal by the Shanga cooks. Reena passed by Safina and said softly, "My child, you should sit somewhere on the outer edge."

Safina obeyed, and Reena followed her so she could hear what father and daughter might say. In a while, a tall, black figure walked across the lawn with a glass cup, a green stripe set all the way around it like the outline of a mountain. Dak's safety visor was down as if he had just been at the fire, but when he reached the girl, he lifted it as he handed her the treasure.

"Safina," he said.

She stayed calm but said, *"Asante sana*, Baba."

§ § §

"Thank you very much, father," the girl had said. Dakimu had turned with his hand on his heart and moved away from her. He thought that no one else would know Safina had meant *Father* when she spoke to him. He had let her see the gold cross as he leaned down to her. He had said her name.

People lined up at the makeshift confessional, lame and sound alike, murmuring to each other and deciding inwardly what they would say, knowing Father Amani had limited time. A pile of gifts swelled near the place he would assure them their sins were forgiven. A couple of military escorts for the Light of the World field trip glanced over when Dak reached the door. *I am known as Shanga's glass blower. I cannot be the black they are hunting*, he thought as he stepped behind the curtain.

"Bless me, Father, for I have sinned," Dakimu said into Amani's ear.

"Dakimu, God be with you. Speak quickly, my friend," the priest said.

"Thank you, oh thank you, for bringing Reena and my daughter here, my sweet Safina. My sin is that today I love them more than God."

"You are still not safe, my son. And this was very dangerous for them. Do not thank me. Thank the God you have put in second place," Amani said.

"I could return to Dar es Salaam. I could pay for my sins," Dak said.

"Self-defense is not a sin. Continue to work here. Share your skill, your passion. God will show you a way for the future," the priest said.

"How will I know it is God who guides me?"

"It will be a voice or a sight that has no other explanation," Amani said.

"Father, listen. If I have to flee from here, I'll send the sea glass rosary to you. The crippled boy won't care. He's happy with anything. Take the rosary to the market and give it to Kiiku's mother. She will know where I've gone."

"How will she know that?" the priest asked.

"I told her once that the rosary meant the misery of Christ. She will only say the Swahili word."

"Yes … yes … in the name of the Father, the Son, and the Holy Ghost. Amen."

Dakimu pulled down his visor and strode out of the confessional toward the glass shop. He thought he saw Safina among the school children holding the hand of a white girl. He stared at them to memorize the sight. They came out of the shadows into the sunlight, and Dakimu felt sick at the sight of the ugly birthmark on the white girl's face. Suzanna Sommers. The child of the man he killed. The grandchild of a man he had killed three decades ago. It was his sin—that mark. And there was his child kissing that cheek!

§ § §

With her heart aching, Reena watched the line by the confessional slowly shorten and Dak's back fade into the crowd of tourists still milling about the grounds. Dar children tumbled on the lawn with Shanga children as if they had known each other forever. Then the sky turned black, and the vendors began to cover their wares or close their stalls entirely. The nuns called to their students that it was time to go, and they climbed aboard the vans clutching their treasures.

Safina and Suzanna were able to find a seat together. Reena told the priest she would go in that van, and she found a place directly behind the girls so she could warn her daughter with a hand on her shoulder if she started saying too much. At first, they shared the prizes that they had bought or been given. They compared colors and sparkle; they tried on each other's bracelets. Then Safina held out the drinking glass and ran her hand around the mountain-shaped ridge of green.

"But why did that black man give that to you?" Suzanna asked.

"I think my … one of the nuns told him I liked green."

"It's the best thing anyone got," she said.

They were quiet for a moment and seemed to be watching the street scenes, which were so different from the scenes in the big city.

Then Suzanna said, "You gave up the sea glass rosary. How could you?"

"Two boys were broken and needed some healing. I am well. Why shouldn't I help them?" she answered quickly.

"One black and one white. Your favorite thing."

"Almost," Safina said.

Reena smiled behind her veil.

Very late that night, they pulled into the old mission at Dodoma and spread their sleeping bags along one wall of the sanctuary. The church had been partially repaired after years of tribal wars, but the sky still poured through gaps in the broken stained glass in the ceiling and behind the altar. Now those empty places were full of stars.

Father Amani said Mass as Reena, disguised as the Sister of Silence, the nuns, teachers, some of the older children, three of the SUV drivers, and a handful of local blacks took pieces of bread, though not unleavened, from leftover sandwiches and sips of grape juice consecrated by the priest's hand.

The parish priest brought incense and swung the smoke in a tin bowl from corner to corner of the shell of the cathedral. He served Father Amani with grace, his gold and white robes shimmering in the light of the few candles that remained. The wind whispered its own blessing through the cracks in the masonry, and Sister Kimya saw a star fall from the heavens through the lattice work of mahogany arches and splintered alcoves. The church breathed again in those moments with its message of redemption and love.

§ § §

Long after the caravan of children had left the village of Shanga, the glass blower lay in his bed weeping. His wife, Baraka, ran down the footpath between the *vibanda* and grabbed the hand of Kivuli, her lover. They stole back to Dakimu's side, massaged his back, and drew their strong fingers down his arms and legs to distract him. They rubbed his forehead with healing oil and whispered to him words of comfort.

"Tell us, husband, what your heart cries for," Baraka said.

"Reena."

"The black nun who was here? That is the woman you have longed for since hiding here?" Baraka asked.

"Yes … and another woman, a white woman."

"Ah," Kivuli said, "a double sorrow."

"With a single name … Reena Pavane," he said.

"A black and a white Reena. Do they know each other?"

"They do," he said. "The black one was named after the white one who was a well-loved missionary in Huzuni. I have chosen the black Reena but cannot forget the white one. I am tied to her still."

"But why, my husband?" Baraka asked.

"She saved my life … she …" He paused. "I can read you the story if you like," he said.

"Oh yes. Reading is better than weeping," Kivuli said.

He reached in a bag where he kept important papers and a handgun and brought out Jim Stone's *Memoirs on an African Morning*, the red leather book that was banned in some quarters, treasured in others.

"Oh, I have heard of this journal," Kivuli said. "You can be put in jail for having it."

"Read to us, husband. It is a long time until daylight," Baraka said.

Dakimu opened the book and began at the place he loved to read most, the scene where he and the white Reena are twenty-three and twenty-one and facing the crossing of the flooded

Rufiji River with malaria medicine for a British journalist the girl adored. He read with dark emotion about how Reena untangled him from a rolling tree limb after they abandoned the jeep, how they struggled midstream to reach the shore, how she held his head while he heaved up the murky water and pounded his fists on the ground because he was indebted to her and half in love.

"We traveled for weeks together after that, having lost the medicine and all our supplies, but the girl would not go back. We took care of each other, bound wounds, caught game, and built fires. Finally, I had been with her longer than she had been with the white man, Jim Stone, but when we reached the camp where he lay sick and terrorized, she fell into his arms, and I was nothing." This Dakimu improvised because the book didn't exactly read that way.

The women's eyes were bright. They held each other's hands but let the fingers of their free hands linger on his shivering body. Then they covered him with a soft robe and wished him soothing dreams. He knew they were afraid to know about the white Reena, and afraid the black Reena could lead the soldiers to him. They both loved him, in a different way, of course, than they loved each other. Dakimu had heard them once when they thought he was sleeping, just a few weeks ago.

"We are Chui, my love," Baraka had said. "Very few women can claim this. We want justice for the poor, the hunted, and the dispossessed. Who is all these things?"

"Your husband," Kivuli answered.

"He has enabled us to have each other. We must enable him to have life," Baraka said.

So now, he knew they hated to leave him caught in his trap of the love of two women and the hunger of soldiers desperate to claim him as their prize. Baraka kissed his cheek and said, "We can stay all night."

But he urged them to go, saying it was his trouble to bear.

"My husband is a generous man," Baraka said, and she and Kivuli left him.

Dakimu dreamed of that great, flooded river of his past, the thrashing in the waves and the swallowing of the deadly water. He felt himself drowning in his sleep and then arms dragging him out of the depths of the raging water. He woke suddenly, sensing a movement against his canvas door. It was still dark. He felt his way carefully across the hard, dirt floor and slid the opening back.

He could not breathe. There, asleep, curled as any cat would, was a huge, male leopard. Dakimu thought he was still dreaming, but no, the animal stirred slightly and slapped his spotted tail against the ground. He did the only thing that came to him in that moment. He reached out and stroked the big cat from the top of his head all the way down his beautiful back, as the women had done for him. The skin rippled. The cat raised his magnificent head.

"*Chui*, what are you doing here?" Dak asked softly. "It is not safe."

The leopard rolled to his feet and looked at Dakimu. Something flickered in the cat's eyes, as though he himself had been dreaming of hunting gazelle and awakened, surprised, by the black man's door. The animal was not afraid, and neither was Dak. An understanding passed between them.

"*Chui*, run off to the coffee plantation. Hide in the long rows. No one will harm you there … unless you eat coffee beans, eh?"

The leopard padded away just before light broke into the haven of Shanga, and workers began to cook their morning meals.

seven

Reena woke with an azure sky cast into the stained glass like an artisan's new work. Local people made everyone a breakfast of porridge, mangos, and corn cakes. Some of the blacks acted as if they had never seen so many white faces in one place and definitely had not seen a white child holding a black child's hand. After Sister Kimya helped load the children and their possessions in the vans, she saw the Dodoma people gathering around to touch the priest and wave at his strange group of travelers, and many of them called out "God's blessings" or "Allah be with you," and the boys and girls waved back.

About two in the afternoon, they stopped by a roadside stand selling packaged food and some local fruit. The children resisted getting back in the vans, so weary of this long, long excursion, but finally, at three, they were on the road again. They entered the streets of Dar es Salaam at the peak of rush hour and didn't reach the schoolyard until almost seven. The next day was Saturday, so all could rest and recover.

Parents retrieved worn-out sons and daughters; teachers and nuns drove others home. Sister Kimya offered to take Suzanna and Safina but of course didn't speak a word until she dropped Farley's daughter off at the Post. The girls hugged each other and promised to call each other in the morning.

"You did well, my sweet," Reena said as they left the military base.

"It was hard, but … I think I saw my father," she said in a reverent voice.

"I think you did," her mother said, and removed the head garment.

Safina held out the remarkable glass that fit perfectly in her eight-year-old hand. "I hope I will never break this," she said.

In the haven of peace on the Indian Ocean, Reena and Safina trudged up their stairs. Sitting on the landing leaning against their front door was Kiiku.

"Oh Lord, I don't think I can handle any more today," Reena whispered.

"I need a place to stay," the young man said.

"You are welcome here, of course, Kiiku. Come in."

"Thank you, mama. I'll be no trouble. Just for two nights, maybe?"

"What is wrong, son?" Reena asked.

"Someone has seen me with my mother. A white man on a horse chased me through the streets, but I circled back behind him and found narrow spaces where the horse could not go. I'm tired and hungry, and I missed my little sister," he said.

"Was it Farley?"

"No … another soldier."

"You stole Farley's horse last year, didn't you?" Reena said.

"Yes. He's a good animal. He's well cared for," Kiiku assured her.

"Still, it was a crime."

"What was a crime?" Safina asked. She had gone to her room to get ready for bed and had come back to eat with them, clutching the leopard.

"I took Major Farley's horse when he left him alone tied to a broken fence on the street," Kiiku told her.

"You stole Resolute?" she asked with alarm in her voice.

"Ah … that is his name. Very fitting," Kiiku said.

"Yes, and you should give him back," Safina said crossly.

"Maybe I will," he said. "But, Safina, where were you today? You didn't come home from school."

"No. Some of us went to Shanga," Safina said.

His eyes lit up, and he looked over at Reena, who was heating some soup. "I didn't know. What did you find there?" he asked, meaning, Reena was sure, what toys or jewelry.

"I found my father," she answered as clear as day.

Kiiku took in a sharp breath. "Did you tell anyone?"

"No. Not even my best friend."

"You are very strong. What did your father say?"

Safina closed her eyes as if trying to remember the exact scene.

"He said my name and gave me a beautiful drinking glass he had made."

Reena had just poured some milk into it and set it on the table with bowls of chicken and vegetables in a coconut-flavored broth.

"Eat, you two. You can talk tomorrow," she said.

They sat in silence, taking mouthfuls of the satisfying soup. She felt as protective of Kiiku as of her own child. Finally she sent Safina off, already half-asleep. The girl disappeared down the hall lined with photos taken by a man who loved Tanzania and its people but who could not help them now. He was far away with his own cherished Reena Pavane, who had loved Safina's father in her own daring way.

"Reena?" Kiiku broke into her reverie. "What will you do now?"

"Do my job at the hospital, raise Safina, worship God, and love Dakimu as long as he needs me," she answered.

"I fear a terrible ending," Kiiku said.

"You must have faith, little leopard. There are many things only God can do."

The next day, Reena left Safina with her brother so she could go to work. "Do not open the door to anyone," she said as she prepared to leave.

"Not even Major Farley?" Safina wanted to know.

"Especially not him. You know your brother is wanted by the police, and the military has been looking for him too. Just mind me, child. You don't have to understand everything."

"Someday I will."

"Yes, I'm sure someday you will. Let Kiiku help you with your homework and listen to his stories."

"Okay, Mama."

"Kiiku, please keep your stories *child appropriate*."

"Yes, ma'am," he said. He was folding the sheets and blankets he had used on the couch.

"Do you think you can fix your sister something to eat?" Reena asked.

"Oh yes. I am a brilliant cook!" he exclaimed.

"Well, I may not have brilliant ingredients, but do what you can."

"*Asante sana*, mama."

"Yes, yes, I must go. Safina? Mind your brother," she called to her daughter, who had gone back to her bedroom.

"Okay, Mama," she called back.

"You trust me, Reena," he said

"After I saw your father again, I knew I could trust his son. Now, I'm going," she said and opened the door.

§ § §

Kiiku washed some dishes that were still in the sink and made a special porridge with maple syrup and fresh pineapple. He fried Reena's last half pound of bacon and started making some coffee. Then, noticing the instant hot chocolate, he made a small pot of that with cream instead of milk. When Safina finally got to the table, she couldn't believe it.

"Is this a holiday or something?"

"It is my first real day with my sister. I want it to start with a bang," he said.

"Well, I don't like pineapple, but I'll pick the pieces out."

"You city girls are spoiled," he teased.

"I don't think a girl who just saw her father for the first time in her life is that spoiled," she said with a small pout.

"I didn't see him until I was about twenty-five," he informed her.

"Oh … I'm sorry, Kiiku," she said, and then ate a large chunk of pineapple without making a face.

"What did our father say to you?"

"Not much. We weren't supposed to know each other. Some bad people are looking for him."

"I think you have things mixed up," her brother said. "Some *good* people are looking for him because he did a bad thing, well, many bad things."

"I don't believe it, and I don't want to know."

"That's good because I'm not going to tell you," Kiiku said.

"I said I didn't want to know *yet*."

"You are a smart girl, little Safina."

"I'm not so little!"

"Little … but with a big heart, I can see already."

There was silence after that. They ate their breakfast.

"Do you want to know a secret?" Safina asked finally.

"I don't know. Whose secret is it?"

"My mother's."

"Oh, I don't think so!" Kiiku said adamantly.

"Well, it's mine too, so it's all right."

She led him into her mother's room, got down on her hands and knees, and began to pry the floorboards loose where she had seen her mother bury things.

"Oh, Safina, what on earth?"

"Mostly they're presents you left for us, but here is a book. I want you to read me something from it."

Kiiku stared at Jim Stone's *Memoirs*. His mother had that book, but even translated into Kiswahili, she didn't understand it. Kiiku himself had not ever finished it. It was surely not for this child to hear. She told him a white man called Jim had written it and had said what he liked about Tanzanians and that she wanted to know some of those things. Maybe someone would write about her in a book.

"And what have you done to be in a book?" Kiiku asked seriously.

"I saved my best friend from a beating with stones when some bullies were hurting her because of her birthmark."

"I'd say that counts for a lot," he said. He didn't tell her he had been watching her that day. "Who is your best friend?"

"Her name is Suzanna Farley, and we love each other, even though she's white and I'm black."

"Farley ... not related to Major Fulsom Farley."

"She's his daughter, and sometimes I get to play at her house on the Post. We brush the horses and do our homework, but we have to be very careful because Suzanna's mother used to hate me."

"Why did she *used* to hate you?"

"Because I'm black."

"No, I mean why doesn't she hate you anymore?"

"I healed her once of a terrible pain in her head."

"Maybe you should have hated her instead," he said, mindful of his own experience with white people.

"No, she's broken, like Jester. She doesn't need any more hate, only peace."

"Who the hell is Jester? You're losing me, girl," her brother said.

"Jester is a horse that was in a sling for a long time because of a broken leg. But he's mended now. So Mrs. Farley can get mended too."

"Do you know what broke her?" Kiiku asked cautiously, thinking, *This child has too much knowledge for her own good.*

"A black man," Safina said matter-of-factly.

"What black man? What's a black man to her anyway?"

"I don't know, but she said, 'He was the ruin of us all,' but I didn't know what that meant."

"Nor should you, Safina. People have their own demons. We shouldn't mess with them."

"I don't see her much. She's *quieted* like Jester and sleeps a lot."

"You mean given a tranquilizer?"

"Yes, that's the word."

"Oh my, little girl, what have you stumbled into?"

"Well, one good thing, Mr. Farley likes me and wants me to be Suzanna's friend, so he is a kind of *mlinzi.* I had to tell him what that meant."

"A guardian, a faithful watchman," Kiiku translated. "That's good if he can be trusted."

"Why wouldn't he?"

"Lots of people make promises and friends they can't keep. They make choices and then find they have made the wrong choice for themselves," he said.

"I will never do that," she said. "I have chosen Suzanna, and I will never turn against her."

"What if she turns against you?" Kiiku asked.

Safina had to think about that for a minute. Then she said, "It's just that I think I understand the world better than she does. She may stand by me not knowing why she shouldn't."

"How did you get so perceptive, my sister?"

"I watch things happening and try to imagine the outcome. Like the day the major put Suzanna and me on Jester. It was muddy, and the horse had been in the sling for a long time. I was prepared to land in the mud long before Suzanna. She was so surprised to find herself on the ground. I expected it."

"I think you can hear the words in this book. Come on. I'll read you a bit of it."

They settled on the sofa where they could see the distant Indian Ocean. Safina snuggled close to Kiiku. He opened the red book randomly and began to read from the memoir of Jim Stone.

"'I met Dakimu Reiman— '"

"Who is that?" Safina broke in.

"Our father. I thought you knew."

"No. Mama wouldn't tell me his name."

"I'll start again," Kiiku said, wondering if he would lose all Reena's faith in him.

"'I met Dakimu Reiman seven days after I lifted Reena Pavane out of her burning village—'"

"Not my mother!"

"No, the white missionary ... 'and into the one British helicopter that had come. She told me she had promised her people that all would be saved, and now I was forcing her to leave them, to save herself when they would surely die. Christians and whites were at the mercy of savage tribes pouring across the land with their chants and their guns.'"

"I don't like this story," Safina said.

"Just wait. There's a good part coming. 'I saw a black boy clinging to the white girl as I tore her away. She begged us to take him, but the pilot said no. She told me his name was Nathan and that he'd be dead within the hour. I forced her into the chopper and turned back for a photo. The boy was holding onto a broken cross.' Look, Safina, here it is," Kiiku said.

"I don't want to see it. Keep reading."

"'In just seconds, it seemed, we were in the air. Below us huts flamed and people fled into the forest. The girl sat very still, but tears streamed down her cheeks. She didn't know how sick I was. Malaria had weakened me of late, and the air was very rough. The noise was deafening, but I couldn't have talked anyway. I tried desperately not to throw up. Suddenly this lovely stranger took my hand and held on tightly, and I thought, *This woman is a healer*, though I did not believe in her god. She was not afraid for herself while the helicopter bucked and dipped in the wind. She was comforting *me*.'"

"I like that lady," Safina said.

"Maybe you will meet her someday," Kiiku said. "She is Jim's wife now, and they have been together a long time."

"Go on."

"'We landed in Dar es Salaam, but Reena didn't let go of my hand. She told me to stay still for a moment and take some deep breaths. Pretty soon I was able to ask her if I could take her someplace. But she had no place to go, so I said she could come with me. We were together in my apartment for six days. She let me write her story, the reason she had been the only white in the mission village of Huzuni, and why she loved Africa and its natives.

"'We walked the streets and visited the markets during the day, and I introduced her to my friends. Most of them were black, which pleased her very much. We ate a small meal at my table in the evenings and met in the hallway before going to our separate rooms. Sometimes we just touched briefly. We seemed to have a connection that was beyond words.

"'Then I was called on a top-secret political exercise, to record the event with my camera and my pen. I was averse to leaving the girl. She was only twenty and not used to city life, but I was told I would return in two weeks. So that night, in the dark hall, I kissed her.

"'The next morning, I walked onto the British Air and Ground Patrol Base, and a gallant and handsome black greeted me and helped me with my bags. He steadied me with an arm once when I felt about to faint. I had forgotten to take my malaria medicine that morning and asked if he could explain to the officials that I had gone back to my apartment for it. He said he'd even tell them that I should not be going on this excursion, as I did not look well.

"'Before either of us could speak again, I was commandeered into the vehicle and driven away by a devious and self-serving man named Colonel Edmund Hahlos.'"

"I don't like him already," Safina broke in.

"No one did, child," Kiiku said. "But the black man's name was Dakimu Reiman."

She clapped her hands. "Oh, read me more! Read me more!" she cried. "But wait. Why was Father's name not African?"

"That's not in this part, but I'll tell you. He was raised in the same village that Reena had taught in, by the first missionaries in Huzuni, the Reimans. They gave him that name."

"Oh. Should that be our last name?"

"Technically, I suppose, but listen. Here's the good part … 'You will hear the details of my trek with Hahlos, my unbearable pain without my malaria meds, my heart's sadness at never saying good-bye to Reena, my horror at how Edmund used the natives to his own ends, but I want to tell you now what that compassionate black, Dakimu, did. He put himself at great risk, suffered and almost died crossing the flooded Rufiji River, for *me*. That young, courageous Dakimu brought to me many weeks later the chloroquine for my malaria and the lovely missionary, Reena Pavane.'"

"I know about that. Mr. Stone told me, but it's nice to hear the words he wrote about it," Safina said.

"He stole a jeep, supplies, and medicine and protected that white Reena so together they could save Jim Stone. It was a harrowing journey. You can read it yourself when you are older, but think of the hero our father was then when you hear about the crimes of which he is accused."

"He will always be a hero to me," she said.

"To me too," Kiiku said. "Now, we should put the book back. Your mother may not want you to hear the story just yet."

"Okay."

Safina placed the red book in the hiding hole under the floorboards. Then she said to her brother, "Thank you, Chui, for showing me a piece of our father's heart."

Kiiku tossed her the stuffed leopard and said, "Don't let anyone hear you call me that."

For a while, he helped his sister with her math and listened to her read the Bible. Kiiku said he was not Catholic but admitted that the faith seemed to have given much comfort to their father. He always wore a gold cross and said he followed the example of Jesus in all things.

"But Jesus didn't kill anyone," Safina said.

"Of course, sweetie, mere humans can never be Jesus," her brother said.

"I saw Father go into the confessional at Shanga. I wanted to run after him and throw my arms around him! Can the police chase him forever?" Safina asked.

"For what he did, yes," Kiiku answered.

"But he saved Mr. Stone. Doesn't that cancel his crimes a little?"

"To us, Safina. To those who love him. To others, saving the life of *one* white man does not justify taking the lives of … four."

"He killed *four* white people? Safina asked, her eyes widening.

"I should not have told you," Kiiku said.

"Well, I don't believe it! He wouldn't have done that without a good reason!"

"I believe two of those were unavoidable and perhaps justified, but the other two were not. And oh, my dear Safina, there were others."

"Is this story in the red book?" she asked.

"Some of the most terrible killing is there. But I don't want you to read it," he said.

"Have you ever killed anyone, Kiiku?"

He hesitated and then said, "No more than any Chui would … to survive," he answered.

"I don't think we have a big enough space to hide you, brother. But I will not let anyone in," she said.

"It's nice to be safe in *someone's* heart," he said softly.

"You are safe in God's heart," she said.

"Hmm … that would be appealing to believe," he said.

He thumbed through the pages of the Good Book. "Hey, Safina, do you think if I stopped and looked right now, wherever my fingers are, God will speak to me?"

"I don't know, Kiiku, but wherever you stop, there will be a meaning. It's for you to decide if it's for your eyes," she replied.

He opened the Bible, ran his fingers down the page, and read, *"Therefore we will not fear, though the earth give way and the mountains fall into the heart of the sea, though its waters roar and foam and the mountains quake with their surging … Oh, that is so beautiful!"* he said.

Just then Reena came in the door. "What is so beautiful?" she asked as she approached the couch where brother and sister sat side by side with the open Bible.

Kiiku took her hand and placed it on the Holy words. She read them and then said, "Those were powerful words for the ancient people of God."

"They are still powerful today, to draw my hand and my heart to them ... but I am a Leopard. I know no god," he said.

Kiiku found a way out of the city the next day and arrived at Shanga in the middle of the night. He went straight to his father's door. Dakimu opened it tentatively.

"It is only your son ... what are you afraid of?" Kiiku asked.

"I'm not afraid, only not wanting to scare it."

"Scare what?"

"The *chui*," Dakimu said.

As if on command, the leopard slunk out of the shadows at the end of the *vibanda*. The two men stood very still. The big cat brushed against their legs, but a noise in the next hut startled it, and it bounded away.

"Baba, what do you think of this?" Kiiku asked.

"I think it is a spirit," Dakimu said.

"No, Father, it was very real."

"I love him," Dak said.

"As you love me?"

"Yes ... like a son."

"Maybe it is a *mlinzi*, a watchman, a thing to guard you," Kiiku whispered, hoping the cat would come back.

"Yes, but it should not be here. Someone will kill it. Oh God, Kiiku. It is my punishment. I will know how David Sommers felt, how Felicia felt, how Suzanna will feel when she finds out who I am!"

"Baba, you have Safina. She may save you all," Kiiku said and led his father back into the hut. "Where is Baraka tonight?"

"With Kivuli."

"Then I'll stay with you," Kiiku said.

In the morning before light, Kiiku found the leopard lying at Dakimu's feet.

§ § §

After the children returned from the field trip to Shanga, Farley knew something had changed. Safina could not stop talking about the adventure but avoided his eyes when mentioning the gift she had received from one of the vendors—a hand-blown glass etched in green.

Farley himself had changed. He almost loved the black child but not just because she was so good for Suzanna and Felicia but because the woman he had secretly claimed for his heart for more than thirty years, long before he married Felicia, embraced all tribes, all colors, all ways of loving.

He had driven in wild circles looking for Resolute and ended up one night in the village a few miles from where his woman lived. Her friends told him she wasn't at home, and he missed her so profoundly that he began to be drawn to others who reminded him of her.

And so, he leaned over to hug Safina as she and Suzanna sat whispering on the couch about their experience in Arusha. He caught words like *Joshua, rosary, confession.* Oh yes, he'd better confess how he'd wept after not finding his love where he'd always found her or retrieving his horse from the hands of a Chui madman.

Safina endured his large, white arms wrapped around her and said, "Are you all right, Mr. Farley?"

He hardly knew what to say. He had the means to destroy her life but hated himself for planning to do it and suddenly released her. "I perhaps have need of your medicine, Safina," he said.

She reached one hand out and placed it over his heart. Blood rushed in his ears, and something like elation swept through his body. What had the girl done to him?

"I have a secret," she said. "And though I can't tell you, I can explain how it feels. When you find something you have longed for your whole life, you want to shout it to the world, but you can't without hurting someone."

"I know that, child. I certainly know that," he said. *She has seen her father*, he said to himself. His chest felt warm where she had touched it, but his heart felt cold. He would have to disappoint her. He would have to break his promise to Reena. The black assassin that was their hope must pay for his deeds.

"You know I have a job to do, don't you, Safina?" he chanced to ask.

"Yes, sir," she said. "And so do I."

"I will not keep you from it," he said.

"What are you talking about, Daddy?" Suzanna asked, with something like alarm in her voice.

"Things that divide my world from yours," he said.

Safina didn't say a word but put her arm around Suzanna and stared back straight into his eyes. He couldn't stay in the room. He couldn't go into Felicia's room just then. So he went out into the dark night and walked across the parade grounds to the stable. There he raked fresh straw into piles of bedding in the stalls of his favorite horses, even in Resolute's empty one, believing in that moment that he would spare the life of Dakimu Reiman to have that horse back.

eight

*A*fter Kiiku left, Reena felt relieved. He brought an unknown element into the life she had carefully worked out for herself and Safina. Yes, she had willingly taken a chance so Dakimu could see his daughter, but it had been under her control. Kiiku was a wild card. She could not control what he did or said. He had told Safina things Reena had not wished her to know just yet. He did not believe in God. He was a Chui.

She wanted Safina to have a life that flowed smoothly and graciously through childhood and into an equally sane adulthood. But already her daughter shared part of her days with the mentally unbalanced Felicia Farley and did increasingly unsafe exercises on that immense horse, Jester. So when Safina turned nine a few months after Suzanna and went off to fourth grade, Reena searched her heart for a tranquilizing—she hated to use that word—factor, something that would pull Safina back from the edge of disillusion.

But before she could even think clearly, one evening after a fourteen-hour shift at the hospital and a midnight Mass at St. Joseph's, Reena found a note tacked to the door of her apartment. She was surprised it was from Major Farley, thinking Kiiku might have come back. The major had written—*Mrs. Patel, I took the girls out of school today and will keep them here until I speak to you. Faithfully yours, Fulsom Farley.*

It was too late to call and impossible to sleep. She poured some cold tea into Safina's green-lined glass and held it in both hands, feeling some peace in touching the treasure Dakimu had made. She wondered if she could disguise herself again and go to him. Then she thought of the boy, Joshua, at the orphanage in Arusha. She wondered if a priest could adopt him. It would be too suspicious for her to do it, but having the boy with their dearest friend, Father Amani, and attending the Light of the World School might give Safina a better focus for her life than constantly dreaming about a father she may never see again or forever hungering for the company of Suzanna, having few other friends. Reena could not name one.

She called Fulsom first the next morning, but Suzanna answered. "Hello, Mrs. Patel. Father is out on patrol, but Safina and I are fine."

"Why aren't you in school?"

"The nuns tried to say Safina and I couldn't be friends, and my father got really angry. He said he wouldn't bring us back until everyone accepted that we were sisters, never to be separated again," she said.

"Well, good for him," Reena said. "Where is Safina?"

"She's reading to my mom."

"Oh?"

"Yes. She's reading the Bible, the parts where Jesus heals people."

"Okay. I'm going to work, but I'll be home by three today. Tell your father to come to my apartment when he can," she told the girl. Reena knew she would be off by two, but she had to allow time to go to St. Joseph's.

"Mrs. Patel?"

"Yes."

"Do you know who Joshua is?"

"I think Safina mentioned him once." Of course, Suzanna could not have known that Reena was there on that field trip and had seen Joshua herself at the orphanage.

"He's an orphan we met on the field trip. I can't forget about him, but my mother could never raise another child, especially a … black one," the girl said.

"I understand, Suzanna," Reena said. "I'll talk to you later about the boy, all right?"

"Yes, ma'am. Thank you."

They hung up. Reena was stunned. Could it be this easy? Suzanna wanting the boy in their lives too? Had Safina saved the boy off of the dark streets of Arusha so he could save them?

Reena went to St. Joseph's as soon as she could after work, different scenarios playing out in her mind. Father Amani took her into his office and made them both some tea. "How are you feeling, my dear?" he asked, after they had sipped a bit of the flavorful liquid.

"Father, there are two things I want to do with the rest of my life," she said.

"Only two?"

"Two significant things."

"Should we be in the confessional?" he asked.

"Probably," Reena said, "but I have committed no sin, at least not yet."

"Go on."

"I want a relationship with Dak and at the same time to keep Safina from her father's turmoil, to give her something important to do with her life besides pining after him and perhaps after Suzanna. She needs something else to focus her passion on these days."

"I believe these things may be mutually exclusive," the priest said.

"But I have an idea. Remember Joshua? The orphan in Arusha?" she asked.

"Yes, I do. Safina seemed to have saved him from a speeding car in the dark, and she and Suzanna could hardly say good-bye to the parentless child. Why?"

"I want you to adopt him."

"Reena! I don't think I would be allowed to do such a thing!"

"Do you always do what's allowed?" she asked.

"You know I don't, but this … this is crazy," he said.

"Just this morning, Suzanna asked me about Joshua, I think hinting that I adopt him. Her mother could never adopt a black child. If you did it, it would be good for everyone."

"I'm not so sure, Reena. You know the first person to question this will be Major Farley and then, of course, my superiors."

"I've thought of that, but Fulsom and I have become … friends. We have our daughters to protect, our daughters who love each other so much. I imagined the child Joshua would give them someone else to love. Their world is very … closed," Reena said.

"I wondered when you would become concerned about the girls' … relationship."

"Father, they are like sisters. I have no concerns about them *that way*, not yet. Do you think I should?"

"I don't know much about these matters, Reena, but girls do fall in love with girls."

Reena thought suddenly of Dak's gorgeous wife and her lover so chastised by their tribes and the Church, so rejected that the one would have to marry a man to have standing in the community. No, she didn't want that for her daughter and Suzanna.

The priest put his hand over his eyes and didn't say anything for a moment.

"I suppose we could go to Arusha and speak with the directors of the orphanage. I know them—Aranya and Lee Park. I've placed a few of their orphans with church families. I could suggest a guardianship, which we could share, to see that the boy gets a good education," he said at last. "Would you find your way to Dakimu on this trip?"

"I hope so, Father. I have never stopped loving him." Reena glanced around the sanctuary where she had witnessed Dak's conversion.

"But is he safe with you?" the priest asked.

"For a little while, I believe. I have to see him again … somehow."

"We'll speak later, Reena. I have confessors waiting."

"Of course, Father."

Amani blessed her, and she rushed back out into the world of suspicions and dangers, planning what she would say to Fulsom. He was waiting at the top of the stairs when she finally got home, and they went into the apartment. They stood at first. There was an uncomfortable silence. Then Farley broke the impasse.

"The girls are well. You would not believe how Felicia responds to Safina. It is a joy to behold. I greatly fear her knowing the truth, but we must put some things in God's hands, I suppose," he said.

"What happened at school? Tell me everything," Reena said.

Fulsom described the scene with the nuns attempting to part their daughters and tell them they shouldn't be so close, that they should have other friends, even friends that are *boys*, and not touch each other. He explained that he had refused to bring them back unless the school honored their special relationship. And then he added that the girls' friendship was vital for his birthmarked child and his ill wife.

"I do agree with you, Fulsom. I was just speaking with Father Amani about this very subject." She hesitated a moment but felt the need to be completely truthful. "If our children did grow to have that kind of love, I would not mind," Reena said.

"Really? I shouldn't be surprised," he said. "Women seem to have more supportive feelings about such love. I would not want my daughter to suffer any more than she has. Being *that way* would surely lead to unhappiness and pain," Fulsom said.

They sat now on the couch that faced the large window that revealed the sprawling city and a range of the Indian Ocean always changing texture and color.

"I think we should trust our children to find the love that is best for them. We can give them our blessing for whatever that may be, can we not, Fulsom?"

"I believe you are right, Reena. Now, another thing. The girls will not stop talking about an orphan named Joshua."

Reena smiled. "The priest and I spoke of the boy. Father Amani might apply for guardianship of Joshua."

"Could he do that?"

"He's considering asking his archbishop. Would you help us?"

"What could I do?"

She looked at him with determination. "You could not follow us to Arusha every time we went to see the boy or let anyone else follow us," she said, taking a big chance on his reaction.

"I think I could manage that, Reena. I do not hate Dakimu so much that I would sacrifice you to the wolves, so to speak."

It was out then between them that she might know where the murderer of his stepchild's father and grandfather might be.

"I thank you with all my heart, Fulsom. You are a good man."

The following week, on a day that Safina usually came straight to their apartment from school, she begged to go back to the Post.

"I am desperately wanted at the Farley's," she explained.

"Why are you *desperately* wanted?"

"Because Felicia's headaches are getting worse. Suzanna told me her mother said, 'That black child is the only thing that makes my life bearable.' I should go to her."

"You mean right now?"

"Yes, Mama. Suzanna passed me a note today saying her mother begged her to bring me home."

"All right, but I'll come with you. I need to speak to Mr. Farley about something."

Thus it was that, even though it held some risks for Reena, she was able to listen to the conversation between Felicia and her daughter. Reena could hear the woman moaning the minute they stepped into the bungalow.

"Oh, thank God you're here," Fulsom said.

"Safina? Is that you? Help me ... help me," Felicia cried.

"Mr. Farley, can you burn those plants again? Put in more red pepper leaves this time," Safina said and went into the bedroom.

Soon the whole house was filled with a tangy smoke, and Felicia's groans softened. But she would not let Safina go.

"Where did you come from?" Felicia asked over and over.

"From Soko Street," the girl said.

"No … whose are you?"

"My mother, Reena Patel, and my father, Sanjay Patel," Safina lied quickly.

"Reena … Reena," Felicia said, whimpering a little. "Why do I know that name?"

"Oh, it's common," the girl replied. "Even I know another Reena."

"Is she black or white?" Mrs. Farley wanted to know.

Uh oh, Reena thought outside the slightly open door.

"White." The girl did not lie that time.

"It's a puzzle," the woman in the bed said.

"Some puzzles cannot be solved, nor should they be," Safina said.

"Do you have a picture of this white Reena?" The woman was unstoppable.

"No, ma'am," Safina answered truthfully.

Major Farley offered Reena a drink.

"No, thank you, Fulsom. I was going to speak to you some more about Joshua, but I can see this is not the best time."

Suzanna had disappeared into her own room, and the dreadful sounds from Felicia's room had died. There were no more questions and shaky answers coming through the sick woman's door, just one last amazing pronouncement for Reena's daughter.

"Your hands are like God's," Mrs. Farley said.

The weeks passed. Dr. Mbulu told Reena he was pleased she had not bounded away again after Safina's father.

"I am dependent on the priest for anything I do from now on," she said.

"What about that major? Aren't you afraid of him?"

She had to think how carefully she should answer that. She folded some fresh towels on a table by the nurses' station. The doctor had stopped to file a patient chart. "I'm afraid Dak or Kiiku might make a mistake. I don't think Fulsom would show much mercy to them. But to me he offers leeway. I know he treasures my daughter. I'm not sure of the other reasons, but because of them, I have to trust him."

"You will come to me if you are in trouble?" Mbulu asked.

"Yes, Thomas," she said. "You are a great friend."

Later that day, she went to the base to watch her daughter and Suzanna ride Jester. At the far end of the arena there was a woman in a white robe leaning against the railing. Reena pulled a scarf over the lower part of her face. Safina brought the horse to a halt and asked, "Why do you look like a Muslim today?"

The riding instructor called loudly to Safina, "Why do you stop when I tell you to canter?"

Reena said quickly, "I feel a little illness coming," and waved at her daughter to go on.

Soon Felicia wandered back to bungalow number eight without even acknowledging Reena. The girls took turns on Jester. He was very obedient, and Reena could see that the children had acquired a supple grace, a confidence that glowed in their every move on the large animal. One time, she heard Suzanna ask the trainer if she could approach Mrs. Patel and talk to her.

"After your part of the lesson," he said and then pointed to a series of low rails Reena later learned were called cavalletti.

Suzanna trotted over them several times with her body forward, her seat out of the saddle, her heels down, and her head tilted up toward the next pole. The horse lifted his strong legs under her. The instructor kept adding these obstacles until the girl passed over them in perfect form. When it was Safina's turn, Suzanna dismounted and helped adjust the stirrup length. Then the girls hugged. The trainer admonished them. "That's enough of that!" and Safina swung up into the saddle.

Suzanna walked over to Reena, and they sat together in a small grandstand. The girl seemed nervous and moved close to her. She was shivering.

"What is it, dear?" Reena asked.

"My mother is upset today and keeps begging us to come in. Father has gone off for a few days, and Mrs. Vinton is in Kenya visiting her son. I don't know what to do."

"Would you like Safina to stay until your father returns?"

"Oh yes! Safina can calm her in an instant! Sometimes Mother can even get by without her pills when Safina's here."

"Where did Major Farley go?" Reena asked, thinking perhaps she could use those calming pills herself.

"I'm not sure," Suzanna said. "It has something to do with the black fugitive, but he doesn't tell us much. He mentioned the Selous Game Reserve. But Safina told me later that that was the wrong way. How could she know, Mrs. Patel?"

"She doesn't know, but she likes to think she could save the man." Reena tried to smile as though this was just her daughter's childish fantasy.

"She would save even *him*?"

"She imagines his heart is breaking … for his family, for his former life, whatever it was before your father began hunting him."

"That sounds like Safina," Suzanna said. She watched her best friend execute a lovely flying change on the willing Jester. "I kind of feel sorry for the black too. Because my father does not give up easily."

Reena pulled the girl closer and said, "Safina does not give up either when she wants to help someone."

"Well, it's a good thing for me."

"Yes, my dear. Now, I'll take Safina home after the lesson so she can gather some clothes for a few days' stay with you. I'll bring her back as fast as I can."

"Thank you, Mama Patel," she said.

Reena wasn't sure she should leave the girls alone with Felicia. Would they have to miss school to take care of her? Would they hear things they were not ready to hear? She would make Safina promise to call her if anything got out of hand.

§ § §

As she followed the horse master's directions, Safina thought of Major Farley traveling south toward the Selous. She knew Kiiku had misdirected him by allowing himself to be seen galloping off that way on Resolute and then disappearing in the bush. He had told Safina this one day when her mama was at work, and Suzanna had stayed after school for band practice. She had learned to play the flute because, she said, when you play the flute, you turn your head slightly to the right and her birthmark would not show on the concert stage. Safina had felt sad that her friend had to plan her entire life around the mark on her face.

Kiiku had come to explain his plan in case he was captured or worse and couldn't ever see her again. Safina cried hearing this but thought the plan was wonderful. Kiiku would leave hints with villagers along the way that he was trying to get to his father. He would race into a town on the black horse, spread rumors, and race out, where down the road a truck and trailer would take Resolute and him farther south, thus maintaining a good distance from the pursuing major.

But the best part, besides distracting Farley from his hunt for Dak in the correct direction, was his ultimate surprise. When the major reached the first fork in the massive Selous waterways, there Resolute would be, tied to a baobab tree with a note tacked to the trunk—*You may not have my father, but you may have your horse.*

Oh, how Safina wished she could be there to see the major's face! She had thrown her arms around her brother and said, "This is the finest thing you have ever done!"

"Maybe next to breaking Dakimu out of jail years ago," he had said.

§ § §

Suzanna was greatly relieved when Safina finally got back to the bungalow after leaving her to cool Jester and face her fractious mother who had been pacing her room, pulling clothes and things she had hidden in her drawers out onto the floor.

"Where is it? Where is it?" the woman kept shouting.

Safina stood quietly for a moment in the doorway.

"Safina, I can't take this anymore! Please help me!"

Suzanna watched her friend enter the bedroom and grab her mother's hands. "Mrs. Farley, Mrs. Farley, look at me," Safina said. "What are you searching for?"

"A book! A red book! It was here, I know it was!" Felicia cried.

"Mama Farley, I'll find it if you'll go to bed. You just rest. You'll feel better, I promise," Safina said. Then she ran her fingers through the desperate woman's tangled hair, whispering something in Swahili and arranging the covers over her as she climbed into bed with all her clothes on.

But Felicia kept mumbling, "He'll kill me too, he'll kill me too."

"Mama Farley, I won't let anyone kill you. You're safe now," Safina said.

The distraught woman closed her eyes, and Suzanna led Safina out to the kitchen table where earlier she had set a plate of sliced mangos and a couple of avocado sandwiches.

"She wouldn't take a bite, just started raving about the red book," Suzanna explained. "Father hid the red book from both of us. I don't know why. He said I wasn't old enough to read it and that Mother shouldn't be reminded of things that were best forgotten."

"I've heard things from that book. I've even met the man who wrote it. He loved Tanzania. Why would your mother fear what it says?" Safina asked.

Suzanna didn't have an answer. She trusted her father to do the right thing for her mother, so she had never questioned the disappearance of the red book. She felt crushed by her whole life. "Sometimes I hate my mother," she finally said.

"No, Suzanna, you shouldn't. Someone hurt her."

"When she screams, my face hurts."

Safina brushed her hair back from the red mark. "I'm so sorry," she said.

"You don't understand," Suzanna went on. "I hate her because she treats you like a daughter and me like something to be withstood."

"Oh. I just want her to *like* me. I thought she *loved* you," Safina said.

"I don't even care anymore. Your love means more than hers now." She pushed her plate away and rested her head on her forearms. She didn't want to say it, but she did. "I think her madness might come between us."

"Nothing will ever come between us," Safina said. "Not even the red book."

Mrs. Vinton came back from Nairobi before Suzanna's father returned. She and Safina did homework together until the neighbor arrived to fix dinner and help Felicia at bedtime. Then Mrs. Patel would come to get Safina, and she and Suzanna would kiss in the doorway as if they might be parted forever.

One Saturday at noon, when Suzanna and Safina were in the barn grooming Jester, a military truck with a horse trailer pulled into the stable area. They raced out to see what was happening. Major Farley grabbed both girls by the hand and said, "Close your eyes for a minute."

When they opened them, there stood Resolute, shiny and glorious in the midday sun. Suzanna shrieked and jumped with joy. That horse had been her favorite after Jester. Safina clapped her hand over her mouth and didn't say a word. As they stroked the glistening, black coat, Suzanna stared into Safina's secretive eyes.

"I suppose you knew about this too," she said.

nine

Reena hardly knew what was going on with the girls. She went to work, confession, Mass on Sunday, and seldom spoke to Father Amani about Joshua as the weeks went by. She heard about Fulsom hiding the red book from Felicia and the mysterious return of Resolute. Farley was briefly ill after his journey to the Selous, and when he recovered, he told her that some of his bitterness toward Dakimu and his son had dissipated. "But I still have a duty," he reminded her.

On Safina's tenth birthday in September 1996, just weeks before the girls entered fifth grade, Father Amani took Reena aside after a church service and said, "The Parks have said 'absolutely not' to my pleas to bring Joshua to Dar es Salaam—no adoption, no guardianship. Apparently the boy has had some problems, and they feel sending him away from the orphanage could exacerbate them."

"Oh no," Reena said in a hoarse whisper.

"But wait." The priest held up his hand. "They did say we could come to Arusha and take him for an outing. Trusted friends of the charity are encouraged to accompany the children on short adventures. We could certainly do that, Reena, could we not?"

"Yes. I suppose that would be something. Mbulu doesn't want me out of his sight, but I am due for a few days off. Can you make the arrangements, Father?"

"Of course. Perhaps you can close this chapter of your life," he said.

"Which one?"

"The one with Dakimu at the heart of it. I have become fearful of the situation."

"This is just where the story gets better," she said.

The next Sunday, the sanctuary was overflowing at St. Joseph's. Even Major Farley had taken his place in the front pew. Reena wondered if he was worshipping God or keeping track of her, contrary to his promises. She had noticed more soldiers on Soko Street and neighbors gossiping about new sightings of the fugitives, but no arrests had been made. She felt her anger rise at the white man who could so easily go back on his word.

He waited in his seat until she reached the communion rail and then got up and knelt beside her. They drank from the cup, one after the other. And the priest said, "The blood of Christ given for you." She flinched ever so slightly when she saw that, even though Amani had wiped the rim of the cup, Fulsom put his mouth in the exact spot where hers had been.

An hour later, Reena tried to reach Father Amani through the crowd. He looked tired, but he was giving blessings and not making any move toward his quarters. Finally, she stood on the steps of the cathedral close to him. He started to say something. But Major Farley drew near, and Amani turned to greet him.

"Are you really going to adopt that orphan Joshua?" the major burst right out.

"No," the priest said. "It has been denied. However, Reena has offered to help me take the boy on an approved outing, if we will not be prevented from visiting the child."

Fulsom looked at Reena with an unfathomable expression. He said quietly, "On Thursday next, my brigade and I are performing our equestrian and shooting skills for the president. We will be on the Post the entire day." He went a few feet away, then turned and said, "The homily this morning was especially insightful, Father."

The priest waited until the major's back blended into the throng of the faithful. He leaned toward Reena as if giving her a blessing and said, "Pack a bag, my dear. We'll be staying overnight."

Reena's heart jumped, and later that day, she began to believe in the possibilities when Safina asked her if she could spend the night with the Farleys on Thursday. "Our history class gets to watch the military games in the afternoon! Jester and Mlinzi will be the star horses because they can jump the highest. Suzanna's father thinks I should sleep over because it will be very late."

"Of course, Safina. I'm always happy for you to be with the Farleys," she answered, already thinking of what she would wear onto the grounds at Shanga.

On Thursday morning at 7:20, Reena and Father Amani sat side by side in the turboprop. The priest fingered his rosary and Reena the colorful beads on her wrist. She had seen a soldier at the back of the plane when they boarded and took their seats. Could Fulsom have tricked her after all?

The priest had noticed him too but said, "Are you going to look over your shoulder the rest of your life?"

"If that's what it takes," Reena said.

The flight was uneventful, and they disembarked on a clear spring day. A driver who worked for the Parks was waiting outside the terminal. The soldier got in a vehicle a few cars behind them, and it pulled out ahead of them. Reena could hardly think of the safest way to see Dak. She would not be disguised as she had been the two previous times she had gone to Arusha. For all anyone knew, she could be three different visitors.

It was an hour to the orphanage. Reena and Father Amani didn't say much to each other. The driver played a tape of melodic, a cappella African music as they passed banana plantations, avocado groves, and villagers burning small piles of trash on the roadside. When they reached their destination, they didn't climb out of the car immediately. Reena was exhausted and apprehensive.

When she opened her door, there was Joshua, two years older, with a direct and serious gaze.

"*Habari*," Reena said to him.

"We're having tie-dye class. Do you want to come?" he replied.

"Why yes, that would be fun," Reena said.

He didn't seem to remember her, so she told him she was Safina's mama.

"The one with God's eyes? The one who saved me?" he asked, brightening a little.

"Yes. She sends her love, Joshua."

"Oh *asante sana*, mama!"

"We should check with the directors first," Amani said.

So the boy led them to a small office and then ran off to his painting class. Reena and Father Amani stood outside a door that had a name carved in it—Aranya Park. The priest had told Reena that Aranya was a black woman who had married a Chinese missionary named Lee who helped her with the business side of things and tried to Christianize the natives. They were both in the office when Reena and Amani entered.

"You're here for Joshua's outing?" Mr. Park asked.

"Yes. Mrs. Patel's daughter befriended him when the children from the Light of the World School were here. We thought we would see how he was doing."

"Befriended him?" Aranya said, her eyebrows raised. "I think she saved his life."

"She seems to have a sixth sense about people in trouble," Reena admitted.

"Well, that is one of the reasons Joshua isn't available for adoption. He has had some problems—learning disabilities and some attachment disorder. You know what that is?" Lee Park asked.

"We do understand such things," Amani replied. "We don't mean to upset the boy, only give him a pleasant day with people who care about him."

"Joshua knows nothing about this outing," Aranya said. "Maybe you can win him over. He likes folks who wear a cross."

They all went out across the well-kept grounds to a room with a dirt floor. Children were busy coloring pieces of cloth with patterns of African animals to sell to tourists. It was very dark and stuffy in the enclosure. Reena felt good about taking Joshua out into the sunlight.

Aranya and Lee singled him out of the group and introduced him to his visitors. "They're here to take you on an adventure," Mrs. Park told him.

"Is it a forever adventure?" the boy asked.

"Just for today," Aranya assured him.

But Reena thought the boy looked disappointed. He reached out and grasped Amani's gold cross.

"*Mungu*," he said in Swahili.

"God … yes," the priest said. "What do you think about God?"

"He made me … and everything in the whole world." He said this with his arms moving in a wide arc. "But he forgot something."

"What's that?" the priest asked.

"I have no mother or father," he said. He let go of the cross and looked down at his feet but just for a moment.

"Maybe God wants you someday to be a father and a mother to others who are suffering," Father Amani said gently.

"Like you?"

"Yes."

"And I could live in the church and be with God?"

"I believe so, young man," Amani said. "Now, shall we go to the Cultural Center and maybe the Maasai Market?"

"Oh yes, please," the boy cried, clapping his hands. "And can we go to the place with the crippled artists?"

"Maybe tomorrow," the priest said, giving Reena a meaningful smile.

When they walked into the Cultural Center, Joshua put one hand in Father Amani's and one hand in Reena's. It was so satisfying to be showing this child the world that Reena didn't mind waiting awhile to look for Dak. This was her disguise—a Catholic woman sharing an act of service with her priest. She relaxed.

Joshua asked how he would know all of the people and the meaning of the exhibits. There was so much he had never seen of his own country—African art; sparkling gemstones from deep in the earth; ancient, hide, hunting skirts and hand-forged bells; and endless displays of beaded baskets, bracelets, dancing collars, wedding collars, clay animals, and carved wood of many shapes.

Father Amani offered to buy him a piece of jewelry, but he kept saying, "Cross … only a cross like yours."

So the priest found a tiny gold crucifix that gleamed against Joshua's black skin.

"Who is on the cross?" the boy asked.

"Don't you know?" Amani said.

"Maybe. Maybe it's Jesus. Baba Park told us this story," he said, running his hand across the shining body of the Savior.

They had lunch at the Maasai Market—roasted corn and lamb barbequed with salt and coriander. Joshua leaned closer to Father Amani as they made their way down the narrow, congested aisles, vendors dangling wares in their faces and trying to draw them in. They turned at the end of one row and began going down the next.

Suddenly, Reena stopped. About ten stalls away from them was the soldier that had been on the airplane. Amani saw him too. He said, "Just keep moving, Reena. There's nothing he can do here."

But when they reached the place where the soldier stood, Reena impulsively spoke to him. "Are you following me?"

"Just to protect you, mama," he said with an earnest voice.

"Thank you, but I believe I am safe with Father Amani," she said, fingering the soft folds of a silk scarf on a rack by the soldier's side.

"No worries, mama," he said.

But she did worry and pleaded with their driver to lead the soldier astray in the crowded streets, dropping her at Shanga, and continuing on by a seldom-used track back to the orphanage. And so they were able to evade the soldier as evening approached. Joshua fell asleep in Amani's lap as they looped in an odd pattern through Arusha and didn't wake when the van paused at Shanga. Reena climbed out and vanished into the falling light of the African night.

She presented herself at the entrance and said, "I am here to pick up some items I ordered from the glass maker."

"Wait here a moment, mama. We are almost closed."

Reena edged into the courtyard. She had worn a traditional tribal dress of many colors, with long, flowing skirts, beaded necklaces, and a headdress of silk. From a wristband she had hung the tail of a go-away bird that she had found on the path that first day at Shanga two years ago. Some of these items she had left in the orphanage taxi and added as they made their way to the handicap center. She looked nothing like the nun that had been her disguise. Her back was turned, and Dakimu did not recognize her.

"Mama, what glassware have you commissioned?" he asked.

"Pieces from the shore of the Indian Ocean," she said as she faced him in the moments before dark.

"Reena! I thought I would never see you again! What are you doing here? It is dangerous," he cried.

"It's not dangerous. I have a *mlinzi*, I told you. I think I am protected, though I have little faith in it. But, Dak, do you think one kiss in a dozen years is all I want? Do you think that is enough?"

"Of course not, but I am not free," he said.

"You are not free of Reena Stone!" she blurted out, not meaning to speak of that yet. "But I am here. I love you. And I need a place to spend the night. Can we not have one night?"

"We can ... but it will not be easy."

"Why? I can be a cousin from Dar, an old friend who needs lodging. Your wife can stay with her lover."

"Of course, all these things are possible, but you don't know about the *chui*," he said.

"Oh, Kiiku is here with you?"

"No, a *real* leopard comes to my hut most nights. He doesn't care for strangers."

"You are joking," she said.

Dakimu laughed softly. "My dear Reena, we have been apart too long. I have chosen a wild life; the leopard has chosen me. You'll have to share me now, woman," he said, touching her cheek.

"Show me this leopard. I will have my Dakimu either way."

It was completely dark now, so they passed undetected across the grounds and into his hut. The *chui* had arrived early and jumped up as they entered the *kibanda*.

"Oh my God," Reena whispered.

"His name is Chui. Chui, here is Reena. You've heard me call her name in my dreams," Dak said to the big cat.

Black or white Reena, Chui? Reena asked in her mind.

"You must love her too, my leopard," Dak continued.

The *chui* flipped his head, made a peevish sound, and flopped in a heap at the end of Dakimu's bed.

"Baraka must have gone to Kivuli's. She won't stay alone with the animal," Dak explained.

"Well, I'm having a hard time staying at all," Reena said.

"Come to bed, my love. If he purrs, you are quite safe. He does not purr for Baraka."

"I thought the big cats didn't exactly purr," she said.

"Well, whatever that noise is, I call it purring," he said.

He embraced her and kissed her and pulled her under the sleeping net. Soon their clothes were on the floor, and Dak sought all those places of old that Reena loved him to touch. Their breath began to come in short gasps. Reena was lost in the passion she had almost forgotten. Chui purred deliriously all the while.

In the morning, a length of purple silk was draped over the leopard's head.

"Too bad it's not green," Dakimu said. "That would be a sweet irony."

They stood looking at each other with a renewed sense of belonging while the leopard rubbed against their legs.

"Chui! It's late! You must go," Dak told him, removing the scarf and nudging him in the side.

"Wait," Reena said, "I must thank him."

"Say his name," Dak instructed.

"Chui … Chui, come here," Reena begged.

The leopard pushed his spotted body along the rails of the bed. She did not stroke him, as Dak had told her he didn't want the *chui* to be a pet, but rested her hand on his withers, massaged a bit, and said, "Good *chui*. You are a good *mlinzi*. Better than my Major Farley … with a different kind of power. I hope you two will never meet."

And the leopard, hearing pots and pans being gathered in nearby huts, slipped under the door flap and was gone.

Reena burst into tears. "Oh, I have been such a fool, Dakimu. I do believe you'd choose that leopard over Reena Stone."

"I believe I would. He came to me with no demands, no expectations. He loved me before he even knew who I was. It is a mystery. I do fear for his life. He hides by day in the coffee plantation as I once did. The farmers have talked of missing chickens and a dog but also see fewer rats and rabbits so don't mind his selective hunting."

"Do they know it's a leopard on their land?"

"I don't think so. But one of the managers told me they don't want to hurt a creature trapped in the city with perhaps no way out."

"Like you," Reena said.

"No," he said. "I have a way out, but I could not take him with me, so I don't think about that day. It hurts too much."

"Where? Where could you safely go?"

"I think you might figure that out. I have a method to tell you anyway when that time comes. Oddly, I rely on Kiiku's mother, who will not see that she is delivering me into your arms. I believe she is past caring how I … misused her. But, my dear Reena, why are you here?" Dakimu finally asked.

"Father Amani and I came to take an orphan in Arusha for a

day trip. There was talk of adoption, but we decided we shouldn't bring a troubled boy into our complicated lives."

"But will I ever see *my* child again?"

"I'm praying to God every day that you will, but the answer seems to be in the hands of a white man," she said.

"Hmm. My fate always seems to be in the hands of a white man," he said.

Or a white woman, Reena thought.

"You know that I loved Jim Stone equally, I mean, with the same passion that I loved his wife," he added suddenly.

"No, I didn't know that. I'm not sure what you mean," Reena said, startled anew by this revelation.

"I'm not sure to this day. Talk about complicated. You have no idea."

"I think I should stay out of that part of your life," Reena said. "I know you needed the Stones desperately at one time. I just want you to need me now. And Safina."

"That is an easy need. That is a saving need. The other sent me far in the direction of the unsaved," he said.

He took her face in his hands and slowly brought his lips down on hers. For her, it was perfect and complete. For him, she could not say.

The sun leapt into the sky too soon for the lovers still tentative in their embrace. It had been a good reunion, Reena thought, and she dreaded saying good-bye. She noticed on her exit from Dak's hut that the leopard had waited just outside. The beautiful cat looked at her with a softness in his eyes and then slunk through the hole in the plantation fence, and she imagined him beginning to hunt for his breakfast.

§ § §

Major Farley gazed at the trooper with a mixture of disgust and dismay. "You lost her! How could you lose her?" he said. "Has all your training been for nothing?"

"Sir, the orphanage driver knows the streets of Arusha much better than I. I commandeered the taxi after we left the airport, but perhaps I should have kept that man. He might have been able to follow the woman and the priest. But, sir, I'm confused. You told me to protect her *and* find her black lover that may be the fugitive you seek. Those orders seem to contradict each other," the young soldier said.

"Well, they seem perfectly clear to me. You don't have to know all the details. Did I tell you to shoot anyone?"

"No, sir."

"Did I tell you to reveal anything you discovered to anyone else, the police or the government officials?"

"No, sir."

"You couldn't very well protect Mrs. Patel if you didn't know where she was, now could you?"

"No, sir."

Farley sighed and altered his tone. "It's just as well, I guess. I'm not quite ready for my final maneuver."

I ought to be, he thought, *after all this time*. But he couldn't reconcile his own contradictory feelings. He cared about that Reena. He loved her daughter. He longed for his mountain lover who had never questioned one of his decisions in her life. He wanted revenge for Suzanna's father and grandfather. He wanted to do his job. But none of those things promised a happy ending. Maybe life wasn't supposed to have happy endings. *We all die, after all*, he told himself.

The girls were having a lesson. Their instructor had come to him earlier complaining about their closeness and their concern for each other when each should be concentrating on her own equitation and handling of the horse.

"Girls will be girls," the major had said.

"Yes, I know about such things," the trainer had said with something like a sneer.

"Would you prefer me to hire another horse master?"

"No. I just expect full cooperation and attention to my instructions."

"I'll see that they comply … without offending them," Farley replied.

His lover had told him once of a young woman who loved women, how she and her lover were almost outcasts from their tribe. She had said, "I would not want a child of mine to be branded for having such a special love."

"But you don't have a child," he had said to her. He was surprised to see tears on her cheeks.

He glanced out now at Suzanna and Safina cooling Jester out, riding together on his bare back. He rather enjoyed seeing the black and white arms wrapped around the reins and each other's hands. They were only ten years old. They couldn't know all the meanings of their immature love. He crossed himself, something he rarely did in the open. Perhaps he would go in and spend some time with Felicia.

§ § §

One morning, a while after the trip to Arusha, Reena looked down at the bus stop. Suzanna had been there all weekend with her and Safina as Farley tended to the floundering Felicia. She could see the girls from the window. Safina held her white friend's hand. She had a drawing in her other hand. Reena smiled. She had seen it the night before. It was a fine sketch of Noah's Ark with a long ramp upon which small pairs of African animals marched toward the ship, which looked a lot like a Tanzanian dhow. The amazing thing was that one animal was drawn larger and with more detail and appeared at the front of the line—a leopard. Over the boat arched a rainbow. The colors were not in the right order, but the arc of green was definitely the widest. Reena wished she could see the nun's face when she looked upon that scene.

She thought of the Bible verse she had found in Genesis when she was searching for a name for her newborn girl—*Make yourself an ark of cypress … I will establish my covenant with you, and you will enter into the ark ... Every kind of creature that moves upon the ground will come to you to be kept alive.*

Then she thought of the Stones. How they would love all this drama, this symbolism of names. Dak's wife's name, Baraka, meant *blessing* in Swahili. "Something we all need," she whispered to the bright morning air. She remembered that when she first met Jim and Reena, they had spoken of their own struggles in Africa, seeking God and love and words to fix their souls upon the planet. Yes, mistakes were made but were redeemed by other acts surely blessed by God, if one believed in God.

Reena had no personal doubts about God, but that he determined the outcome of conflicts and desires, she was not so sure. When he created the color green, could he have known it would become the symbol of rebellion and grief among disenfranchised Tanzanians? When he created the leopard, could he have foreseen the animal treading softly toward the ark of a little black girl?

She drove to work slowly, trying to banish her doubts. She took the first parking space she found and walked reluctantly toward a job she usually loved. But she was distracted now by the ache in her heart. Dak still hid at Shanga, and she could not see him. Weeks had gone by, and the man she adored seemed farther away than ever. Was he feeling the absence of her voice? Her touch? He had his wife, his glass blowing, his son, and now his leopard. Who was she? What need could she fill that the others did not?

Safina. Of course. He'd want his daughter in his sporadic and strange world. *I will give him his daughter*, she thought. And then she had an even more frightening and brazen idea. *I will give him his white Reena!* She would outmaneuver God himself and have her heart's desire, counting on Dak's exhilaration at her selfless gift.

But God could not have known what would happen next. Reena had seen a few patients. Going back to the nurses' station for some meds, she saw a familiar figure emerge from Dr. Mbulu's office—the still beautiful and openhearted Reena Pavane Stone.

They approached each other in the hallway, and the white woman held out her arms. Reena Patel fell into them without a second thought.

"I was just thinking about you!" Reena said with some guilt.

"My dear Reena, I have missed you," Mrs. Stone said. "I wouldn't have come, except ... it was Jim's dying wish ..."

"Jim is dead? What? Why?" Reena had to sit down. She felt as if she were in a terrible dream. He had been so loyal to her. To Safina. He couldn't be gone.

"I'm sorry to bring such bad news. I'm not quite used to it yet myself," the widow Stone said.

"This will be very hard on Safina too. She always talks about Jim. I think Kiiku has been reading to her from his *Memoirs*. She seems to know a lot about his past ..."

"Wait, she knows Kiiku?"

"They are very close. It's a long story."

"Wow," Reena Stone said.

"So what was Jim's last wish?" Reena could not believe what she was hearing. Jim had so much heart that it seemed it would go on beating forever.

"'Spread my ashes in the green hills of Manyara where Dakimu carried me when I was sick coming back to Dar es Salaam,'" his wife quoted calmly, the words seeming to give her strength.

"I don't know what to say," Reena told her old friend. "How ... did he die?"

"His life was extremely compromised by the malaria drugs he'd taken for so many years. Very hard on the liver and the heart," she said. "I held him until the very end. We had been together thirty-six years, a wonderfully long time. But he was only seventy, after all. Sometimes I can't bear it. But I can do what he wanted."

"When did he—"

"Two weeks ago," she said. "I have not been to Manyara. I've been staying at the Imperial Arms—I still call it that. I didn't feel like seeing anyone."

"Father Amani?"

"Not even him," she answered. "I came here to see if you wanted to go with me."

"I … don't think I can. There are many reasons."

They looked at each other in silence for what seemed like a long time. Finally, Reena Patel said, "Will you come see me after you return from the hills?"

"I will."

Reena started to turn away to resume her duties, but she stopped and said to her mourning white friend, "I'm so sorry. God be with you on your journey. Be sure to visit the Shanga Center in Arusha on your way."

"Yes."

Did she know Dak was there or just then take Reena's suggestion as confirmation? But Mrs. Stone answered that question without reservation, "I figured out the clue … but I didn't want to go while Jim was alive."

"But you'll go while I'm alive," Reena said, hating herself for being so petty.

"What do you think I should do, my friend?" Reena Stone asked.

"Follow your heart," Reena said.

She went into the nurses' lounge fighting tears. She wanted to cry for Jim. He had surely suffered … but died in the arms of the only woman he had ever loved, as far as she knew. She would read his *Memoirs* again. The first time she had read it she had felt his love for Africa, for Tanzanians, and for Dakimu. Dakimu! She should be the one to tell him that Jim was gone! *But when he sees Reena Stone standing in the courtyard at Shanga, he will know. What emotions rise from his heart only his white Reena will see,* she thought with jealousy.

Reena was plagued with the irony that the malaria had finally taken his life since that dreadful disease had brought the young missionary Reena and then Dakimu into his struggle as long ago as 1960. The three had bonded against almost insurmountable odds. It was all in Jim's red book. People would be mad for that book now, autographed copies selling for thousands, and the characters in it revered and hated. And remembered. Whites like Hahlos, the Sommers family, Jim and Reena, and the Christian missionaries. Blacks like King Kisasi, Dakimu, Kiiku, Kiiku's mother, and Father Amani. Reena could only hope the news would not travel too fast.

But she was shocked when she returned home to find Safina curled in Kiiku's arms. "Mama, Mama, Mr. Stone died," she wailed.

"I know, sweetheart ... but how did you know?" she asked her daughter.

Kiiku answered, "My mother told us. I took Safina and Suzanna to the market after school for some supplies for their sewing class. My mother was waving Jim's red book in the air for all to see, crying, 'Amekufa! Amekufa! He is dead!'"

"But why would she ... even know him ... or care so deeply?" Reena asked.

He told her with his eyes trained on the window, as if staring into a perplexing past. His mother had revealed to him in her muddled way that she had known a white man, the man who had later written the red book, who had lain weak and sick in a prison hut before Dakimu and the white missionary had reached him with his malaria drugs. She had kept him clean, his bedding dry, had ground the quina bark or made tea from the sweet wormwood plant, if she could find it, for medicine, and stayed outside his door at night, his *mlinzi*. Jim had told her she was an angel, something she had never heard being an untouchable of sorts, although she was the king's daughter. Jim had touched her hand, which no man had done with gentleness or respect.

"Of course, later, Dakimu would have his way with her."

"What?" Reena gasped. Is that what Dak had meant by *misused*?

"Oh, yes. You didn't know?"

"But why? Why would he do such a thing?"

"He married her in exchange for her father, my grandfather, King Kisasi, releasing the prisoner and letting Dak take Jim back to his white world. When my father returned, as he had promised, she had borne a child by another man, a daughter."

"You have another sister?" Reena asked, totally caught off guard by this new information.

"I did ... she drowned in the river by our village. But my mother never forgot the generosity of Jim Stone ... or the cruelty of Dakimu."

"Does your father know about Jim?" she asked with a catch in her throat.

"I don't think so. I need to tell him," he said.

"I'm going with you," Safina announced.

"Kiiku?" Reena implored.

"No, Safina. It's too dangerous. I can't take a chance on losing another sister."

"You may be too late anyway," Reena said. "Jim's wife is on her way to Manyara with his ashes. She was the first to get the clue to where Dak was. She should be the one to tell him."

"She'll be followed," Kiiku said.

"Maybe not." Reena reached for the phone. Safina was lying on the couch holding the leopard. When Fulsom answered the call, Reena just said, "It's me."

And he said immediately, "She will not be trailed. Let her scatter her husband's ashes in peace. Keep the black's son with you. I can't always protect him. His Chui clan has been robbing tourists and stealing horses and weapons."

"Thank you," she said. She hung up but left her hand on the instrument, unable to move. Finally, she said, "Kiiku, you cannot go either, not right now. You are safer here."

"I will never be safe," he said.

Safina got up and came over to her brother. "Kiiku, I will be like *two* sisters to you."

"Yes ... I believe you could do that," he replied.

Reena said, looking back to that day when she first saw him down on Soko Street, "Are you sure you did not come for us?"

But he couldn't answer. Reena thought he must be trying to imagine how his father would feel losing his white brother to the African malady.

ten

$\mathcal{E}$very day that Dakimu passed by the poor boy with the sea glass rosary around his neck, he was reminded of the day he and Reena had wandered along the tide line on the Indian Ocean, and he had pledged his love to her. She was the same lovely woman that she had been over ten years ago. Beautiful and loyal and the mother of the equally beautiful Safina. Why could he not let the white Reena go? She haunted him and sparked memories of running through acacia forests and hills of strangler figs and mahogany trees, bathing in rain pools and struggling across hot, dry washes and tall grass plains.

Had those days barely surviving in their search for Jim Stone bound them so strongly they could not come apart? He had sent her the clue first. But the black Reena had found him and brought him his child one unforgettable afternoon. But if he were free, which Reena would he seek?

Lately, he lived for the companionship of the wild leopard, although fearing for the animal's life and hating the long nights when he didn't come. There was a close call one night when the *chui* was purring so loudly the sound spilled out of the hut. Someone passed by and said, "Hey, man, whatchu got in there?"

"A leopard," Dakimu said.

"Oh yeah, oh, a leopard," the man said, drifting off in fits of laughter.

Dak put his fingers to his lips and said, "Shh," to the cat. The leopard turned over on his back and purred even louder.

"Ach, Chui, you are going to be the death of us," Dak said and kicked him playfully.

§ § §

Reena Pavane Stone sat in the turboprop with the mahogany box, holding the remains of her dear husband. Dakimu had married them twelve years ago, but they had met twenty-five years before that, the year they had met the beautiful, passionate Tanzanian black under troubling circumstances. There were pieces of the story in Jim's *Memoirs*, in articles in British journals, in essays published by Peacetime Publications in New York City, and perhaps in diaries of Africans touched by the love of each of them, black and white.

But at this moment, it seemed the story was over. There would be no more poetic and moving words from the pen of Jim Stone. He could never embrace Dakimu again or drive through the parks and villages of Tanzania that had defined his life. She would spread his ashes over the wild forests where Dak had carried him to safety; she would put this box in Dak's hands, or maybe not; she would hold Dak for a moment, or maybe not.

She gazed down at the country below as she had done many times. The last few months had been so hard. She had wanted to bring his black friends to him, but many of them were no longer living, having been older than Jim when they helped him through his first attack of malaria in the early fifties. Once, in his delirium, Jim had called out for Dak. She had lied that Dak was coming, to hang on, knowing the black could not have come, even if he had known how ill Jim was.

She thought she might write about those years since 1970 when they said good-bye to Dakimu at the airport in New York and then threw his gun in the Hudson River. Oh, she could say it now. Who would be dredging up that river for a gun that old?

She could finally reveal the secrets of that disaster of a man, Colonel Edmund Hahlos, the damage he wrought in the serene Tanzanian land, pitting warriors against peacemakers, blacks against blacks, blacks against whites. Only four people had ever known that Dakimu had killed him, and now, she was the only one still alive, besides Dak himself, who knew it. She could tell many things that were not in Jim's *Memoirs*, but she only had the strength to tell Dakimu why she was back in Africa and empty the mahogany box over the trails that had witnessed their betrayal and their love.

The plane banked sharply as it turned into the wind and prepared to land at the Kilimanjaro International Airport. It was an hour's drive to Arusha, but she didn't feel up to it. She hired a driver, who tried to take the urn from her hands, not knowing what it was. She gripped it and said, "*Siyo!*"

"*Samahani*, mama," the Tanzanian said in apology.

Reena had her own duffel and two suitcases full of items for the orphanage. She let the young man put those in the car.

"Where shall I deliver you, mama?" he asked.

She hesitated. There was a comfortable hotel in Arusha where she could rest and prepare herself to meet Dakimu, but she said, "Shanga," and did not think of changing her mind. The fields flew by. Mt. Kilimanjaro rose as tall and lonely as ever out of the plains. Mt. Meru was cloaked in haze, the way her imagination clouded as they approached her destination, her rendezvous with the unknown.

"Someone watching for you at Shanga, mama?" the driver asked.

"Yes," she said, but she knew Dak could not possibly be aware of how close she was to where he was hiding or that she was even in Africa. The last time they had been together, she had kissed him in his jail cell, trying to pour her faith, her passion, and her love into his soul. For her, it was not sexual, although she had never told her husband about that kiss. For Dak, it had seemed more than sexual. It had a hunger. She did not want to kiss him

151

again, but the fire was there, would always be there between them.

Arusha had been a small village over thirty-five years ago when she and Dak passed through searching for Jim. Now, it sprawled out toward the foothills of the famous mountains, and boys rushed out from alleyways to wash vehicle's windows if the car or taxi had to stop for any reason. Reena gave one teenager five American dollars because he was so polite and genuine.

"You shouldn't do that, mama," the driver said.

"Oh, I know, but these are my people too," she said.

She was sure he questioned that, but he just smiled. She could see his handsome face in the rearview mirror. She got out her own mirror and checked her hair. Silver strands ran through the golden-blond but still curled softly in waves down her back. Her face had a few lines around her eyes and mouth, but she smoothed those with a little mineral powder and brushed some light peach blush on her cheeks and lips. She had not taken this much care with her appearance since Jim died.

"You see someone special, mama?"

"Someone special," she said.

The gates of Shanga stood open and welcoming. Handmade wind chimes jangled in the afternoon breeze, and hand-woven scarves rippled with a myriad of colors from the first vendor's stall. Reena walked slowly, carrying the mahogany box. Then she called to a Shanga guide and asked if her box could be put in a safe place for a while, that she was looking for a friend who lived or worked there.

"What is friend's name?" the guide asked, taking the wooden urn from her hands.

But she did not have to answer because she saw Dakimu striding across the compound and entering the glass blower's shop.

"I see him now," she told the guide.

He moved with the grace of a leopard. Her heart pounded. *Oh, God, please let me do the right thing*, she prayed. Dak pulled his safety visor down and began to shape the stem of a glass. His arms glistened in the light of the fire. Sweat poured down his face from under the shield and fell like tears to the ground. Another worker tapped him on the shoulder, and he raised the visor. "You have a visitor," the artisan said.

Reena wanted to touch him before he looked into her eyes, to soften the blow. She reached out and wrapped one hand around his that did not hold the glass. She put her soul into that grip.

He closed his eyes. "There is only one reason you would come," he said, and then in a choked voice, "I feel joy and sorrow … maybe not in that order. But I am beyond words."

"It's safe to acknowledge me. No one followed," she said.

He put her hand to his lips and held it there for a long moment. Finally, he said, "This is so impossible … that you are standing here. How can I believe it?"

"Believe that I am here to return Jim to the land he loved. I just couldn't do it without telling you, in case you wanted to go with me … or wanted to hold the box … with his ashes," she said.

"Oh God, Reena, I'm so sorry. I know how you loved him."

"And I know how you loved him," she said.

He let go of her hand but leaned over and kissed her cheek. She tasted his tears. "Where are you taking him?" he asked.

"Manyara."

"I must go with you. It was our country, his and mine. You and I did not travel that way, but when Jim and I stumbled on the trail, you were surely there."

"I think I was in the air over the Atlantic," she said.

"Hmm … there too."

Some customers wanted glassware, and his fire dwindled precariously. He went back to work after asking her to collect her box from the guide and sit on a bench by the creek behind the restaurant. "I will have a hard time shaping the glass with your eyes on me," he had said. "You may find some peace there out of the crowd."

It was getting late. Many vendors had closed. Reena took her mahogany urn and searched out the resting place near the creek. As she crossed the wide lawn and wandered down the brook, the day flew from light to dark. She had seen the Shanga-built swing before the light was gone. She sat gratefully and breathed in the fragrance of flowers she barely remembered the names of. Jim would know.

She caressed the polished box and thought of the day she had received the clue from Dak, the poem with the words *a twisted pillar of wax*. She knew instantly that he was at Shanga, but she didn't believe she would ever be here with him, so now she let the reality of it fill her and steady her for the task she had come to do.

She could still hear the chimes singing up by the entrance. The breeze had increased, and the willows swayed along the bank of the brook. And then she looked across the water from the place where she rested straight into the face of a crouching leopard. She had seen leopards in the wild, but this one did not threaten her or shy away. It lay its head down on giant front paws and returned her gaze.

"*Chui*," she whispered.

He rolled onto his side.

What an amazing thing, she thought. *Perhaps this is how Dak felt watching me across his forge.*

"Reena, don't be afraid," Dak said behind her.

"Oh, I'm not. Do you know him?" she asked.

"I think it's more like he knows me," he said. "Come, I'll show you."

She followed Dakimu across a small bridge, along a row of huts, and entered the fourth one on the left. He lit a candle and took the urn from her hands.

"This I really cannot believe," he said. He set the box by the candle and put his head in his hands. "Was it very bad?"

"Bad, but not too long," she told him. "Dak, I don't think I can talk about this until he's … where he asked me to … you know."

"Bury him."

"Yes."

"That's okay with me. Listen, I can fix us some supper or call for Baraka," he said.

"Baraka?"

"My wife," he said.

"Dakimu, I return after eleven years, and you have a daughter, a wife, and a leopard!"

"Things change," he said.

"Do they?"

"Well, not all things."

And in the silence that followed, the leopard came under the door flap in his usual way and jumped into Dak's sleeping net.

"He only does that now when a new person is in here. With Reena Patel, he slept at my feet. The first week he was here, he curled up outside the door."

"What does he want?"

"I think he wants Safina."

"Your daughter? Why?"

"I think he got trapped in Arusha. Maybe he has a mate someplace. His heart is broken."

"In that he is not alone," she said.

"But I think he needs someone to show him the safe way out, of the town and the broken heart," Dak added.

"Safina is just a child. You shouldn't let her near the *chui*," Reena said.

"I don't know. If she finds out about him, she'll drive her mother crazy until she can see him. What worries me is that she's getting old enough to find her way out here by herself. And there's a deeper problem. The first time I saw her, she was with her best friend, the daughter of David Sommers."

"Oh Lord. She couldn't know ..." Reena began.

"No. She doesn't know who I killed. I believe Suzanna's stepfather knows, of course, and he knows where I am but is protecting the girls' friendship for some reason."

"How could he know where you are?"

"Something Safina or Reena said, I'm not sure," Dak answered.

"But how did Reena find you?"

"Kiiku hid the clue in a stuffed leopard and gave it to Safina. Reena must have opened the toy up and discovered the verse. And then Kiiku brought her here during a time that I had abandoned Shanga. I wasn't ready to see her anyway."

"Jim called Reena after he came back from Africa and read her the poem."

"I suppose that's how she put everything together," Dak said.

The leopard stretched and slung one paw over the side of the hammock.

"Do you want to touch him?" Dakimu asked.

"He's so beautiful … but he came to you, to your family. I shouldn't interfere," she said.

"You are my family too. You always have been."

Reena looked at the *chui* in Dak's bed. He was purring as he exhaled. The dim candlelight muted the spotted cat and gave a glow to the shadows so it seemed just a painting on the wall.

"Why is he so tame?" she asked.

"He is not tame … but he loves me. That I cannot explain." He traced one finger over her lips. "As other love cannot be explained."

"Dak …"

"I need to tell you something, Reena," he said. "All these years, from the first day we met, I would have taken you away from Jim if I could, but now that he is gone, I shall never do it."

"It's kind of hard to make a promise to a handful of ashes," she said.

"He lives in my heart," he said, removing his fingers from her still beautiful face.

"Mine too," she said.

There was a low whistle at the door. The leopard lifted his head.

"It is Baraka," Dakimu said. "My wife. She accustomed the leopard to that sound so she wouldn't startle him."

Reena was startled herself by the exquisite beauty of the woman who entered the hut.

Baraka said immediately, "Ah, the white Reena."

Dak slid the urn out of sight and then said, slightly embarrassed, "I forgot Baraka and Kivuli had invited me to dinner tonight."

"You are welcome too, Mrs. Stone," the gorgeous woman said in accentless English.

"I'm terribly tired," Reena said, "but thank you. Maybe Dak can bring the *chui* and me some leftovers. That would be a gift."

"I like this white Reena," Baraka said. "But I don't think we should leave her with the leopard, as sweet as he is. Kivuli and I will bring the meal to you. Now, light some more candles. I'll make the cat wait outside."

She opened the flap slightly and glanced up and down the rows of *vibanda*. "Come on, Chui," she said. "Come with Baraka."

The cat jumped down obediently and followed her to a large inverted crate Dak had built for the leopard to hide from strangers or get out of the weather. Dak told Reena how he and Baraka would laugh to themselves when evening visitors would sit on the structure not knowing there was a leopard right under their feet.

"You have a good life here, Dakimu," Reena said as they arranged his small table with plates and utensils made by Shanga artisans, his own forge-blown glasses, and linens woven by women watching over disabled children, letting them untangle thread or group shades of color.

"I was happy having my son for many years. He was a great strength and forgave much of my past. But he became a warrior, just as I had done, a Chui. And then he told me one day about Safina. I was languishing, not eating. There was no church I could safely enter."

"Jim saw her, of course, when he answered that cryptic note Reena put in the *Tribune*. He told her a little about you and then met me in Amsterdam for a study we did together on climate change. When he began to be sick, we didn't think of anything else. And your Reena chose a different path too. I'm sorry, Dak."

"No, my dear, it is I who defined the paths for everyone."

Dakimu's wife and Kivuli soon brought a savory meal to the

kibanda, and they all ate quietly. No one spoke of Jim Stone. The women could not have known about the mahogany box hidden nearby or the errand Reena was on. Dak would probably tell them later. She was not sure of the women's relationship. They deferred to each other in all things—the seating in the best light, the sharing of the last serving of food, and the answering of questions. Baraka's English was much better than Kivuli's, but Dak's wife always let her speak first if she could. So when Dak stopped eating for a moment and rested his head in his hands, Kivuli looked at Baraka, who nodded almost imperceptibly.

Kivuli said, "What could be your trouble, baba?"

"My heart is heavy with grief. A friend who was like a brother to me has died."

Baraka leaned down and kissed his hands and said with sudden understanding, "We will leave you then and your friend's … widow." And the women retreated from the hut.

When they had gone, Dakimu told her how he had met Baraka when he was hiding at a spring in the hills outside of Arusha, soon after Kiiku had broken him out of the jail cell in Dar es Salaam. "I was so exhausted and thirsty. I lay by a pool of mountain water and did not hear her footsteps on the path. She spoke to me in Swahili, asking if I needed help, was I sick. I said in English that I was sick of running; I was a fugitive from the law; I had killed people, thinking she wouldn't know what I meant. 'Then it is a good thing a Blessing has found you,' she said in English. She took me in, showed me the safe trails, and told me about a woman that she loved but was not allowed to visit. So I married her. She and I were both under less suspicion, and we were able to have some peace."

"I could not have written a story like that! Does she sleep here?"

"Usually, but I'm sure she won't return tonight. So, Reena, will you stay with me? You can sleep in the other hammock."

"I'll stay and be glad of it. You are the only one who knows my heart."

But in the night, when the *chui* stole in and lay at her head, she thought perhaps the leopard knew her heart too.

Baraka brought them breakfast. She whistled first at the door, but the *chui* had disappeared in the night. She served them buttermilk crepes with Shanga raspberry preserves and hearty coffee from the plantation next to the center.

"I will leave you now," Dakimu's wife said. "I need to help pick the corn while the air is still cool."

"Baraka, thank you," Reena said. "I hope we will meet again."

"Yes, madam. I hope I will know your story. Dakimu says it is in the red book written by your husband, but I have been afraid to read it," she said.

"I have come here to scatter the ashes of my husband in some country not far from here."

"Oh … I will be pleased to read it in his memory then." And she passed between the curtain of the door and the wall of the hut as silently as the leopard.

The widow put down her fork. She was reluctant to speak, but she said, "Dak, do you still love Reena?"

He hesitated, but he too was able to find his voice. "I do," he said. "But she wants me to love her as I love you … and that I can never do."

"You have never said that to her!"

"God, no. I told her once she was the only woman I loved, and maybe it was true at that moment. But I am never going to get over what I felt in your arms on the bank of the Rufiji River."

"Nor I, Dakimu."

They looked at each other across the Shanga-hewn table, across the millenniums of evolution between black and white, across the lies and betrayal that had separated them, and across the truth that had brought them together again, intensely aware of a thousand burnt fragments in a mahogany urn under a chair nearby.

§ § §

In Dar es Salaam, the black Reena sat on the couch with the startling view of the Indian Ocean. That day, it revealed layer upon layer of white curls churned up by storm winds and a recent earthquake off the Asian coast thousands of miles away. But Reena's eyes were not on that turbulent scene for long. They were drawn back to the red book she held in her hands and Jim Stone's powerful words.

Today we entered the forests at Manyara. It was a place I had always loved but had not been to for many years. Its mosaic of green, blue freshwater pools, red-limbed mahogany, stands of evergreens and yellow-barked acacia, here and there an ancient baobab, herds of zebra, elephant, golden jackals, flamingoes on the lake, and many other animals among the trees and grasses had always calmed me, blessed me, even though I could not name God as the creator. The place had always been a refuge, a vision for the lens of my camera, not a place to worship.

But today, I collapsed at the shadowy entrance, feverish from the malaria and weakened by months of imprisonment in the camp of the militant Vitani, in the territory controlled by King Kisasi. I could not even lift my Rolleiflex, read my light meter, or focus the images before me. We were taking the longest route from where I had been held—for ransom, so to speak—by the blacks who were waiting for arms and medicine promised them by the British. The shortest route would have been the most dangerous for the black who had been allowed to guide me back to Dar es Salaam, to the arms of Reena Pavane.

Reena Patel closed the red book. She thought that Mrs. Stone might be releasing Jim's ashes into the wind at Manyara at that moment and with the black man who had comforted him and then carried him for many miles through the canopied forest and down the dusty, red tracks. The white woman could be leaning on that same black man now for her own strength. How far might that need go, with her husband drifting down upon the emerald and gold earth, the two mourners alone in the forest?

She looked again through the pages of Jim's *Memoirs* to distract herself from these disturbing images.

Dakimu Reiman, my guide, my guardian, my friend, walked behind me for a while after we had argued about trust—the ambiguous nature of that value between nations, between races, between men and women, and between the two of us. That move told me that he didn't trust me, but I loved him. The strange thing is that if he had been white, I would not have loved him. I loved him because he was a Tanzanian, because he was risking his own life to evacuate me from the ruthless Kisasi warriors. But there was a lie between us. And I loved him because he did not let that lie destroy our friendship.

All this I realized in the forested gardens of Manyara, in a malaria delirium and deep pain. We still had hundreds of miles to go, unsafe villages to steal around, terrorized black Christians who ran from us, and British patrols who would kill Dak on sight. But there, in Manyara, I understood the meaning of love more than in any other place. There, I wish to be buried if there is anyone left who reads these words and can grant me this wish.

§ § §

The widow of Jim Stone and Dakimu Reiman stood in the heart of Manyara with the mahogany urn between them. They had been driven there in a jeep caravan guided by the Chui clan. The men had peered out of the open-topped vehicles with rifles pointed in all directions. At one point, a military helicopter had flown over and then veered quickly away. A massive tree blocked the road, and while the young warriors worked to clear it, Dakimu and Reena got out of the jeep and made their way through the broken branches.

"Can we find a place where you carried Jim?" she asked, suddenly feeling how anguishing that time must have been for the men.

"I don't know. Everything has changed. Jim fell by a pool of fresh rainwater, but it has not rained in a while," Dak said.

"Was there a place where you suspected he might betray you, but you loved him anyway?"

"Many places, Reena. Those have surely become overgrown and inaccessible. But wait … here is a meadow we crossed. I remember the fallen mahogany on one side. It's still there. We used the branches for a fire and slept under a curve in the big trunk. How resilient that wood is to withstand the storms all these years."

"That will be the place," Reena said. But she held back for a moment, not wanting to let her husband go.

§ § §

The eyes of the black Reena found these words—*Dak and I were cold and hungry. It had been raining, and I stumbled in a shallow pool. Dakimu caught me and somehow lifted me onto his back. Ahead of us across a wet meadow was a downed mahogany. He struggled toward it, carrying me and our few provisions, and laid me on my sleeping pallet under an arc in the huge trunk. He made a small fire, cooked the last rabbit he had snared, and held my head up so I could drink a cup of fresh water from a spring in the nearby woods. Then he gently let my head back down on my blanket-wrapped camera case, where I had hidden the film I had promised to destroy, photos of his warrior tribe murdering and pillaging in the name of King Kisasi.*

Reena stared again at the actual photos right there in black and white on the next few pages. They were shocking, and what they portrayed, unforgivable.

Dak rested his hand on my forehead. He said, "If you die, my friend, I am going to leave you where you are and go back to my people. I will still love you, but I will not die for you." I thanked him for his care, in case I died that night, and said, "If I live, I will still love you, wherever I go, whatever I do." Later, of course, we doubted that love from time to time, but in that moment, we seemed helpless not to love each other.

§ § §

By the ancient mahogany still sprawled in the meadow, the white Reena and Dak spread the ashes of Jim Stone. The black's fingers were wet from wiping tears from his face, and some of the ashes stuck to his hands. He bent over and wiped them on the old trunk. "Here," he said to the red bark still clinging to the tree, "hold onto my friend for the next one thousand years. I can carry him no more."

Reena did not cry. She felt a certain joy at fulfilling Jim's wishes, at seeing him become part of the meadow and the tree in the country he loved, in the place where he suffered to have a chance to be with her again. On the way back to the jeeps, the black and the white did not touch each other. But for their vows to the deceased Jim and to the mother of Dakimu's daughter, they walked with some distance between them.

Dak rode in a truck with Chui compatriots, and Reena rode alone with the empty mahogany box on her lap. At Shanga, in the *kibanda*, Reena did embrace her friend and said, "Dak, I'll leave now for Dar es Salaam. The sooner I'm gone, the safer you'll be. I'll miss seeing Chui tonight, but think of this—I'm going to spend some time with Safina if her mother will let me."

"Oh, then let me hug you again, for Safina!"

They could not stop hugging until the long-remembered Rufiji flooded their regrets and their pain and swept even grief far down the river from the place where they had come up alive on the shore.

§ § §

Reena Patel wept when she closed the red book. She wept for the widow of Jim Stone; she wept for Dakimu, torn between black and white, friends and enemies his whole life; she wept for Safina, who could not ever know the beauty of her father without knowing the ugliness of his acts. She even wept for Felicia Farley, drugged and shielded from a truth she knew but of which she could not speak. And then for Fulsom too, caught in the middle of justice and injustice and the friendship of their children.

The phone rang. It was Fulsom. He merely said, "It is done. Everyone is safe."

"Thank you," she said.

She placed Jim's *Memoirs* in the hiding hole, but his words would stay with her, as well as the image of Dakimu watching his friend's ashes fall around the mahogany, if he and Reena had found that meadow, in the beautiful land called Manyara. She took out the bracelet with the green beads that Kiiku had brought from Shanga for Safina and slipped it on her arm. She would wear it for Kiiku and for the real *chui* that slept at Dakimu's feet.

A few days later, Reena opened her door to the white widow. She beckoned her in and then said, "I have been reading your husband's book."

"I thought you had read it years ago," the white woman said.

"Yes … I did. But today it is more beautiful than ever, though the full meaning is beyond my poor mind."

"Reena, you have the child of the man my husband loved! I came to see her. There are things I can tell her about her father, things she should know."

"I have forbidden her to read the red book until she's older. Please don't tell her those things," Reena begged.

"No … what I want to tell her are things about friendship … and sacrifice."

"I only want you to tell her what she desires to know," Reena said.

"All right," the white Reena said. "Shall I wait for her?"

"She'll be home from school soon. I'll make some tea."

Reena wanted to hug her for her terrible loss and shake her for the truth of her time with Dak. Instead she asked, "Did you see the leopard?"

"Yes."

"Did he sleep at your feet?"

"No … at my head," the widow said. "Baraka was there too … all night."

"She's lovely, don't you think?" Reena asked.

"I do. And Dak seems to feel protected having a wife … and a leopard."

"I know," Reena said. "Were you able to travel to Manyara without trouble?"

"Yes. I believe thanks to you."

"My friendship with Major Farley has helped me sleep at night. But I don't know how it's going to end. He must uphold the law, you know."

The widow said, "Whatever will be the end, Reena, I won't be here to see it. I have said good-bye to my friend Dakimu … if that matters to you."

Reena looked away, her eyes seeking the comfort of the blue sea beyond the window, beyond the response she might have made. She said, "I will light a candle for Jim, though it won't have the power of what you and Dak did for him."

"I guess we'll never know that," the widow said. "My plane leaves tomorrow, but if you need me, I'll come back."

"That's what Jim said."

"And now he is here," Reena Stone said.

No more words passed between them. A death can do that, but then, so can love.

Safina came in just then, her hand in Suzanna's. "We have a school assignment, Mama," she said and then became aware of the white woman.

"Who are you?" she asked in her direct way.

"I am Reena Stone," she said.

"Oh, Mama Stone. Jim's wife!"

"Yes, darling."

"I remember him. I can still feel him here in my heart," Safina said. "He had a black heart too, did you know?"

"I did know that … but how did you?"

"It's a secret," she said.

Reena guessed that Kiiku had been reading her daughter more of the red book than she had approved. She suddenly resented that Safina was caught in this web of adult drama.

"This is my best friend, Suzanna," Safina told the widow.

Reena interrupted before Jim's wife could say anything. "Suzanna, come with me for a moment. You can help me with the tea. She knew there were things Reena Stone might say that Suzanna should not hear. But she herself could not help listening at a small opening in the kitchen door.

Safina asked immediately, "Have you seen my father?"

"Yes. He went with me to scatter Jim's ashes in a special place," Reena said.

"Why was it special?"

"Because it was the very place your father carried him to safety a long time ago, when they were friends, when they loved each other."

"But how can a black man love a white man?" she asked.

"How can a black girl love a white girl?"

Safina sat down suddenly next to Reena and grabbed her hands. "It's okay then, the way Suzanna and I love each other?" she asked almost desperately.

"Why wouldn't it be?" Reena asked.

"The nuns at school and some people at church don't approve."

"Safina, when you grow up, would you want to marry Suzanna?"

"Oh, no, ma'am. She is my sister. I'm already thinking of marrying Keiti Doude who is a black boy two grades ahead of me."

"That's lovely, Safina. When Jim deeply loved his black brother, your father, even when there were secrets between them that could hurt, Jim wanted to marry me. There are different kinds of love, but you shouldn't be afraid of any of them."

"Oh, Mama Stone, I think I understand now … but about the secrets, I am not sure. I don't think I should keep secrets from Suzanna."

"No, probably not, but what is the worst thing that could happen?"

"She would stop loving me," Safina said.

"Today, when your father and I let Jim go into the African wind, your father still loved Jim, with all the secrets revealed. Just think of that friendship when you need to know what to do."

"Mama Stone, can you tell me a secret about my father that will help me know him better?"

"Your father has a wild leopard that sleeps by his bed."

She gasped and seemed reluctant to let go of the widow's hands. "Who else knows?"

"Kiiku and your mother."

There was some silence. Reena shut the door and placed some ginger biscuits on a tray with the tea Suzanna had made. But when they went back into the living room, Mrs. Stone was gone.

§ § §

Reena Stone spent her last night in Africa at the Imperial Arms, now called Travelers' Inn. She did not sleep. The weight of Jim's absence was heaviest there, and she wanted to feel it. She wanted it to drive everything else out, the sensation of Dak's arms around her, the sound of the leopard purring in the hut at Shanga, the conversation with Dakimu's daughter who was on a collision course with her own history. She could not be part of these things. They were beyond her now, gathering a momentum she could not stop.

When she boarded the plane that would carry her far from Africa, far from the ashes of her indefinable love that nourished a nameless meadow in the heart of Manyara, she did not whisper *kwa heri* to the land that she loved beyond any other. She did not have the heart to say good-bye.

eleven

The week after Reena Stone left, and Dak felt certain she was out of the country, he became aware of an increased presence of the military in and around Arusha. He remained hidden behind his glass blower's mask and didn't speak to anyone. He remembered both Reenas telling him they were not being followed and the helicopter veering away from him and Jim's widow as they journeyed toward Manyara. Had Farley tricked them all into letting their guard down? The children were safe now. Would that tempt the major into continuing his manhunt in the places Reena Stone, Reena, and Safina had been?

He began sleeping at Baraka and Kivuli's hut, but he hated to leave Chui at the mercy of the soldiers. The cat might escape, or he might lead the troopers to him. He was glad Reena Stone was gone. How could he shape his existence on the power of one kiss? Only his daughter and her mother could complete the part of his vision that had always been missing—a family to love and take care of and die for, if necessary.

And yet, he trembled at the memory of the day Jim and Reena had walked back into his life in 1985, into the meadow at Huzuni, and he had said, "In all my life, I have loved only you." They were there in his heart now; even though Jim was buried in Manyara, and Reena was in a distant land across nameless seas, those words were still true.

One morning, he sent Kiiku, who had finally made it safely back to him, into the streets to find out what was going on. His son, disguised as a woman, returned with distressing news. Major Farley had been at the Maasai Market brandishing a photo of him cut straight from the pages of Jim's *Memoirs*. Of course, he looked nothing like that photo now, and he had never been in the Maasai Market. But there was another thing. The major was offering a reward.

"What will you do?" Kiiku asked.

"I must send something to Father Amani. It will go with the regular shipment from Shanga to St. Joseph's. The priest will give your mother the package. She will know where I can be found. Reena and Safina will come or not."

"But how does my mother know where you're going?"

"A long time ago, I taught her the name when she kept pointing at the Catholic missionaries who tried to convert us after the Massacre. She wanted a rosary. She cried out 'What means? What means?' I told her the only word I remembered that connected me with Christians. One day, a nun gave her a rosary, and she called it by that name."

"Maybe she's forgotten it," Kiiku said. "Shouldn't I know it? Shouldn't I come there?"

"If your heart is breaking without me, follow Safina ... just follow Safina," Dakimu said with a heavy weight on his own heart.

But Dakimu hesitated, ran away from Shanga, and almost a year passed before he put the sea glass rosary in the mail to Father Amani.

§ § §

Fulsom Farley emerged from the house of his lover far from the village of Shanga. He had driven away from Arusha on his own after a disappointing and thorough search of the tourist town. He had left a small contingent of men to question anyone who behaved suspiciously and trail vehicles that left the city at odd hours.

He knew these men were bored and yet eager for the reward money he had been authorized to supply. He didn't entirely trust them without giving them direct orders. They drank too much when he was absent and were not opposed to bending the law, thinking they were *above* the law.

But he needed a break. His nurturing woman always brought him back to considerations of peace and mercy. She had no rancor in her heart. She believed the black man had suffered enough. He had been deprived of his family and could never sleep securely in his own abode.

"Dakimu has not suffered as Felicia has. How can you defend him?" Farley said.

"I'm not defending what he did. But how many more people will die in bringing him to justice?" she replied.

"I don't care," the major said. "I have a duty. He broke the law."

"Are you not breaking God's law taking me in your arms all these years?"

"Oh yes, and every minute was worth whatever price God makes me pay," he said.

"Tell me something *good* about these blacks," she continued, seemingly in their defense.

"The older one once saved a white man from some very vicious warriors. His son returned my horse Resolute in fine condition. But he had stolen him in the first place!"

"Ay, Fully, your bitterness does not become you. I know a different man under that blue jacket with the three gold bars," she said.

He clutched her to him. She smelled of burning eucalyptus and goat's milk and corn cakes and their night's lovemaking. She was all things to him. He never thought of Felicia when he was with her, but he always went back to Felicia. Because of the children, he told himself, even if neither one was his. He felt responsible for their happiness, the peace of Suzanna with her awful mark, the joy of Safina to know her own father, and, he had to admit, to lay her magical hands on his demented wife.

The children seemed to need each other to find comfort for their little woes and everyday disappointments. But Safina was always in the middle, putting herself up against the world for Suzanna, for that rascal Kiiku, for Kiiku's mother, for Reena, for the horses, for Felicia, and, of course, for her well-hidden father. How could she be the daughter of that fierce and troubled Dakimu? But there was no doubt that she was, and he had misdirected his troops and resisted the final orders over and over—to imprison the ruinous man.

He stood in the soft wind of the high acacia forest beneath the bluest of skies and resisted the return to Dar as Salaam. Whatever awaited him could never be as wondrous as this. A tawny eagle soared down, searching for his own satisfaction.

"Fully, you must go back now," his lover said.

He found that he was gripping her tighter as these random thoughts filled his mind.

"I will always come to you. I will always treasure you above the confines of my duties. I will keep all this madness away from you."

"If you can, Fully. If you can," she said gently, but still he did not release her.

He kissed her as he had never kissed Felicia. Then he said, "We are a strange couple, you and I. No one would believe this."

"No one ever needs to know," she said, caressing his back and turning her lips to him again.

When he drove off, he knew, as soon as his jeep rounded the curve in the red dirt road that led to his other life, that she would weep.

§ § §

One morning very early, just after Safina's twelfth birthday, she opened the door to harsh pounding. Kiiku burst into the apartment. He was looking for Reena, but she had left for work. "What is happening?" Safina asked.

Kiiku grabbed her arm. "Safina, listen to me. Your mother needs to go to the market and find my mother," he said.

"Why?"

"There is something my mother will only tell your mother. I'm not sure of the message myself, only that Father Amani delivered to her that sea glass rosary that you gave the crippled boy at Shanga. No one else is supposed to know."

"But, Kiiku, I have to get to the bus stop in a little while. What if I can't reach my mother at the hospital?"

"I already tried to find her, even disguised as a priest. They wouldn't let me have any contact with her, some new security rules. It's up to you," he said.

"I'll try, but wait, Kiiku, I have to ask you something. I have been reading the red book, and I want to know about a name I've read there that is also in my history book at school. The stories do not match up," she said.

"What name is that, little sister?"

"King Kisasi," she said.

He looked out the window at the dark Indian Ocean.

"He was my grandfather," Kiiku said.

"Your grandfather? Not my grandfather?"

"No, my mother's father. But our father knew him when he lived in the camp of the Vitani. The king called him his *mwana*, his son," Kiiku told her, letting go of her arm where his tight grip had left a mark.

"In my history book, it says he was a ruthless king but had no sons, only a daughter raped by his own warriors."

"My God, Safina, that can't be in your history book!" Kiiku cried.

"Not exactly," she admitted. "The nun told us the word *ravaged* meant raped, that the king was a very evil man and that some of his warriors from the sixties Massacre are still alive and killing people! *Our* father was a warrior. It says that in the red book. There are pictures of him with a spear in his hand. I have to know what this means."

He said, "This means you may have to grow up faster than any of us want you to."

"Is my history book true or is Mr. Stone's book true? Our father saved Jim when he could have killed him. Maybe he was even ordered to kill him … by your grandfather!"

"Would you like to take *me* to 'show and tell,' Safina? Would your nun believe *my* history?"

"I believe you, but you must tell me more," she said.

"Your mother will kill me," he said, "but get me the red book."

She dug it out and heard from Kiiku's own lips that part of the story that revealed how their father had agreed to marry the king's retarded daughter if he could be allowed to take the white prisoner, Jim Stone, back to Dar es Salaam, that the journalist was sick and had a woman there who could take care of him. When Dakimu returned to the Vitani camp, his wife had had a child by another man. In anger, he took the unfaithful woman without her consent. Jim never knew if a child had come from that forced union.

"But he did know!" Safina interrupted. "That child was you!"

"Jim didn't know that when he wrote his *Memoirs*," Kiiku said. "He didn't know everything that happened after Dak took him home to England. Some of these things I have read to you were added as they became clear, in this second edition. But my existence was not known. Safina, many hearts were broken. There is nothing you can do."

But there was. She stood up in her seventh-grade class that day and looked the nun right in the eyes when the history book said that the king's men ravaged all the women and killed their children. She said, "That is not true! King Kisasi had a daughter and two grandchildren that lived!"

"Safina, sit down! You can't make up stories like that. This is history," the nun said.

"The history is wrong," she said. "One of the children of the king's daughter is my half brother!"

"Safina, you will not tell these lies," the sister said, raising her ruler.

Then Safina said very calmly and softly so everyone had to strain to hear, "The man who married the king's daughter is my father. I have a book that proves it—*Memoirs on an African Morning* by Jim Stone."

The nun shook her head as if fighting a bad dream. "The red book! How could you have a copy of the red book?"

Safina knew she was in trouble then. Her own mother didn't know she had read any of it, only that when she was younger, Kiiku had read to her the description of the beautiful landscape and the magnificent people. Then out of nowhere came a terrible thought. *What if the black man that was the ruin of Suzanna's family is my father?*

She slipped into her desk. They would hear nothing more from her that day. But the principal saw her in the hallway later and informed her he had called her mother. Even though she had told lies against her will, she didn't seem to be able to lie about this—her father's history. It was her history too.

Later, she sat stone-faced in the main office. She knew what she knew but would not repeat it, no matter what anyone said. Her mother entered the room and shook hands with the headmaster. She said right away, "Master Keppler, my daughter does not lie. What is going on here?"

"Mrs. Patel, Safina has challenged the facts of her seventh-grade history book, specifically the chapters about the Massacre in the sixties."

"What has she said?"

"She said her father married King Kisasi's daughter who had a son who is also her half brother! This is just a fabrication we cannot allow."

"How do you know what Safina says is not true?"

Safina smiled, sitting stiff-backed on the hard timeout chair.

"Well, surely Mr. Patel did not marry King Kisasi's daughter!" the headmaster said.

"Perhaps Mr. Patel is not Safina's father," Reena suggested.

"But your records clearly state Sanjay Patel as her father."

"School records are the least reliable source of information, don't you think, Master Keppler?" Safina's mother said.

"So who is her father, Mrs. Patel?"

"I don't believe that's something you need to know, sir," she answered.

"Well, whoever her father is, I'm sure he's not in the pages of the history text," he said.

"It was a long time ago. There are many warriors from those days that have changed their names. And many warriors to whom Kisasi could have married his daughter, don't you think?"

Safina could see that her mother was leading the headmaster right out of the conversation. Later she would have to tell her mother she had been reading the red book and discovered her father's name all on her own. His name could even be in the history book in a chapter they had not covered yet. But she would never say his name to anyone.

But it was not the end of the conversation for Safina. Suzanna caught up with her on the way to algebra class. "You were so brave to contradict Sister Zahra. But why did you do it? Is your father mentioned in the history book?"

"I think so," Safina said, braving the consequences.

"What's his name?" Suzanna asked.

"I promised my mother I wouldn't say his name," she said, which was true. "Oh no! I forgot to tell Mama something really important. I'll have to go home today after school. You don't mind?"

"No."

"I might have to help my mother with something," Safina said.

"Can I help?"

"Maybe … I will always ask you first. I think there's something strange going on."

"Me too. My father said they knew where the killer was …"

"What killer?" Safina broke in.

"You know, the black man my mother is so afraid of, I think," Suzanna said. "Anyway, all the jeeps were loaded last night. I snuck outside and watched. There were a lot of guns and big trucks."

Safina's heart leaped almost out of her body. She had to find her mother. The phones were off limits for students. The bell rang, and Suzanna disappeared into the classroom. She saw nobody she knew well or trusted in the hallway. She ran out of the building. From the corner of the playground, she could see the Post. Her mind whirled. Jester!

As Safina willed her legs off of school property, she believed it was the only thing she could do. It took her fifteen minutes to reach the stable. Men and trucks crisscrossed the area hurriedly. No one noticed her. She lifted Jester's bridle off the tack room wall and stepped quickly into his stall. The gelding swung his head around from the feeder and jumped a little when he saw the girl he knew so well with the headstall in her hand. She slipped the bit easily into his mouth and the leather over his ears in one motion. She led him to the mounting block where she vaulted onto his bare back and trotted down the long aisle and out into the yard.

Most of the vehicles were gone, and the front gate had been left open. She stole through while the guard turned to answer the phone. Then she galloped him down the narrow alleys and across weed-choked, dirt lots with an eager purpose that even the horse could feel, reacting to Safina's body shifting at this corner and that, until her apartment building came into view.

"Mama!" Safina cried out, hoping her mother could hear the sound of Jester's rubber-shod hooves on the cobbled stones, that she had gone home after the meeting with the headmaster, and that Jester wouldn't get scared and unseat her.

But Reena was downstairs when Safina came through the ground-level door, still holding Jester's reins. "Mama, oh, Mama, I forgot to tell you what Kiiku said. You must go before it closes!" she cried breathlessly.

"Go where, child?"

"To the market! To Kiiku's mama!" She could barely get out the words but went on. "He said you'd understand, but he couldn't explain it to me. Hurry, Mama! I passed by vendors already heading home!"

"Okay, okay. How did you escape the Post on that horse?"

"Everyone was busy preparing for a long march to arrest the bad black man. Maybe Suzanna's mama can sleep better now."

"Oh my God, child, you don't know what you're saying. But never mind now. Can you take the horse back by yourself?"

"Oh yes, I've had many lessons on him, and he respects me," she said.

Her mother helped her remount Jester, and Safina started for the base more slowly now that she had delivered Kiiku's message. She would ask later about the urgency of the things happening around her. The pieces of the puzzle would not come together in her mind, so she merged her spirit with Jester's and looked at the world through his eyes as she wound her way through the maze of colors and streets of Dar es Salaam.

§ § §

Reena drove carefully toward the market not to attract any attention. Mostly people watched the black child on the shiny, brown horse weave through the late afternoon traffic. But she was nervous about what it all meant and stopped at the first pay phone to call Father Amani.

"St. Joseph's," the priest answered.

"Father, it's Reena. Can you talk?"

"Yes. Don't be alarmed. I have sent your sea glass rosary to Kiiku's mother. It is a sign. You must go to her."

"Kiiku gave Safina the same message, but I didn't trust it. What has happened, Father?"

"I believe Dakimu has had to move. Kiiku's mother will tell you where. Kiiku was probably afraid to tell Safina, afraid she'd try to find him, if he even knows himself.

"I'm on my way to the market. I'm so scared, Father."

"God will be with you," the priest said.

She hung up and parked her car as close to the market as she could. She bought a nice green and purple reed basket to appear to be a late afternoon shopper and to put Kiiku's mother at ease when she noticed the green on her new purchase. But Kiiku's mother had her head down in her usual posture when Reena hesitated by her stand. Reena did not know her name. All she could say was, "Do you have a sea glass rosary, mama?"

The aging, mentally slow mother of Dakimu's son reached under the table heavily laden with vegetables and brought out the sparkling rosary strung with the sea glass she and Dak had collected on the shore of the Indian Ocean. Did Kiiku's mother know who she was? Did she know she was helping the man who had raped her? Would she speak?

"Huzuni," the woman said and vanished behind a curtain without another word.

Huzuni. Reena put the rosary in her basket, bought some mangos and white corn in their husks from the stall owner, a local farmer, to spread on top of the elegant, silent message from Dakimu.

Reena sat in her car and reflected on the situation that seemed entirely out of her control. Huzuni was a questionable place to go. It was a mere hundred miles from Dar es Salaam and closer to main roads. Did Dak think the military troops would fly by that place, certain he would have moved even farther out into more hostile territory?

It was a place of extremes for the now fifty-six-year-old black. He had grown up there when it was a Christian mission and given the founders' last name and probably a taste of their dogma. He had met the white Reena Pavane soon after she had been evacuated from that same place as it burned to the ground in the first of the uprisings that led to the Massacre. He had returned to Huzuni after a terrible crime spree in the United States and lived there for twenty years until the day Jim Stone and Reena returned to Africa. And he had married the two whites under a new altar fashioned from the charred timbers of Huzuni's tortured past. He had told her this that very day when he brought the ailing Jim to the Hospital of the Good Samaritan. It had been a turning point in her life.

She drove straight to the military post. She hoped the guard knew her by sight now, knew she was a friend of Major Farley's, and would let her right in. There was no problem at the gate. She found Safina washing down the magnificent Jester and hand-feeding him oats mixed with watered-down beet pulp.

"Mama!" the girl cried. "What happened?"

"I found out that your father has left Shanga," Reena said. "But I know where he is."

"Oh, Mama, we must go to him."

"Safina, I promise you when it's safe, I'll send for you. But today can you go to the Farleys'?"

"Mrs. Farley will be very happy to have me. She said just last week that I could have been her child. She would not have minded my black skin."

"Oh, Safina, what have I let you do?"

"It's okay, Mama. You are friends with Mr. Farley. I've heard you call him Fulsom."

"Yes, we are deeply involved with the Farleys now. We will have to see it to its end."

"Why will it end? Because we're black?" she asked.

"No, my love, it's much more complicated than that, but I will ask Ful … Mr. Farley if you can join his family for a while. I will say I have to accompany a patient out of the country. Dr. Mbulu will back me up."

"I'm so glad for you to be with Baba. I will long for him all my days … but the leopard calls me too."

"Oh, Safina, you can't save everyone," her mother said.

Just then, Major Farley came into the barn striding purposefully down the long aisle. When he reached them, he said, "Safina, I heard about that trick you pulled, taking Jester off the base. What were you thinking, child?"

"It's my fault, Mr. Farley. I was supposed to pick her up from school early for an appointment, and when I didn't, she got worried," Reena said.

"And what would have been wrong with the school bus, young lady?" he said to Safina.

"Sir, I'm sorry, but the first thing I thought of was the horse."

He sat down heavily on a tack trunk nearby. "Well, be sure you thoroughly clean that bridle."

He seemed to be too weary to be angry, so Reena jumped in. "Now, Fulsom, I have to ask you a favor. I have been assigned to travel with a patient to Johannesburg. I don't know how long I'll be gone. Would it be possible for Safina to stay with you and your wife?"

"Yes, I think that would be acceptable, Mrs. Patel. I have to be ... on an assignment myself, and I fear leaving Felicia alone. Her doctor, of course, is on call, but with your daughter here, she will be all right. Safina knows just what to do ... to handle the situation. I don't quite understand it, but maybe God understands it, so who am I to doubt what has occurred between Felicia and your child. When are you leaving?"

"I think as soon as I can pack a few things," Reena said.

"I need to get some clothes and books," Safina said. "Should Mama bring me back on her way to the hospital?"

"Yes. I may be gone by then. Can you and Suzanna take care of Mrs. Farley? The neighbor wives have promised to help too while we men are ... trekking," he said.

"Suzanna and I together can do anything," Safina answered.

"I believe that. My daughter got home a little while ago. She didn't seem to know where you were, Safina. I'll go and explain what happened and that you'll be back," he said.

"Thank you, Fulsom," Reena said, but this time she could not meet his eyes.

Reena and her daughter were quiet in the car going home, but finally Safina said, "Mama, I think I should know where Baba is."

"It is a big secret for a little girl to keep," Reena said.

"I've kept all the others," Safina said.

"Well ... almost," her mother said. "This is the biggest one of all."

"Where is he, Mama?"

"In a village called Huzuni."

"Misery," she said in English.

"Yes. A place where he was healed once. A place he trusts."

"Will the soldiers look there?"

"I don't think so. There are many hiding caves close by and many people who would give their lives for him."

"So he is not a bad man?"

"No, Safina. He regrets his crimes, and God has forgiven him," Reena said.

"But have the people he hurt forgiven him?"

"I'm afraid not … but I think there is someone who has begun to heal them," Reena said.

"How?" Safina asked.

"With love," Reena said. "With a love that they have never known."

"I believe in love like that," Safina said.

"I know you do. Now, let's hurry."

At the apartment, they packed quickly. Reena put on the nun's outfit that Father Amani had provided her. She was sure no one would stop her. Huzuni would be a place a sister might visit. She left all the symbols of her relationship with Dak and Kiiku in their safe well under the floorboards. She would have to drive in the dark to a place she had never been, even though her own mother had lived there before she was born. She could ask natives the way. Even soldiers would probably help her without suspicion.

She let Safina out of the car a block from the Post. It was still light, but by the time her daughter reached bungalow number eight, it would be completely dark.

"Be assured in the Lord, my child," she said as Safina opened the door.

"I will, Mama … and you. *Upendo* is all," she said and lifted her suitcase out of the backseat.

"Love is all," Reena whispered back.

She had let Safina keep the sea glass rosary that she had

sacrificed for the sake of the white boy on the Shanga field trip almost four years before.

"How did you get it back?" she had asked her mother while they were packing.

"I can't tell you, Safina, but the glass was collected and made into the rosary when your father and I were very much in love."

"And now?" Safina questioned.

"We love each other … but many things have changed. You can't always get back the precious things in life from which you have been estranged."

"But now you have a chance, Mama," the girl had said.

It took Reena four hours to reach Huzuni. She was stopped several times at roadblocks, but when she showed the soldiers her ID stating her name was Sister Kimya, they assumed she had taken a vow of silence and asked her no questions. The roads were bad. It was March, and the long rains had not lessened. She took one wrong turn and had to double back, searching for the track that led to Huzuni.

Finally, she saw lantern lights and small fires in the area the map noted as Huzuni. She hid her car and walked into the village, still primitive by modern standards, with dirt streets, mud and straw houses, and the mission church freshly painted chalk white. It was getting late, and she was hungry.

Suddenly a voice behind her said, "Sister, whom do you seek?"

"Dakimu Reiman. He sent me a sea glass rosary."

"Yes. He is in the church. We have built a safe room in case soldiers come and a special place for Chui."

"For his son, Kiiku?" Reena asked.

"No, for the real leopard," the man said with a slight tremor in his voice.

Oh dear God, Reena thought.

There was one light on in the church. It was not a Catholic church. The missionaries welcomed all faiths, but Dak had told them that she might appear as a nun. She entered the building.

Dakimu was sitting in the last pew. At his feet on the floor was the leopard.

"Is it you, Reena?" he asked softly.

"It is I. And I will never leave you."

"And Safina?"

"She is with the Farleys," she said. "I pray we can be reunited soon."

"Jesus," Dak said with a swift exhalation of breath. "You trust that Major Far—"

"Fulsom ... yes," she said.

He still had not looked at her. "That much," he said.

"Do you trust that leopard?" she asked.

He laughed. "About as far as I can throw him."

To show *her* trust, she stepped carefully over the leopard and sat down next to Dak. "How did you get him here?"

"I was going to leave him. I shooed him into the coffee plantation, but when I got in the jeep, he leaped in the back, which I had not yet closed."

"And Baraka?"

"She did not leap in the jeep. Her love for Kivuli is too strong, and I did not have the room or the strength for two passengers. I have asked Father Amani for an annulment, since she and I never consummated our marriage. He's working on it," Dak answered.

"You called the priest?"

"I wanted to be sure he got the rosary and that, ultimately, you would get it," he said.

"So he knows where you are?"

"Yes. He's always known that this is where I would make my last stand."

"That makes more sense than anything. I should have guessed," she said.

Reena told him then about Safina riding the horse Jester, which she *borrowed* from the Post, trotting and galloping when she had a clear space, to give her the message to go to Kiiku's mother in the market. "She didn't know why, just that her brother had made it seem so urgent. And she was worried because she had forgotten to tell me earlier when I was at school … on another matter," she said.

"What matter?" he asked.

"Apparently, her seventh-grade history book has played a bit loosely with the facts. She felt called to correct the nun."

"Is my name in that book?"

"I don't know. Maybe as *Alama*," she said.

Dakimu reflexively grabbed his arm.

"Does it bother you still?" Reena asked. She knew he had been branded with a cross by King Kisasi, who put that *sign* on his Christian enemies. But the king himself had burned the mark to splinters in a tortuous ceremony when Dak became a pagan warrior in the early sixties.

"It seems like yesterday," he said after explaining that scene again to Reena, who knew it very well and had not forgotten it.

She put her hand on his where it trembled on the ruined flesh. "Jim and Reena had the cross too, but you suffered the most for it."

"And Colonel Hahlos. He had the cross, but he paid the biggest price. I killed him."

"But no one is looking for you for that," she said.

"No … but I should not have done it," he said.

The leopard rolled his head over onto Reena's foot. "And what do you think, Chui?"

"Sister Kimya, you are not as quiet as I remember," Dak said.

"I have been quiet for too long. I hid behind the name Reena Patel. I told lies. I asked our daughter to lie. Something has to change," she said.

"Does she know where I am?"

"Yes."

"She should not have to grow up without a father," he said.

"Suzanna is growing up without her father. Pray God she will never know why."

twelve

*I*n Dar es Salaam, in bungalow number eight, Safina arranged the medicines Major Farley had given her for his wife and thought of the last words they said to each other.

"Are you going to get the black man?" Felicia asked.

"We will try. He is very stealthy. Like a leopard. It will not be easy. I hope to be back in a few days. Will you be all right?"

"With Safina ... I will be all right."

"And Mrs. Vinton will check in on you when the girls are at school," he promised her.

Safina got worried when Felicia didn't respond. She filled a glass with water and moved toward the bedroom. Then the woman began another track.

"Why have I not ever seen Safina's mama?"

"That I cannot answer. She's gone to South Africa for a while."

"Where is her father?"

"In India."

"The child is an orphan ... or maybe a hallucination. But her hands are real."

"Yes, Mother. I'll be going now."

After Farley left, Safina sat on the edge of Felicia's bed. Suzanna was fixing her mother some dinner, which would only be half-eaten, if they were lucky.

"Do you think someday this fog will be lifted?" the white woman asked.

"Maybe the fog is protecting you," Safina said. "Sometimes when you see things clearly, it's more painful."

"You are a good child," Felicia said.

Suzanna set a tray with an exotic and tasty dish on the bedside table.

In the morning, it was as cold as stone.

Major Farley had been gone for three weeks. His wife stopped asking every day when he would be home and settled into the routine of the girls feeding her and reading to her and bringing Mama Vinton over to play card games and wash her hair. A couple of times, Safina held Felicia through near-seizures of despair, her steady black hands easing the tremors with uncanny power. No one spoke of what the soldiers were doing so long in the field.

At school one day, the history teacher, the nun Safina had already defied, Sister Zahra, said, "All right, children, we're going to skip to page 209, which starts with the process of ousting the British from our country, which was still called Tanganyika in 1961."

"But what happens from page 184 to page 209?" Suzanna asked.

"Just more of that awful Massacre. We don't need to dwell on that," she said.

But Safina was already looking through those pages and almost cried out when she came to a photograph of a young warrior holding a long knife in one hand and the head of a white child in the other. The caption read—*King Kisasi's most honored warrior shows no mercy.*

It was her father. The footnote at the bottom of the page said that this tribal leader was called *Alama* for the sign of the cross that had been burned into his arm and then slashed to an unrecognizable scar later in his transformation from Christian to killer.

The page with the photo began to darken and rumple with Safina's tears. This man could not be the father she had believed in all her life. It could not be the man whose gold cross had touched her cheek when he leaned over to give her the green-ridged glass or the man her own mother had given up everything to be with. But this could be the black man that Felicia Farley had declared *the ruin of us all*. Safina could not imagine why, but it was possible. She turned to page 209, thankful Sister Zahra had decided to pass by that part of their African history.

Her stomach started to hurt, and she thought she might throw up, but with her usual grace under fire, she composed a little prayer, which she said to herself while the nun began outlining the good things and the bad things the British had done in their country. *Holy Mary, Mother of God, bearer of the Light of the World, take this darkness from me, from all who suffer carrying their crosses. Show me how to redeem my father beyond the redemption he has already received from the Lord Jesus Christ, your son …*

"Safina!" the nun cried out. "Please read the first paragraph on page 210."

She looked over to the correct page and read, "'The photojournalist Jim Stone was among the most influential reporters of African affairs at that time, but what set him apart from many of the white rulers in Tanganyika was his indefinable love for our people.'"

And then Safina challenged Sister Zahra's patience once again. "I knew him," she said.

"Whom did you know, child?" the nun asked.

"Jim Stone. He was a friend of my mother's. He died last year, and his ashes were spread in a meadow in Manyara." She was sure that's the place her mother or Mrs. Stone had told her Jim wanted to be buried.

"Safina Patel, why are you telling these stories?" the sister asked.

"This story is true!"

"You will stay after school, young lady. We'll talk about it then," the nun said.

Safina panicked. She and Suzanna were supposed to have

lessons on Jester. And who could vouch for her? Who else knew about Jim? Kiiku? No telling where he was. Her mother, of course, but she didn't know how to reach her. And then, she knew— Father Amani! But the lesson had continued, and she couldn't say anything more.

At lunch, she clutched her stomach, which really did hurt, and was allowed to go to the nurse's office. Sister Abigail opened the door. "Safina? Are you sick?"

"No, but I need to call the priest at St. Joseph's."

"I guess that would be all right," the nun said.

Amani answered the phone right away.

"Father, I need your help. It's Safina."

"As I thought," he said.

"Can you come to school at three? I'll be in room fourteen, the history class. The nun thinks I'm lying about something, something you know is true."

"Is it something safe to speak of?"

"Yes, Father."

"I'll be there, child."

When Safina went into room 14 at the end of the day, the priest was waiting for her.

"Well, now, what's this about, Sister Zahra?" he asked.

"Tell him the lie you told in class today, young lady," the nun ordered.

"When I read aloud from the history book, there was a name I recognized, and I said I knew him. Sister wouldn't believe me."

"What name, Safina?" Father Amani asked.

"Jim Stone."

"She definitely did know him, Sister Zahra," the priest said. "She spent an afternoon with him in her mother's apartment several years ago. And perhaps saw him a few times after that. The Stones were very good friends of her mother's. Why do you doubt this girl?"

"I know she lies. There are things she has said that don't make sense," the nun replied.

"Maybe they don't have to make sense to you," Amani said.

"I do lie," Safina spoke up, "but only when adults tell me to. I never make up a lie of my own. I hate lies. And one day, all the truth will be known. Then God can judge if the lies were necessary."

"I just don't understand you, Safina," the nun said. "But, of course, if Father corroborates your story, I'll have to believe it."

Safina turned to the priest. "Father, can you take me to the Post? I have missed my bus now."

"Yes, I can do that. Sister, please feel free to call me if you question anything Safina says. She carries a heavy burden and needs our support. As you know, her mother is in Johannesburg, and communication has been difficult. The child is helping Suzanna Farley care for the frail Felicia Farley."

The nun just shook her head.

On the way back to the Post, Safina told Father Amani she had seen a picture of her father in the history book. She was still holding her stomach.

"Yes, my dear. Your father fought for his tribe during a very bad time in our country. It has nothing to do with you. You must let it go," he told her.

"Father, there is something that does have to do with me, but no one will tell me. Can you tell me?"

The priest did not answer for several moments but at last said, "I have made promises to shelter you from some truth, just as you did to protect your brother and your father. You must trust God to show you what you need to know in time."

"I think I'm going to throw up."

"Oh, baby." Father Amani pulled over and stopped. He got out and ran around to the passenger door just in time to catch Safina as she leaned out of the car, heaving into the dusty road. "What has the world done to you?"

She rested against him gratefully. His arms felt like God's arms, strong and adoring. "I'm sorry, Father," she said.

"I love you as if you were my own child. You have nothing to be sorry for," he said.

"I can go to the Post now," she said. "Suzanna will be worried about me."

The priest got her some bottled water from his backseat and didn't start the car right away. "Can you handle the time with Mrs. Farley?" he asked her.

"She says I am her only hope now."

"Really? Hope for what?"

"To accept the way things are … but I don't know what that means," she said.

"I think it is a lesson for all of us," he said.

Later that night, a messenger brought word from Major Farley. He had sent notes for the children and a colorful bracelet for Felicia with a handmade card. Safina knew immediately those things had come from Shanga, but she kept quiet. The notes reminded the children to keep up with their schoolwork, obey the nuns, and have patience with the delays in his mission.

Safina changed the sheets on Mrs. Farley's bed while Mama Vinton gave her a bath. Suzanna had already gone to bed. It was easy for Safina to unfold the brown parchment that lay on Felicia's nightstand and read the words her husband had written to her— *Darling, I hope you are well and that the children are not too much trouble. The black man was not in his last known hiding place, so we are traveling north for a few more weeks. I love you, Farley.*

She felt a little leap of power within her. She knew so much more than they did. She knew where the black man was. She tried to think what she should do. She could open the history book to that terrible page and show it to Felicia, see how she would react. But when she remembered the sight of her father holding the white child's head, she had to sit on the edge of Felicia's bed, doubled up against the pain in her belly.

Finally, she was able to turn down the sweet-smelling sheets and smooth a few wrinkles in the pillowcases before calling goodnight through the bathroom door and going into Suzanna's room, where the two girls slept together. Suzanna turned over and woke up. Safina looked down at her and thought suddenly that the awful thing her father had done he could have done to her white friend. She was afraid to move, afraid that she might be sick again, but Suzanna reached out to her, pulled her close to her in the bed, and cupped her hand gently against Safina's churning stomach.

The next day at school when the girls parted to go to different homerooms, Safina leaned over and whispered in Suzanna's ear, "Thank you." No explanation was needed. Now they each had a birthmark—one girl's on the outside and the other's on the inside. In history class, Sister Zahra asked Safina to talk about Jim Stone, what else she knew about him that was not in the text. She went to the front of the room and told things she mostly had read in Jim's *Memoirs* without mentioning the red book, about how he had been healed by his Tanzanian friends when his malaria flared up, about the missionary girl he had saved and then married years later, and about the way he had lied in the courtroom to prevent one of his best friends from an unjust sentence. She knew that was going too far, but no one pushed her for any more details. The nun was very pleased.

"The history book seems to have left out a lot of interesting facts," Sister Zahra said.

School and life proceeded in this manner, nothing to scare or surprise the girls as long as Mr. Farley stayed away. Safina ached for her mama but believed with all her heart that when it was safe, she would be allowed to go to her. They went to church when they could, and Father Amani would whisper to Safina that everything was all right. She didn't know how he knew that.

Safina used her whole strength to keep her friend comforted, and they grew closer. They rode Jester after school and lured Felicia to the supper table. She would come with her hair tied back severely from her pale face, her clothes not matching, sometimes one sock on and one off. Soldiers came and went, but no one told them what happened in the savannahs and forests far from home.

At last, Major Farley returned, a thin, bearded version of himself in Safina's eyes, with bad news for his wife. He and his men had not found the black killer of four whites, one of whom had died in 1961 with a knife in his throat, which Felicia appeared to have forgotten.

"What *do* you remember, my dear?" the major coaxed.

"I remember that I used to hate blacks until Safina came here. Something that happened that far back can't have anything to do with me."

Safina was brushing her teeth and heard the Farleys talking about her father.

The major said, "I don't know how he could elude us for so long. Even bribing the Chui warriors got us no closer to the man."

"Why don't you let him go? Maybe he isn't so bad anymore," Felicia said.

"*You* can say that?" Mr. Farley paused and then said, "What is the point of laws if we let him get away?"

"I don't know. I don't want to think about it."

"Of course you don't," he said. "I'm going to check on the children."

Safina dropped her toothbrush and raced into Suzanna's bedroom. She feigned sleep. She felt the major's hand rest briefly on her head. He whispered, "Forgive me, Safina." And for the first time, she thought she knew what he meant.

In the morning, he asked Safina outright, with Suzanna sitting joyfully in his lap, "Why isn't your mother back from South Africa?"

"I don't know, sir," Safina answered.

"If she doesn't return soon, I will have to send you to Father Amani," he said.

"No!" Suzanna cried, leaping up. "I'll go with her!"

"You most certainly will not. Your mother needs you. I am only here for a few days. We are picking up fresh horses, as the new territory we'll be searching is not accessible to vehicles, and resupplying our camps with food and ammunition. We are returning to the campaign with renewed vigor. I can't be worried about children in my house who are not mine! One of which is not mine, of course," he amended.

Safina wondered briefly at the significance of *that* statement but said, "I don't mind going to Father Amani. School's almost out. Maybe Suzanna can stay at St. Joseph's once in a while, like a sleepover. Mama Vinton has offered many times to care for Felicia."

"It's settled then," Farley said.

Suzanna did not get back on her father's lap. "Can Safina still come and ride with me? You're not taking Jester, are you?"

"I thought about it," the major said, "but he's earned a longer rest, and I know you girls delight so in him. I guess I can't take *everything* away from you."

The next day, Safina walked up the steps of St. Joseph's through the big wooden doors and into the sanctuary. Major Farley assured her he had called the priest and explained that he could no longer keep her, as he had expected Reena back weeks ago, and he had too much on his mind to deal with her.

But when Father Amani greeted them, Farley started right in. "Where *is* Mrs. Patel, Father?"

"I'm not sure. I did hear that the patient took a turn for the worse, and Reena was committed to standing by," Amani lied, crossing himself as though adjusting his robes.

"It's a bit difficult to believe, don't you think, Father?" the major said.

"Probably ... but Reena will do the right thing," the priest replied.

"I used to think that, but some doubts are creeping in," Farley admitted.

"May God deliver you of your doubts," Amani said.

Before he left, Major Farley thanked Safina for all she had done for Felicia and then asked her suddenly, "When did you last see your father?"

Safina did not miss a beat when she answered, "Four years ago," knowing he did not mean Sanjay Patel.

§ § §

Suzanna felt lost. She did not know how to help her mother in the ways Safina did, and half the time she felt as if she had no mother at all. She tried to get closer to her father, but he seemed to draw away, always busy with his military duties and the final push to deliver the black man to justice. She shadowed Safina at school and longed for the closeness they had shared since the day they met in the stables on the base when they were seven years old.

After school, Suzanna wandered around the barn and rode Jester for hours, trying to remember the feeling of Safina's body pressed up against her on the bare back of the horse. It was then that the two had moved as one. Jester did not care about the birthmark. It seemed that Safina didn't even see it anymore. Without Safina in her bed at night, she tossed and turned and could not get comfortable.

Her discomfort was magnified by the actions of her father. When she noticed him slipping handguns amongst his clean shirts, lining up bottles of his favorite whiskey to be fit into small spaces in his saddlebags, she panicked. She followed him from room to room in bungalow number eight and then out to the vehicle shed, aching for his attention.

Finally, her father turned to her and spoke in a dismissive voice, which alarmed her even more. "What is it you need from me, Suzanna?" he asked. "Be quick."

"Father, please let Safina come back. She is my sister."

"No, she is not."

"But her mother is missing!" she cried, desperate for his sympathy.

"Somehow I doubt that. Two months, almost three now, in South Africa! Please. These people have lied to you."

"Safina doesn't lie," Suzanna said.

"Everyone lies, my dear. Even that priest, Father Amani. You'll find out."

"Then let my friend come back."

"Never."

"Father, what is wrong with you? Can't you do this for me? Don't you love me?"

"Oh God," Farley mumbled. "Of course, I love you, Suzanna. I have cared for you, sheltered you, given you my name, but some things I cannot do, even if I were ..."

"Even if you were what?" she demanded.

He leaned against a camouflage-painted truck.

"Even if I were your father," he said softly.

"What?" Her eyes flashed. "You're not my father? That can't be!" She looked at him in disbelief. "Then who is? Tell me!"

Farley's courage failed him, and he looked away from her incredulous gaze. "Oh Christ," he said. "Go ask your mother. It is not my story to tell."

Suzanna turned and raced across the parade grounds, her golden hair flying out behind her, her long, dancer's legs barely touching the surface. She reached the Farley bungalow and flung the door open.

"Mother? Where are you? Mama?" she called out.

"In here," a faint voice replied. "In my bedroom."

Of course, Suzanna thought, *the place you have spent most of the last thirteen years.*

Suzanna took the final steps toward the truth, her heart pounding as she entered the dim room. The curtains were pulled, but there was one light on the nightstand casting a weak beam on the woman in the bed. She was sitting up, a grimy bathrobe wrapped loosely around her thin frame, hair disheveled, face distorted. She had definitely gone downhill since Safina left.

The mattress had no sheets but was covered with news clippings, old magazines and photographs, a baby's bonnet, and the red leather book. It was like the one Safina's mother had, the one she didn't want the girls to read and always kept hidden under the floorboards. Safina had shown her long ago. That was no secret. It was the one her ... father ... had tried to hide years ago.

Suzanna grabbed a yellowed page from an old Dar es Salaam

Tribune and began to read. It didn't make any sense at first. Then she saw the picture—a pretty, young woman leaning on, yes, it could be Fulsom Farley. The white woman looked pregnant. Part of the article had been torn, but she could make out the words "trial begins today for the black man, Dakimu Reiman … in the killing of David Sommers, son of Major John Sommers who was also … in the tribal uprisings during the early sixties … base near Manyara by this same Daki … knife down his throat. David was shot in the face at point-blank range the night of …"

She could read no more. This Dakimu must be the black man her mother always said was *the ruin of us all*, but there was more to this terrible piece of information, something her father knew but she didn't. Something maybe her mother knew but never told her.

"Mother … who am I?"

"Why, silly, you are Suzanna Farley," her mother answered readily enough, but before Felicia could prepare herself for her daughter's next question, Suzanna jumped up on the bed, papers scattering, a baby cup breaking on the dirty floor, the red book tumbling with the headlines naming *four* men known to have been murdered by the violent black, Dakimu. There were some white people in one picture, but she ignored it and grabbed her mother's face roughly, though she knew her mother had suffered a secret and nameless grief as long as Suzanna had known her.

She reached down and picked up the news clipping again. Yes, it said that the trial was scheduled for some date—the words were blurred—in 1985, the year before Suzanna was born.

"Mother!" She shook her again. "Who is my father?"

"Why, David Sommers, of course," she answered without hesitation. "Oh, he was a handsome man, just like his father, John. Major John liked these blacks, never did any of them harm, but that monster killed them … then he got away, got away."

She was fading, mumbling incoherently, filled with sorrow and perhaps delusions, Suzanna thought. How could she believe her? Safina had blurted out in class that her brother had a warrior father! She hadn't said *which* warrior or recognized a name in the history book. The name Dakimu Reiman was not in the history book, Suzanna was sure. She must find Safina now.

She tried to stay calm. She went back outside and, avoiding the man she had called father from the beginning, told a trooper that Major Farley wanted him to drive her to St. Joseph's. She gave the soldier no reason to doubt her, so he signed out one of the jeeps not being loaded for the campaign and drove her off the Post. When they arrived at the cathedral, the soldier asked if he should wait for her.

"Yes, thank you. That would be good," she said.

Since it was getting late, she knew Safina would not expect her. Earlier, they had had a nice lunch together at school and studied side by side in the library. They had made plans for a weekend of riding, after Major Farley left on his second mission. Now, Suzanna called out in the empty church in a panic.

Safina came from the priest's quarters. "Suzanna, what's wrong?" were the first words out of her mouth.

"I think something is going to put a wedge between us that is not of our doing."

"Here is the only wedge I know. I'm not staying in Dar any longer."

"But why?"

"I … I wish I could take you with me. I have to do something that … you wouldn't like."

"What are you talking about? I like everything you do! Everything you think! I thought we were bound forever, friends forever," Suzanna cried.

A cloud passed overhead and muted all the colors in the stained glass.

"How shall we be bound forever?" Safina asked.

"We could each tell a secret that is breaking our hearts," Suzanna said. "Then if we get separated, we will carry a part of each other no matter where we go."

They sat in the last pew of the sanctuary. They watched the light suddenly stream back in through the windows, illuminating the frescoes of Jesus and Mary, Judas and Peter, lambs in the arms of shepherds, and in the old, wooden pew, their own black and white faces.

Safina spoke first. "My father is not Sanjay Patel."

"My father is not Fulsom Farley," Suzanna said quickly.

They threw their arms around each other in the silent sanctuary and held on tightly for the awful power of those revelations. There was no time to explain the secrets or comfort each other as they had always done.

"You need to say good-bye, girls," Father Amani said from the shadows.

But they did not let go of each other for another long moment.

"I must know where you are going," Suzanna begged.

"Now that he is not your father, you won't tell Major Farley?"

"No. I promise on the name of my real father," she said.

"Huzuni. I tell you in the name of my real father."

"We need to leave, now, Safina," the priest said.

Suzanna whispered in Safina's ear, "I will find you."

Father Amani led Safina away to the vehicle disguised as a safari van that would take her to Huzuni, while Suzanna could only watch in despair that the truth had come to this.

In school the next day, Suzanna poured over the maps in geography class looking for Huzuni. It wasn't too hard to find, but no major roads went there that she could see. It seemed that only game paths stretched out from the little mission one hundred miles from Dar es Salaam. She wondered if Jester could go that far. It might take five or six days, and no matter what time of day or night she rode, she would have to hide him when she slept so he wouldn't be stolen or shot for food. She could dress as a soldier and put on his finest saddle and bridle. She would say she was Fulsom Farley's daughter, even though she wasn't. People would help her.

But why was Safina going to Huzuni? Did it have something to do with the father who was not Sanjay Patel? Was her missing mother there? Suzanna decided to stop her father—it was hard not to call him that—from his terrible mission, but when she got home, Major Farley was gone. Her mother was crying in Mama Vinton's arms. The old newspaper scraps had been cleaned up, and there were fresh sheets on the bed.

"Suzanna!" her mother cried when she saw her in the doorway. "Your father tried to find you before he left. He said to say he was sorry and that he loved you very much."

Suzanna's anger diminished. Of course, it wasn't *his* fault that he wasn't her real father. He had raised her as his own. He had gone beyond what most stepfathers would do, with the child's mother being so unpredictable and ill. And how predictable was Safina's mother? Running off to who-knows-where and leaving her daughter. Mrs. Patel, or whatever her name really was, had never been near the bungalow or attempted to make friends with Felicia. Something was missing in the story. She should have looked more carefully at those courtroom photos.

Suzanna collapsed on the couch in the empty living room with a final terrible thought, *Is Reena Patel with the man who killed my real father?* And then she knew clearly the path she would take. She would go to Huzuni.

thirteen

*D*akimu and Reena woke up at the same moment, at that time when night became day in an instant. They were lying in Dak's narrow bed in the rectory that he had been given for a safe room. It had taken a long time for Dak to get to that place, to make love again without restraint. They had spent many weeks walking in the montane forests on the northwest side of the valley. There were scars in the groves from the torching in the sixties; there were scars in their hearts from the cruel separation almost fourteen years before and the one thing that lay like a surgeon's swift slice to the bone, the kiss of Reena Pavane Stone, the kiss that *this* Reena knew nothing about.

Dak had taken that kiss from Reena Stone as a sign of farewell in 1985, but it had lingered for years in his memory. In his dreams sometimes, he could feel precisely the way her mouth fit on his, open and wet and inviting, sexual but holy at the same time. Dak believed he could not love his black Reena perfectly if he did not tell her about that kiss. So they had slept with their backs to each other, Dakimu struggling to find a way to explain that last day in the jail cell in Dar when the white Reena had reached for him as no woman had ever done and given him that life-wrenching kiss. But one night, Dakimu slipped under the covers and found his black companion naked. He kissed her wherever she would let him, and that other kiss that had haunted him, sleeping or waking, was almost entirely erased.

He knew he might be torn from her at any moment and their lives thrown into chaos. He could be shot on sight if he tried to flee in the face of Farley's troops. Reena had lately wept over having to leave Safina. He knew if she tried to go back for their daughter, she surely would be tracked and forced to give him up. Dakimu saw that she could not go down any road safely, except the road into his arms, and so he promised her the world, even though he knew it was not possible.

There were rumors of troops on the march in heavily armed trucks and horses in long trailers being transported for use in the wild lands when the vehicles bogged down. Travelers to the mission said the soldiers had dug into every corner from Arusha to Manyara and west and north of there, that at Shanga a woman was shot when her partner would not say where Dakimu had gone.

This news devastated Dak who was not sure if that meant Baraka or Kivuli was dead. He mourned for the two women who had virtually saved his life when he had first escaped from Dar es Salaam to the hills outside of Arusha. Reena told him she didn't believe Fulsom would have allowed such a killing, that it must have been done by a civilian gang out for the reward. It didn't soothe his grief.

Then it was said the forces were turning toward the southeast, scouring every valley, riding high up into the forests, and that they could be near Huzuni soon. Villagers boarded their *vibanda*, their simple, dirt-floored huts, and stole away from the mission fearing for their children. The mission pastor stayed and a couple that had cooked for Dak for many months. A few strong, young men refused to be driven from their homes and believed God would protect them. But Huzuni began to be a lonely place.

When the sound of a jeep was heard grinding up the long valley, the remaining villagers hid or fled into the hills where there were caves. Many had stored food and weapons there. But soon, the single vehicle pulled into the opening where a rough-hewn cross had been restored a few years after the sixties Massacre, and Father Amani stepped out with the hesitant Safina.

Dak and Reena rushed from the church and swept their daughter into their arms. Dakimu thought the girl looked sick, but he suddenly felt whole again, even though he barely recognized his daughter. He had not seen her since she was eight years old.

She stepped back and said, first to her mother, "Were you ever coming for me?"

"I was afraid for all of us," she said.

Then Safina stared at him. Her face was a mask. She said, "I need to know your name."

"Which one?" he asked.

"The one in my history book that no one, not even I, thought could be my father."

"I am *Alama*, adopted son of King Kisasi," he said, knowing he could never lie to her.

She stepped back even further. "I have heard your other name from Kiiku, but now I need to hear it from you."

"Dakimu Reiman," he said.

She seemed unable to speak. Father Amani put his arm around her and pressed one hand to her stomach. Dak thought it an odd gesture, but a noise startled all of them. The leopard had been hunting for three days but just then loped out into the open field. Safina saw him and called out, *"Chui! Chui!"*

The cat came straight to her. Her father tried to move between them, but Safina said, "No, Baba, he knows me."

Safina knelt on the ground, so instead of a big cat greeting, the leopard made himself lower in stature and finally put his head on the ground almost touching her knees. Then he let his haunches down, and she said, *"Chui,* I knew you would come to me."

"Don't touch him, daughter. He is not a pet," Dak warned.

"No, he is not a pet," she said as the leopard licked her hands, "but *he* only kills to survive. How *he* kills does not make my stomach hurt."

Ah, Dakimu thought, *she has seen* that *photo. Even Reena has not seen that one.* Jim had left that one out of his *Memoirs.*

Father Amani said, "I have heard the story of this leopard, but now I believe it."

"Reena told you? After she came to Shanga the third time?" Dak asked.

"No, it was your son, Kiiku."

"We have not seen Kiiku," Dak said.

"He is safe … in Dar es Salaam with friends of Dr. Mbulu, who is lying for Reena still. Your son thought he could discover what the authorities were planning and get word to you, but I begged him to let me bring Safina instead, even though she has not been feeling … well. Kiiku would be recognized with me. I think there is only one person who knows Safina is your daughter," the priest said.

"Who?"

"The man who hunts you," he answered.

The only sound that could be heard was the purring of the leopard.

"Father, please stay and take a meal with us," Reena said at last.

Some villagers were drifting back in as they realized who had come up the valley.

"It's the priest from St. Joseph's," someone said.

"And the child of Dak and Reena," another said.

They pressed around the Father and Dak's family, but the leopard would not let them get too close, swinging his head and flicking his tail in annoyance.

"I'll stay for a while and talk to the people, but I must return tonight to St. Joseph's," he said.

They all began walking toward the church. Dakimu held back a little to be with Safina but did not get too close. "I cannot take back what I did, Daughter. It was many years ago, but I live with it still today. Perhaps we can help each other bear it," he said softly.

"I don't want to be sick over it, Baba, but I can't stop it. My stomach just rebels."

"I know. Mine too.

"Really?"

"Yes, my child. There are times when I cannot keep anything in my stomach," he said.

"I didn't know. I'll take care of you," she said, and then she reached over and took one of his hands. Under her other hand, the leopard bumped his head as they went along.

Everyone crowded into the little church, and Father Amani stood in the front and gave blessings and tried to remember prayer requests. Dak showed Safina where the leopard could come and go through a swinging door cut just for the cat in the north wall of the rectory. Reena brought cushions the women had made for some of the pews and some soft linens that had been trade goods and made Safina a place on the floor next to her side of the bed. The *chui* was pacing around, adjusting to the difference in the room. Finally, he stepped through the opening and disappeared, apparently satisfied with the arrangements.

Soon, Father Amani poured over his map looking for a different track. He told Dak he was afraid someone might have noticed him heading toward Huzuni earlier with a black child in his jeep. The priest left gifts for the villagers—beads and cooking pots, leathers and building materials, some bags of lentils and barley, and a few crystal rosaries. He said that next time he would bring books.

"Next time?" Dak questioned.

"There is a lonely, white girl who wishes to be with Safina more than anything in the world," the priest said.

"Who would that be, Father?" Dak asked, thinking he might already know.

"Suzanna Farley," Amani said.

"No, Father, you cannot bring her here," Dak said.

"Her heart is breaking. Would you turn her away? Your daughter's best friend?"

"For her own sake, yes," Dak answered. "She should forget about Safina."

"As you wish, Dakimu, but don't be surprised if she makes her way here."

"How would she know to come here?" Dak asked.

"I believe Safina told the girl where we were going. They made a promise as a bond between them not to tell the secrets they shared at the last minute. I don't believe you'll be able to keep them apart for long. But I will try to keep an eye on Suzanna."

Much later, as Dak tucked a light blanket over Safina, the girl said, "There's no room for the leopard."

"He'll find a space," her father said. "He's a cat."

He felt her eyes on him in the dark room. "We could take Suzanna and run away to a new country and start over," she said.

"And do you think Major Farley will let his daughter just change families so easily?" he asked.

"Suzanna is not his daughter," she answered. There was silence in the room, a quickening of everyone's breath. "You knew," she said.

Dakimu spoke softly, "We knew, my child, but there are only so many broken hearts one little Safina can mend."

"I'm afraid to ask any more questions," Safina said. "Afraid of the answers, afraid that you won't answer."

"Perhaps there are certain answers you will never need," Dakimu said.

"Are there many of these unneeded answers?" she asked.

"Not many," her father said. "Now, go to sleep. We will all be stronger for it."

In the morning, the leopard was stretched out full at their feet, one giant paw resting on Safina's legs.

§ § §

Suzanna searched through the tack shed at the Post and found some old saddlebags. She took them home to repair them and started fitting things in as she collected them—a knife, maps, fire-starter, rain slicker, nutrition bars that Mama Vinton made for Felicia, painkillers, which were plenty easy to come by, and water purification tablets. Sometimes her mother's caretaker, who had been officially hired now since her own husband was out with Farley's brigade, asked what Suzanna was doing.

"A school project," the girl would answer and continue preparing for Huzuni. She had looked up the name and learned that it meant *misery* in Swahili. *Why would anyone name a village Misery?* she thought, not understanding that it referred to the misery of the Christ upon whom the village was founded by missionaries long ago. *I will bring joy to Safina.* After that, she had no idea what would happen.

She had been putting muscle on Jester, working him over jumps and up and down hills in the nearby nature park. He was already fit from the hours of lessons carrying her and Safina, but Suzanna too became strong and supple, her nearly fourteen-year-old body outclassing everyone her age at school, and boys who didn't know her or were new at the Light of the World would follow her whistling and gaping until she turned her face and revealed the birthmark. She didn't care. She had more important things to think about.

One day, five weeks after she was separated from Safina at St. Joseph's and two weeks after school closed, she went out with the now stuffed saddlebags to the barn, tied Jester to the grooming ring, and set his brushes and saddle close by. She had told Mama Vinton she was going to a riding camp for a week and not to worry about her. The woman looked skeptical, Suzanna thought. She had gone into her mother's bedroom with a vase of fresh flowers and a bowl of the best porridge Suzanna could make. She set both things down carefully because her hands were shaking.

"Mama?"

"Yes. What is it? What is it?" Felicia asked feverishly.

Suzanna wondered if her mother could possibly feel the trembling that went down to her very soul. "Just your breakfast. Mrs. Vinton had to go to the market. She'll be back soon, but I wanted you to know that I'm going camping this week."

"No! Where? Where will you be?"

"With Safina," she answered.

"Oh … that's all right then. Safina will watch out for you," her mother said.

"Yes … she will," Suzanna said.

Now, at the stables, a dark fear overtook her. One hundred miles seemed an impossible distance, but the thought of Safina came crashing into her self-doubts—Safina, who took those rocks for her on the playground, who held her head when she was sick, who taught her how to be around Jester and the other horses that she had been wary of before that first day in the barn with the black girl, who healed her disturbed mother, who gave a precious sea glass rosary to a cripple, and never, never shied away from kissing her birthmarked cheek. One hundred miles was nothing compared to those things.

She cinched down the girth and rebalanced the bags. She made sure the breast collar didn't pinch Jester's skin and that there was a comfortable space in the throatlatch. She had brushed the gelding to a high shine and loaded one side of her pack with cut-up apples and carrots. It was the season of ripening wild oats and grass, so the horse would have plenty to eat. She had a short picket line that she could tie between trees. She knew where all the streams and rivers crossed the land on their way to the Indian Ocean.

When she rode out of the compound, no one knew what was in her head. She was a familiar figure on the recovered, brown gelding, galloping on the exercise field, flying over the military post-and-rail obstacles, and heading for the nature park to cool Jester down. This day, she raced through the park and out the north end onto the sparsely treed savannah that spread up toward the hills, forests of whistling thorn and acacia, and then fig and mahogany.

Every six miles she walked the horse, counting ten or fifteen minutes and waiting for Jester's deep recovery breath. Then she urged him to canter again. At creek crossings, she let him drink his fill and then galloped on. If the footing became difficult, she broke to a trot. The first day, she made twenty-seven miles.

At a bustling village on the edge of the savannah lived a black man that was a good friend of Father Amani's. He did not know she was coming and barely knew who she was. But he was the first to greet her as she trotted down the long, dusty main street calling out his name.

"Jonathon Makusaro! Jonathon Makusaro!"

He stepped out of his house and caught the reins as she half-fell off the sweat-covered horse.

"What are you doing out here, young lady?" Jonathon asked.

Suzanna saw his surprise but knew he probably put her presence down to the usual strange things white people did.

"I'm on a journey for God," she replied, letting him take Jester. "I'm a parishioner of Father Amani's. He sends his greetings," she lied, still breathing heavily.

The horse seemed to have already recovered and gazed ahead at the trail.

"A friend of Father Amani's is a friend of mine," he said. "How can I help you?"

"I have food for myself and the horse, but if I could have a meal with you, a groom for the horse, and a bed for the night, I would be more refreshed for tomorrow's climb," she said.

"And where are you going?" Jonathon asked.

"I am seeking the truth of my life from a lifelong friend who was taken from me. She whispered the name of the place as she was leaving, but I promised not to say it," Suzanna answered.

"Is the friend black or white?" he asked.

"Black," she said. "Does it matter?"

"No," he said, "but I am proud you would take this dangerous journey for a black. It must be a great friendship indeed," he said.

Jonathon called a boy over who had been watching the birthmarked white girl speaking with the elder.

"Taki, unsaddle this horse and use cool cloths to wipe him down. Put the goats out and give him the corral," her host said.

"No cold water on his haunches," Suzanna reminded the boy.

"Ah, an educated horsewoman," Jonathon said.

The magic moment from daylight to darkness occurred, and Suzanna thanked God for the good luck of the first passage. Jonathon led her to his house where his wife, Marion, heard her story and prepared a hearty meal for the white traveler.

Suzanna had packed rosaries to give as gifts, thinking if the villagers weren't Catholic, she would cut the strings and offer them the beads or the gemstones. But she knew this man was a Catholic, as Father Amani had told her of Jonathon's conversion when the man was lost in a dust storm for two days. She dug in her bags and found the most beautiful chain of tanzanite and white quartz that ended in a tiny but real gold cross.

The woman's eyes lit up when Suzanna put it around her neck. "Oh, bless you, child. The colors of Mary!" she cried.

And for the first time in weeks, Suzanna slept in welcome comfort.

The next day was not as easy. Suzanna was tired from that first hard gallop, but Jester was not. He pulled on the reins, eager for a faster pace. The boy Taki had cleaned her saddle, breast collar, and bridle. She gave him some money, American coins, which were more valuable than Tanzanian. He took them gratefully but shied away from her hug.

She cried for the first few miles, feeling lonely and vulnerable, but then put that behind her. Ahead lay rougher country. Many times they had to pick their way around downed trees and forge deeper streams. Her map was not clear here, and she knew she would have to tell someone the name of the mission village where she was going.

She rested after about ten miles, ate one of Mama Vinton's nutrient bars, and offered Jester a pile of carrots as the grass was sparser under the canopy of strangler figs and birch. She trotted five more miles and rested again by a pool of spring water where she felt safe filling her canteen. Jester took a long drink, and Suzanna fell asleep holding his reins. The horse suddenly snorted, and she bolted awake. Some animal was browsing in the woods.

She looked at her map. If she could cover eight more miles, she'd be halfway to Huzuni. The temperature had dropped. If she rode Jester too hard and got him hot, it could be dangerous for him, especially if the cold deepened.

Suzanna mounted and worked her way back to the most traveled trail. She passed the elephant that had spooked Jester and picked up a slow trot. It began to rain. She stopped again and put on her slicker, but now, for sure, she could not push Jester too much. After about four miles, she came to an abandoned hunting camp and decided that was far enough.

She started a fire and found a place with good cover for her horse. The picket line would keep him from venturing out into the weather. She pulled grass from the open area until her fingers ached and piled it where Jester could reach it easily, adding apples to the thin meal. They were both restless that night, and Suzanna hoped for more open country for the next day's ride. She liked being able to see for miles around and not being closed in by thick undergrowth and heavy stands of trees.

The third day, she was able to ride twenty miles. She had given up her plan to ride some of the way at night. She just couldn't see the country well enough and feared getting lost. She and Jester broke out into lush valleys with plenty of water and places to rest where Jester could eat healthier grasses, and Suzanna could study her maps without constantly looking over her shoulder. She felt stronger because she had passed the halfway mark, but she longed to see a human that could give her better directions. She ate and drank as much as she could and held onto her rosary through the night. She dreamed of Safina and the way they had learned to ride, clinging to each other and Jester's mane, sometimes falling in a heap in each other's arms.

In the morning of her fourth day, a black hand woke her. A handsome, tribally dressed youth said, *"Hujambo, mtoto?"*

Suzanna knew enough Swahili to answer, *"Sijambo"*—she was fine, but could he speak English.

"Hah! As well as you, I think," he said.

"Then I will tell you I am *msichana*, a young, unmarried woman! Not *mtoto*, just a child! I am Suzanna Farley, from Dar es Salaam," she said, wondering if this were still part of her dream.

"And I am Askari," he said.

Suzanna jumped up. That word meant *soldier!*

"Yes, my name means *soldier*, but I am not a soldier. If I were, I would steal what looks like a soldier's horse! Did you steal it?" he asked.

"Not exactly," she replied.

"So, *not exactly*, what are you doing out here?"

"I'm on a mission," she said.

"Are you going to convert me?" he asked.

"I'm a Catholic, but I'm not trying to convert anyone. I'm trying to get to Huzuni," she said, hoping this far out she would not arouse suspicion.

"Huzuni? What is there?"

"My best friend and maybe a different kind of salvation," she said.

"Did you pray to your god to show you the way to Huzuni?" he asked.

"I have prayed for safety. I always knew the way," she told him.

"Well, you may be safe so far, but you are about to lose your way. Pray again," he said.

She bowed her head and then looked up at him. He gave her a beautiful smile. He had not flinched at the birthmark.

"Your god is very powerful, because *I* am going to Huzuni, and I definitely know the way," he said.

She crossed herself. "Oh, Askari, can this be true?"

"Yes, and I know shortcuts that are not on your maps," he said.

"But why are *you* going there?" Suzanna asked.

"To see a leopard that lives with humans without fear or aggression."

"That I know nothing about. Do you mean a person of the Chui clan?" she asked.

"No, I mean a living, breathing leopard that is *not exactly* tame and *not exactly* wild."

"How do you know this?"

"I had a sister who lived at Shanga. She saw it, but it disappeared with the black man who befriended it," the boy answered.

"But how do you know the man went to Huzuni?" Suzanna persisted.

The lithe and sensual youth fell to the ground and dropped his head as if praying to his own god. Then he said softly, "My sister was killed because her lover would not reveal the name of that place to some angry soldiers. So her lover told me in the memory of Kivuli, my sister."

This name meant nothing to Suzanna, so she asked, hoping to learn more, "What was Kivuli's lover's name?"

"Baraka," he said, still pressed to the ground that was soaking up his tears.

"*Blessing*," Suzanna said. "It was a woman."

"Yes, but Baraka was married to a black man to give him more respect and so the soldiers wouldn't harass him," Askari explained.

"What had he done?"

"He had killed some white people many years ago."

"Oh God," Suzanna said and knelt down next to the boy and grabbed his shoulders. "Tell me the black man's name," she begged.

"Dakimu Reiman," he said, as if it were no secret to him.

Suzanna collapsed in his arms, and he stroked her back as if calming an injured puppy. It was the first person besides Safina who had ever held her like that. The boy didn't ask her to explain her emotion. He just let her feel it. So she said, in barely a whisper, "One of those white men was my father, and another my grandfather."

"So you are going to Huzuni to kill the black then?"

"No. I am going to be with my best friend, Safina, who is his daughter."

"Ho, *msichana*, you are a brave one," Askari said with his arms still around her. "That friend must be very special."

"She is the first person in my life who didn't run from me … You are the second," she said.

"Why would I run? I think you are beautiful," Askari said. "I see those well-shaped legs, firm breasts under that riding shirt, your clear, green eyes, and your loyal heart. How old are you anyway?" he asked.

"Almost fourteen," she said.

"I am sixteen. Perhaps *we* shall become best friends. How many miles do you think you have left, Suzanna?" he asked.

"About thirty-five," she answered.

"I should like to have those thirty-five miles with you, but I know a way ten miles closer," he said.

"But you have no horse," Suzanna said.

"Ah, but I can run," he said. "I can stay with the horse most of the way. When we get close, I'll let you go alone. You can tell everyone I am no threat, to let me onto the mission grounds, maybe tie up the leopard," he added.

He helped her to her feet, smothered her dwindling fire, and lifted the saddle onto Jester's back. "Fine animal," he said.

"If we make it to Huzuni, he is yours," she said.

"That is too large a gift," he said. "I would be happy with a kiss."

"Maybe you can have both," she said. She put her foot in his hand to mount the horse.

He said, "Follow me. I'll slow down if the trail gets rough. Don't want to hurt *my* horse! Just call out if you need to stop."

"*Asante sana,* Askari," she said.

"*Karibu sana,*" he replied.

Oh, he could run all right. His long, muscled legs covered the same ground as Jester cantering! The three of them traveled along in wild landscape, crossed the Ruaha River, and then turned north. *This must be the shortcut*, Suzanna thought because she didn't remember her map showing a turn there.

The track narrowed; leafy swaths of branches slapped her face, tree roots tried to trip up the sure-footed Jester, and waterfalls spilled over their steep banks and made the ground slick. Askari sped on. The horse seemed to understand they were with the youthful, black runner. Suzanna barely had to use the reins to guide him.

Finally, she had to call out, "Askari! Askari!"

He wheeled around and came back to her.

"How much farther?" It was past noon, and she didn't think she had it in her to spend another night on the trail.

"About eight miles. Shall I send you on alone? I could walk for a little bit. Your horse seems fresh still. You'll make better time without me now. You will arrive before dark, which is safer in these times. I will come in the morning light," he said.

"Askari," she said, "my friend and I each told the other a secret before we parted, as a sign of our love. Could we do that?"

"What if we ask a question instead?" he said.

"Okay."

"Suzanna, do you love your friend like my sister loved Baraka?"

"No, it's never been like that," she answered but thought of the time she had put her arm around the half-sick Safina in their bed at the bungalow. She had felt a raw and strangling emotion, something more than sisterly affection. She might have lied to the innocent Askari.

"Now, you ask me something," he said.

"Did someone send you to track me?" she asked.

"No," he assured her. "Sometimes a *mlinzi* appears when you least expect."

He was a guardian beyond expectations. Suzanna hated to leave him. He showed her the trail to follow and described a place to bear right and then look for a break in the trees. "Through that gap is a valley about four miles long. You should be able to gallop the rest of the way then. You'll see a large cross and the *vibanda* and a white church."

"You have been there before."

"My grandfather was led to Jesus in Huzuni by a white girl a little older than you. Her name was—"

"Reena Pavane, then Stone, after she was married there in 1985," Suzanna finished.

"How do you know *that*?" he asked.

"Safina told me, after keeping it a secret for a while, that her mother was named after that missionary. I only learned the name Huzuni recently, but I have been fitting in pieces of a very strange puzzle."

"Do you have all the pieces yet?" Askari asked.

"Not quite. But I believe Safina's mother is there now too."

"Be careful, Suzanna. Remember, the horse might be afraid of the leopard. Call to the villagers as you enter the mission. The cat won't like a crowd."

"*Kwa heri, rafiki*," she said.

"Good-bye, friend," he replied in the English translation.

Suzanna struggled through the thorn bush and vine tangles along the river but soon came to the break in the forest and passed through, walking the horse to bring his heart rate down. When she started up the valley, she broke into a canter and searched ahead for signs of the mission village. The uneven track climbed uphill a ways and then descended. As she came over the rise, she saw the tall cross and the huts arranged in a circle around the church. There, children played in a field nearby, and women came from the river with water vessels on their heads. She did not see a leopard.

The villagers began calling, "Horseman on the road! Horseman on the road!"

Dakimu ran out of the church with Safina close behind, and Suzanna could hear their cries. "That's no horseman! That's a girl!"

"That's Jester!" Safina screeched.

Suzanna flew up the worn path into the churchyard and vaulted from the horse. Safina grabbed the reins and then the whole of her much thinner-than-she-remembered, exhausted friend.

"Where have you come from like a spirit out of the heavens?" Safina cried.

"I have come from Dar es Salaam. No one knows I am here, except a black boy I met on the trail. He'll be here in the morning," Suzanna said.

"He's not a tracker or advanced trooper for your ... for Farley?" Safina asked.

"No. He's coming to see the leopard," Suzanna told her.

"How does he know about the leopard?" Safina asked.

"His sister saw it at Shanga, but I should let him tell you the story," she said.

Then the girls looked over at Dakimu and Reena, who seemed to be waiting for them to calm down. Reena said, "Suzanna, you have taken an awful chance."

"Yes ... for friendship, for love. That's worth a big chance, don't you think?"

"I guess I have to say that I do, since I am here and not in Johannesburg as everyone believes," Reena said.

Dak reached for the reins and said he would take care of the horse so the girls could get out of the sun. "I'll bring your saddlebags in with me," he said to Suzanna.

"Thank you," she said. She felt hot and cold at the same time in the presence of this man.

He led Jester away to a shelter he had designed for the animals to keep them safe from the leopard but was soon back following them up the slight rise to the church. Safina and Suzanna walked arm in arm into the rectory. The two friends sat on the small couch in the entry room, the only place a couch would fit. Suzanna would probably have to sleep there. Reena brought them glasses of mango juice and extra water for Suzanna.

"Tell me everything," Safina said.

"Jester was wonderful," Suzanna began. "I was so scared most of the time, but he wanted to gallop, and the miles went by fast. There was some rain, and I almost got lost a couple of times. He swam through a river and parted a herd of zebras like he knew what he was doing!"

"Crowd control in the extreme!" Safina said.

"He never tried to pull away from the picket line or out of my hands if I accidentally fell asleep at a rest stop. And then we met Askari."

Suzanna did not want to say much about the boy who would arrive tomorrow. Maybe he would see Safina and fall in love with her. Besides, she had her true mission to think of—facing the killer of her real father. She knew the lean, handsome black that led Jester away was Safina's father, but she didn't know for sure if his name was Dakimu Reiman. How could she find out without hurting Safina, who may have guessed part of the truth but not all of it?

The choice was taken from her because when Safina's father entered the rectory, he said to her, "Suzanna, when you have rested, we can talk, no?"

"I'm rested enough. I'm long past waiting to talk to you," she said.

"Let's take a walk, shall we?"

Safina stood with her friend and said, "What could you have to talk about that I can't hear?"

"I think your friend is trying to shield you from grief," her father said to her.

"If she has grief, I want to share it. If it is mine, I want to feel it," Safina said.

"Then let's stay here in the shade of the church. Come, girls. We'll sit in the sanctuary."

They moved into the larger part of the building. The first thing that Suzanna noticed was that people of many faiths had decorated the pews, windows, and the altar. There was an old piano in one corner. Its sides had been blackened by fire. There were places to light candles, hymn books in Swahili and English, a crucifix and a plain cross side by side. The pews were of different sizes and could be rearranged, so Safina's father turned one around and sat facing the girls, who clasped hands on another bench.

"I need to know your name," Suzanna said, looking directly at the black man.

"I am Dakimu Reiman," he said in the same voice he had used when Safina asked him the same question.

"You. You are the black man my mother said was the ruin of us all," Suzanna said barely above a whisper.

"Yes … that I am," Dakimu said equally subdued.

But Safina asked, "What did my father do?"

Suzanna said simply, "He killed David Sommers … and David's father, John Sommers."

"Who is David Sommers?" Safina asked.

"My father," she said.

Safina looked from one to the other. "No," she said. She released Suzanna's hand and pressed both of her hands to her stomach.

Suzanna embraced her ardently. "Let me hold you now for all the times you held me. I know you have been sick over something. I was afraid to ask you in case it was something I said or did."

Safina told her, "My stomach has hurt for weeks because of a picture in the history book, in that section Sister Zahra skipped over. But it was only a photograph taken long ago. What will I do now in this place where my father sits only a few feet away? And you have said he killed *your* father?"

"You may have to choose between your father and me," she said.

"Oh God," Safina said.

There was a sound, a rushing of feet, a shadow on the church wall. No one moved. The leopard came down the aisle and rolled on his side between them, panting from a hot pursuit through the green and silent hills. No one touched him. They watched his limber cat body fit itself between their feet on the hardwood floor. They let their eyes take in his splendid markings and unruffled coat and finally, looked into his gray-gold eyes just before he closed them.

The leopard slept.

fourteen

Reena could not bear the pain in the faces of Dak and Safina and Suzanna, the ones she never imagined would ever know each other, much less love each other. She'd had a big part in bringing them together but now a small part in their reconciliation. How could this be? She even had to add a fourth soul to her list of those she cared about—Fulsom Farley himself.

Where was the man? Word had come that he had made a mistake in his reckoning. Had he done that to give them time to escape again? He could not know Safina and Suzanna were here or even she herself, so no, he must be closing in now on Dakimu. Perhaps he had already caught Kiiku. Perhaps he had already shot Dak's son down like he had Kivuli. No, she would not accept that Fulsom was that heartless.

She wandered out onto one of the leopard's trails. The trees grew close there. She felt their embrace. She knelt by a rumbling stream but was unable to pray. She removed her rosary and dragged it through the clear water, washing away all the broken promises it had seen.

The outline of a leather boot appeared at the opposite edge of the rivulet. She raised her eyes and stared into the eyes of the soldier she had confronted in the Maasai Market months ago.

"Are you here to protect me now?" she asked but seemed unable to get to her feet.

"Yes, mama. I was sent ahead to this place in case you were here. I was to ask you to come out with me and be safe behind the lines."

"Why would I come? I am just visiting some old friends who were saved at this mission and still live here," she said, wishing she could cross herself for the lie.

"Mama, we know who is in the village. Why do you put yourself in danger?"

"I love him."

"Ah," the young black said.

"Why do you follow the orders of the British major?"

"I am a soldier before anything, but I love justice more than revenge. I grew up hearing tales of the warrior but didn't know of his loves, his sacrifices, or his heartaches."

"Will it make a difference now?" Reena asked.

"It's why I'm here. Give me your hand," he said. "There are a thousand men approaching. The fugitive will not survive ... nor you."

"I'm not afraid to die, but there are things Major Farley needs to know—" A sound cut her off—the soldier's horse stamping and nickering. Then the man was gone.

Reena slipped the rosary back over her neck and looked down again into the stream. *Come ye to the waters* ... She retreated to the church. She heard voices inside the entryway where she had made a place for Suzanna to sleep. She listened outside the door.

Dak said, "I am beyond sorrow, my dear child. If it helps at all, I have suffered much for what I have done."

"But you have suffered *alive*," Suzanna said.

"Only alive for brief periods since I killed your father," he said. "When I found my son, Kiiku, when I learned that I also had a daughter and might have a chance to meet her, when I found the leopard curled up outside my hut one morning at Shanga, when I was reunited with Reena, and other moments. I may not have deserved any of those gifts, but I accepted them as signs that God had forgiven me. That you might not forgive me ... is true justice."

Suzanna said, "I have to remember that if my father had killed you, which may have been his intent that night up at the Point, there would never have been a Safina to befriend me, a Safina for me to love."

"I'm not sure that's true, Suzanna. Reena might have already been pregnant," he said.

"But wouldn't my father have killed her too?" she asked.

"I don't know. I can't fathom that. But that would have been my fault too."

"Why?" she asked.

"Because I had killed his father, he wanted to destroy me and all I loved."

"Did you know my grandfather?" Suzanna asked.

"Yes," Dak said. "He was very honorable toward me in a time when blacks were often alienated. I worked for him at the British Air and Ground Control base in Dar es Salaam. He defended me in many circumstances and praised me for doing whatever he asked without complaint. I liked him."

"Then why did you kill him?" she asked.

"I have no excuses or even reasons. I began to abhor whites during the Massacre. Major Sommers was in the wrong place at the wrong time. I am so sorry, Suzanna."

"It's just that I have no family. I feel like an orphan. My mother hardly knows I exist," she said. "My father is not my father."

Reena went in then and said, "There was a soldier in the woods. We can still flee. Farley is a few days away."

"Why did the man not take you?" Dak asked, reaching for her hand.

"I refused to go," she said.

Reena woke first in the morning and watched dawn break over Huzuni, that sudden spear of light on the hills and fields, the animal pens, and the white church, the terrors of the night stripped away in a handful of seconds. Everyone ate porridge in silence. Suzanna shared some honey from her pack, and the questions that lingered were unspoken.

Later in the day, a cry went up. "Runner on the road! Runner coming in!"

Reena went after the girls as they ran down the trail, afraid for them. Askari strode on his long legs toward the church. Suzanna greeted him first. "My *mlinzi*!"

"I'm not exactly prepared to see you," he said. He glanced down at his dirty breeches and sweaty arms.

"You look beautiful to me," she said.

"Have you seen the leopard?" he asked.

"Yes. Oh, he's so magnificent. He fills your heart," she answered. "Come, meet my family." She said it so easily that Reena couldn't believe those words had slipped out of her mouth.

"This is Askari," she said to them. "Askari, this is my sister, Safina, and her mother and father, Reena and Dakimu."

"I am at your service," the boy said. "I can clean stalls, paint the church, carry water, anything to stay here awhile."

"Why did you come?" Dak asked.

"Originally, I wanted to see the leopard, but now I am happy to see Suzanna again," he said.

"Someone at Shanga told you about the *chui?*" Dak continued.

"My sister. She knew you and the leopard at Shanga … but she was killed as a punishment when her lover wouldn't say where you'd gone."

"Who is your sister?" he asked in a dark voice.

"Kivuli," he said. "My only sister."

Dakimu put his hand against the cross at his neck. He seemed unable to speak but finally said, "Who told *you* where I'd gone?"

"Baraka told me in Kivuli's memory," the boy said.

"Why do you want to see the leopard?" Dak pressed on.

"In my sister's memory," Askari said.

"A worthy reason," Dak said to him. "The *chui* comes into the church some nights, but he may stay away now. I am being pursued by those same soldiers who killed your sister."

"Then I'll wait for them with you … and for the leopard," Askari said. "What do you think of this leopard, sir?"

"I think it is God showing me a way in the wilderness," Dak answered.

"So the *chui* is a Christian god."

"Any god who cares," Dak replied.

"Well, god or not, I will watch for him," Askari said. He drew Suzanna closer to him in a protective gesture. She did not resist.

Reena saw the look on Safina's face, but her daughter spoke up quickly. "You like this soldier, Suzanna!"

"I do. He appeared when I had almost given up, when I didn't know what path to take. He was not repulsed by my mark," she answered.

"A youth who sees the soul," Safina said.

"Like you," Suzanna replied.

The recent storms died, and the tracks began to dry up. There was a restlessness in the very trees. The ground trembled with an unknown force. A week after Askari arrived, Reena went out with the girls to check on Jester. They approached the tightly fenced corral calling the horse's name. There was a ladder resting against the high wall. It was normally not left there for fear that the leopard or another big cat could quickly figure out how to get to the horse.

The girls climbed up cautiously and peered over. Reena watched through small cracks in the solid fence. There was a white soldier trying to catch the gelding, but Jester was spinning and kicking out at the intruder. Safina and Suzanna jumped down into the pen. Reena cried *No!* in a silent plea to heaven.

Suzanna said sweetly, "Here, let us help you. He knows us," while reaching in her waist pack for the knife she still carried there.

"You're Major Farley's daughter," the man said.

"Not really," Suzanna said. "But where is he?"

"Not far. A day's drive, some horseback miles. I was sent on one of the best mounts to assess the fighting capabilities at the mission, but the mare collapsed an hour ago. If I could ride this horse, I could turn the infantry sooner," he said.

Does he think Suzanna is being held against her will and would welcome that news? Reena thought in amazement.

"Apparently," Safina said, "we are not prepared to fight, but neither will you be returning to Farley on *this* horse. Say your prayers."

Suzanna plunged the knife into the soldier's heart coming from behind Jester, who was shielding her. She looked at Safina and said, "One enemy down, a thousand to go." And then she screamed.

Askari came running and pushed his way into the hidden gate that the soldier never would have found. He looked at the dead trooper with astonishment.

"We have killed a spy," Safina said.

Reena knew they couldn't leave the man. The smell of blood would draw predators and be intolerable to the horse. They all worked to get the soldier out, and then Safina went back to calm Jester.

"You are brave warriors," Askari said and tried to hold Suzanna, but she lurched from him and stumbled toward the rectory.

Reena ran after her, wanting to protect her from the enormity of what she had done. But Dakimu caught her just as she reached the sanctuary. She held out the bloody knife and said in an unsteady voice, "Now, we are equal. Now, I can love you."

"Whom have you killed, my girl?" he asked.

"A white spy of my ... Fulsom Farley's," she said, "He is a day away. Shall we flee?"

"No, Suzanna. I will meet him. It is I he wants."

A warning was sent out to all the villagers who did not wish to see Dakimu led away in chains or shot before their eyes. The animals were herded to a high pasture where random shots could not wound or kill them. Suzanna, still shaking and unfocused, was able to tack up Jester for the last time and handed the reins to Askari.

"Take him and yourself to safety. This is not your war," she said.

"I will be back for you. You know I will," he said.

He kissed her on both cheeks and then on her lips by way of promise. She watched him gallop down the valley she had ridden up just days before.

Reena married Dak that night in the sanctuary of the two crosses in the presence of the only two children left to them. They had no communion. They had no confessor. They had no leopard to guard the door. He was off on his own mission. Safina wore a strip of green cloth about her waist for the other Chui, her half brother, Kiiku, one hand in one of Suzanna's.

The sound of men and horses lapped like an irrepressible tide against a meager refuge, but there was an ark on the hill too. Reena knew there would always be an ark. She sat down at the scarred piano and turned the pages of a tattered hymnal, the melody she wanted already singing in her head. Just before she put her hands on the old, yellowed keys, she heard Dak ask the white girl whose birthmark had bled into the brown of her tanned skin, "Do you need forgiveness?" and Suzanna answer, "No. I'm not sorry I killed the soldier. He would have run Jester to death. I couldn't let that happen. I'll never be sorry. Let my … father … put handcuffs on *me*."

§ § §

Major Fulsom Farley sat in the woods by a small fire. He was exhausted but exhilarated by the possibility of success. His outrunners had reported seeing the black and perhaps his son building corrals and reinforcing the walls of the church rectory at Huzuni. He had halted his troops for the night and unloaded the horses from the stock trailers. The vehicles would have to be abandoned. They would be too noisy and could not move as well as horses in these last few miles.

He put his head in his hands. The months on the trail had altered him. Even though he was surrounded by vital and companionable men, he had come to understand true loneliness. He missed the chatter of the girls in his kitchen and even the whining demands of poor Felicia. He had felt needed … and loved. He could make mistakes and be forgiven. He could order those people around at the Light of the World and watch the girls' eyes brighten at his defense of them. On these long marches, he was expected to perform, to find that damn Dakimu and his errant son and never go down the wrong road.

The men were settling for the night. The wind had quieted, and the horses quit their pawing and nickering. Then he heard the most amazing thing—a piano. He had felt the vibrations in the air before he heard the music. Higher up in the forest, someone was playing the piano. The sound drifted down through the wild land and stabbed at his heart. It was in his power to stop that music forever, to freeze those fingers in the middle of that lovely hymn. Were they black hands or white? Did it matter? Once he had started on his dreadful course, all the music in the world would not save them.

His campaign had been far from perfect. Soldiers had defected. He'd have to deal with that. Many had been wounded in skirmishes with blacks who loved that fugitive—his Chui brothers, the coffee plantation owners, the Shanga artists, and who knew how many others who had absolved him, Farley's own priest among them! One soldier had not returned from his patrol into Huzuni. Horses had stumbled and died. He did not know how his wife fared or if his … stepdaughter would ever speak to him again. He had not solved the mystery of the missing Reena Patel. He felt defeated. But he felt angry too. *I will kill that black as sure as I'm waiting for dawn's light to lead me to his door,* he thought, trying to shut the sound of that piano out of his head.

He had been a generous father to Suzanna, but he didn't know how to love her, didn't know what to give her to replace what David Sommers would have given her. He had given her his name but could never sign the adoption papers. First, he wanted his own child. He had no idea when he married Felicia that she would turn him out of their bed. And so, he supposed, he resented the child with the terrible birthmark, a mark that had reminded him daily of her real father's death. The truth of David's death exploded in his dreams but in other times got buried in the course of military matters, in the confessional, and in the arms of his long-secret love. What changed was the coming of one little black girl into their lives—Safina.

Now there was an enigmatic child, hands like a healer's and an instinct for the truth. But he hated her father, who certainly had been the ruin of them all. He should take the man in, but he wanted to put a bullet in his heart. He was so close to his quarry he could see the man's blood spilling out of his chest, the shock in his eyes at losing all he had lived for, and maybe, just maybe, a spark of remorse.

When light began to fill the forest, Major Farley signaled his men to saddle the horses. His aide handed him Eagle, the white stallion reserved especially for these difficult campaigns. The horse was fearless and gave Fulsom courage beyond what he naturally possessed. The soldiers trekked up the valley, spreading out through the thick trees and slowly encircling Huzuni and its fugitive inhabitant. The troopers, black and white, lined the fields and footpaths, rifles and handguns swinging from their belts, the horsemen's weapons half-released from their scabbards and ready to be drawn at a prearranged signal.

Major Farley rode at the head of the first column on the dancing Eagle right into the open ground a few hundred yards from the church. There were no villagers in sight, no animals. The piano was silent.

"Dakimu Reiman!" he called. "There is no escape! You must come out and be arrested for your crimes, or we will come in and get you. The church is no sanctuary!" Farley cried out in his best commander's voice. He read off the list of Dakimu's crimes, partly to give the men on foot time to close in with the riders and partly to reveal to the people who had been protecting him how violent this man was. Farley felt the immensity of the force behind him. He felt the righteousness of his cause.

"Dakimu Reiman! This is your last chance!"

There was some motion at the main doorway. Fulsom urged his stallion forward but ordered his men to stay back. He reached for the pistol in its holster on his thigh. He prepared himself to see the tall, black figure of the man he had seen in the courtroom in 1985. His anger was at a boiling point. Suddenly, he knew he didn't want to see even a hint of remorse, only the man's pain, and he reined Eagle fiercely toward the closed, white church.

Then Safina and Suzanna stepped out into the sunlight. Farley took his hand off his gun, and his heart lurched. There was a leopard crouched between them. The girls held hands across his back. A black leg on one side and a white leg on the other brushed against the cat's shimmering coat as they moved toward the major on his white horse. Eagle was as disbelieving as his rider. The leopard was unleashed and disdainfully eyeing the infantry poised to attack.

The men closest to Farley rammed bullets into their chambers. They did not wait for the cue. Soldiers in the woods crowded in toward the children and the cat, their fingers on triggers, their aims steady. Major Fulsom Farley spun his horse around to face his elite guard, his manhunters, his loyal troops who had followed him tirelessly to the sanctuary of the most wanted black and raised his hand.

He raised his hand against the chasm that yawned between his soldiers, the harrowing, futile marches, the loss of decent men and horses, and his enlightenment. He raised his hand against the gulf between these children and their leopard and his love. He raised his hand against racism and the hostile acts that had been committed in this heavenly land, against the rift these things had caused with his wife, who would never bear his own children.

And he said in a powerful voice, for all the world to hear, "Hold your fire!"